AGENT KEYS STEPS OUT

by

Mike Downs

ISBN 978-0692926529
Copyright 2017 Mike Downs
All rights reserved
Published by MKD Publishing

Books by Mike Downs

The Artimus Box

Novac's Race

Novac's Run

Bobo's Raid

Sounds of Deception

Agent Keys Steps Out

Author's Note

Please keep in mind that this is a work of fiction. the names, characters organizations, dates, and events in this novel are a product of the author's imagination, or are used fictitiously. Any resemblance to actual events or persons living or dead is purely coincidental.

This book is available in print and digital formats at most online retailers.

For Miz K always

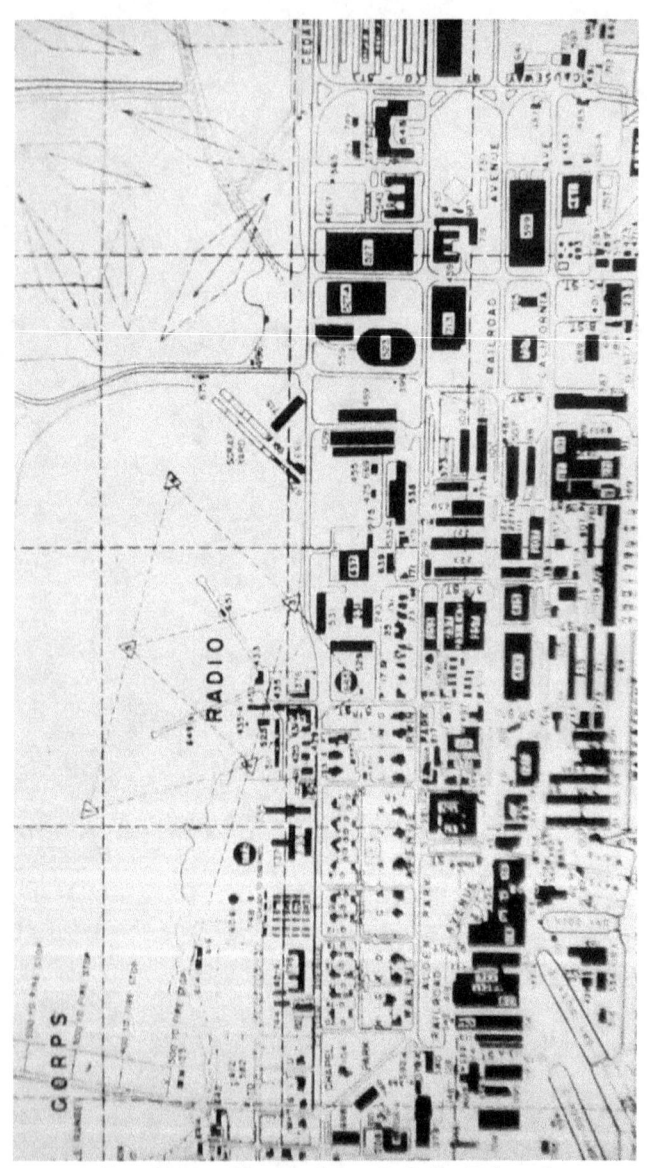

Setting of novel on Mare Island

Prologue

1942 San Francisco, CA

FBI Agent Barry Keys wakes to a familiar voice in a drab ward at San Francisco's City Hospital. Keys' brain struggles to bring his eyes into focus on the worried face of his wife, Mary.

"What's wrong, Mary?" Keys' eyes go wide. "What time is it? Did I oversleep?"

"Oh, thank God. You've been shot, Barry. You're in the hospital. We couldn't find you; I just knew you were hurt. I've been frantic; I…I thought you might even be dead."

Mary releases her grip on Keys' hand; her hands fly up to cover her face as she convulses in tears.

Keys struggles to get up and hold Mary in his arms. It is only when overwhelming pain shoots through his chest that he realizes this isn't a bad dream. Keys' memory flashes back to the night he was shot.

He was following what he thought was a minor criminal. Another agent at the Bureau identified this man as someone who was passing counterfeit twenty-dollar bills. The agent thought the man was a minor member of a gang who might lead them to the head man. The man was, in fact, the gang's leader.

Suddenly feeling cold, Keys shivers involuntarily under the covers of his hospital bed. The vivid memory pulls him back to the lights, sounds, and damp chill of that night when death almost took him.

On that night, a wet mist swirled about the streetlights. Keys pulled up his collar as he followed the man on foot to Montgomery and Pine. There had been little traffic until a car's headlights suddenly stabbed through the darkness to splash Keys' silhouette against a building. The brilliant flash of gunfire was the last thing he could remember before his body hit the cold, wet concrete.

Mary Keys woke alone that night with a terrible, sickly feeling filling her head with fear. She knew, could sense, her husband was hurt and alone. After a day of worried calls to the FBI, Mary called Keys' partner, Jerry Walsh. She was frantic. She begged Walsh to find Keys; she said she knew he was hurt.

Walsh checked hospitals—walked through scores of hospital wards—searching for Keys. Burning more shoe leather, he braved the horrors of the morgues in San Francisco. He spent hours phoning adjacent counties. Not one of the facilities had admitted an FBI man.

Days later Walsh found him at City Hospital tagged as a John Doe. There was no identification found on him when he was brought in. Walsh immediately called Mary who rushed to Keys' side.

While Keys convalesced Mary urged him to quit the FBI. Keys said with the war on he could not.

Mary said she could not stand not knowing if he would come home at night or be found dead in an alley somewhere. She was going to leave him.

"I love you, Barry, I always will. I have worried about you every night you're not home with me. All of the good years we've had together, I've had a nagging feeling you would be taken from me. I'm so sorry, Barry, but now, with all the horrible war news, it's all just too much for me.

"I want to do my part in this war. Marinship wants women to work in the shipyard, and I need something to get my mind off all of this. I'll be moving to the women's housing complex in Sausalito. I'll come back and visit you here..."

Unable to finish her sentence, tears came fast; she leaned down to kiss Keys, then rushed out.

3

***

Keys returned to the FBI after a period of recuperation.

The Bureau was changing, or maybe he was just beginning to notice the changes. He was a senior agent, but rarely the lead man anymore. Keys wasn't kidding himself: Mary leaving had left a void in his life, a pain in his heart.

With the country at war, some cases he was assigned to just seemed too menial. Keys thought perhaps he was being pushed out. He and his FBI partner, Jerry Walsh, were sent out after a man suspected of black-marketing beef.

Walsh, riding with Keys in an old Dodge, spots the man coming out of a little market on Castro in Noe Valley.

Holding up the suspect's picture, Walsh says, "Hey, there he is, Keys."

As Keys pulls to the curb, Jerry yells at the man to stop where he is. The man takes off running.

Walsh looks over at Keys, "You gonna get 'im?"

Keys yanks up the handbrake. "You missed 'im, you chase the horse's ass."

"You gettin' too old for this, Barry?"

"Not too old, just too smart. You chase 'im down the alley, I'll meet you at the other end."

Walsh jumps out to chase while Keys lurches the old Dodge off down the street. At the end of the alley Keys waits for the man they spotted to show up. He sees him a moment later and ducks down behind the car's dash panel.

The black marketer is confronted by a high chain-link fence at the end of the alley. He looks over his shoulder to see Walsh maybe 30 yards behind, pounding down the alley after him. Panicking, he scans around frantically, then pulls a garbage can over to the fence. He mounts the can, then reaches up to pull himself to the top of the fence.

Straddling the top of the fence, his panic subsided, he stops to thumb his nose at Walsh. He drops down, hears a car's engine rev and is pinned to the fence by a huge, rusted-chrome Dodge bumper.

Keys is sitting behind the wheel, smoking a cigarette, enjoying the man's discomfort when Walsh gets to the fence. Keys gets out of the car, handcuffs the black-marketer to the fence, then gets back in the car. He backs the car up, gets out to release one cuff, and puts the man in the back seat of the Dodge.

Walsh is bent over, hands on knees, cheeks red, gasping for air on the other side of the fence. Keys leans on the Dodge's fender. "So, who's too old, Jer?"

Back in the FBI office Keys sat at his desk waiting for his next assignment. The small cases he was getting were setting him on edge. He had twenty years in and knew quitting was the only way he was going to get Mary back. He was wrestling with making a final decision when he was assigned to lead a case that involved a German spy ring.

It started with a sailor stationed at Mare Island who came to Keys with a wild story about being kidnapped. The sailor claimed the kidnappers wanted submarine secrets and would kill his adopted shipyard family to get them.

Keys hoped this would be the case that would bring back the pride and excitement in the FBI he was missing. At the end of the case that took Keys to Mexico, he found the Mexican FBI man was involved with the spies. As Keys concluded the case, he received a note luring him to a supposed informant. The place was dark and deserted; he knew then it was a trap set by the Mexican agent. A bandito came into the light from an industrial building. His gold teeth caught the light as did the long blade of his knife. Keys drew his gun, taking a bead on the gold-toothed bandito.

A second bandito threatened his back. The one with gold teeth taunted him; Keys had cocked his pistol, ready to take him down, when Jerry Walsh raced to his side. Both banditos scurried off into the night.

When he returned to the 111 Sutter Street FBI headquarters instead of receiving a "job well done", he was under suspicion. The Mexican agent had wired ahead protesting his innocence. The man accused Keys of running guns into Mexico.

AGENT KEYS STEPS OUT

His San Francisco FBI boss, Frank Gray, told Keys he had messed up the entire case. Washington wanted answers: was Keys dirty? Keys told Gray the Mexican agent was dirty, not him, and if Washington wanted his badge they could have it. Gray ordered Keys to calm down. Keys threw his badge and gun down and stomped out the door slamming it so hard the glass shattered behind him.

***

North of the city, Mary found the work at Marinship extremely rewarding. At first, she was caught up in the excitement and thought little of anything else. But the shipyard was filling up with new workers every day. Her job was becoming redundant and Mary missed Keys terribly. Some women she knew at Marinship lost their husbands and lovers in the war; still they held their heads up and continued their work.

Keys and Mary had been apart almost two years. The turning point was Nick Devin, the sailor caught up in the espionage case Keys was assigned to. Devin, who shared the deadly adventure with Barry, told Mary he knew how badly Keys needed her, and that she and Barry belonged together.

Mary enjoyed an emotional reunion with Barry at a party in John's Grill where Keys announced his retirement from the FBI.

Chapter 1

On a cool March 1944 San Francisco morning, the 5-foot 11-inch, 42-year-old ex-FBI agent Barry Keys and his wife, Mary, look out across Mason Street to a street-level office. From their third-floor apartment both look down with fresh anticipation at the letters on the office window below.

"Keys' Detective Agency" in gold leaf boldly announces the couple's new venture.

1944 has been an unusually wet year, but the morning rain does not dampen the Keys' spirits as they trot across the street to their new office. The new business is not the only reason for their optimism. The nation's spirits also received a much-needed lift after months of bad news about American defeats at Japanese hands. San Franciscans, once sure of an invasion, rejoiced with the recent good news of naval victories.

AGENT KEYS STEPS OUT

Our American military was turning the tides of war in both Europe and the Pacific. Now the offensive war efforts raise the hopes of many that the end could be in one or two years instead of the five or more years some notables had predicted.

A little before lunch time, Mary Keys shows Jerry Walsh, Barry's FBI ex-partner, into Keys' new office.

"Look who I found," Mary says.

A broad smile is also reflected in Keys' pale blue eyes as he comes around his desk to shake Walsh's hand. Even after a fresh shave Barry's five o'clock shadow never seems to leave his square-jawed face.

"Hey, buddy, how's it goin'?" Keys asks.

Walsh takes a moment to look over the office. "Pretty impressive digs for an old worn-out gumshoe. This is the broom closet, isn't it? Well, at least you've got a pretty secretary to brighten the place up."

"Ha,ha. Whatta ya got in the bag, Jer?"

"I brought you a present to celebrate the new business."

Walsh pulls a bottle of scotch from the bag. "All the hot detectives I've read about have a bottle in a desk drawer. I didn't want you to be embarrassed when a client asks for a drink. How's it going? You got any big investigations yet?"

Keys takes the bottle, making a show of putting it in the desk drawer.

"Thanks, Jerry, have a seat. All I've done so far is spread the word I'm in the business. I did have a young boy come in the other day wanting me to find his lost dog. I couldn't find the mutt so I bought him a puppy."

Mary goes to Keys, resting her hand on his shoulder. "I told Barry we would probably need the tax break after the business gets going anyway."

Walsh chuckles. "Oh yeah, I can see that. You'll be rakin' it in. I hope Mary keeps you out of trouble with all the femmes fatales you private dicks always get involved with."

"Not while I'm here. He's *my* private dick." Mary covers her mouth with her hand, blushing with embarrassment. "Oops, that's not how I meant that."

Walsh looks at Keys, trying to keep a straight face, but as soon as their eyes meet there is no holding back and both break up, laughing like school boys.

After Walsh stops chuckling, he leans forward in his chair. "You did good apologizing to the boss, Barry. I know that wasn't easy for you."

"No, it wasn't, Jer, but I need to make a living. I still remember what happened to Melvin Purvis. I can't afford to get railroaded like that. I like what I do and I'm good at it, so eating crow was less important than lookin' for a night watchman's job."

"The boss said you turned in your FBI gun and ID. He was totally surprised you gave him typed reports on all your existing cases along with the twenty bucks to pay for the window you busted when you slammed his office door."

Keys smiles up at Mary. "Yeah, I had a little push to fix up the reports. Good riddance to the pistol; I never liked that short-barreled gun anyway. I'll take my model 27 with the longer barrel any day. I still say you can't hit the broad side of a barn door with that short barrel. I'm not gonna miss it.

"Anyway, I think I smoothed things over enough that they'll let me work. I may never make much money at this but I am my own boss now."

"I'll leave you boys to it," Mary says. "I've got some ads to place in the papers."

"Don't go yet Mary," Walsh says. "I may just be able to help out a little. The commandant at Mare Island Shipyard asked the boss for Barry to investigate the loss of materials at the shipyard. So, Frank Gray sent Barry's replacement out. The commandant called Gray to ball him out because the replacement guy pissed off the workers.

"The commandant says he has the shipyard working at peak levels: three shifts, 24 hours a day, seven days a week. So, our new FBI guy barges in, threatening to arrest people if they don't stop work and answer his questions. The commandant was pretty frustrated and called the base commander, Morsey, to ask what he thought. Morsey recommended that the FBI retain you because you worked with him on the Nick Devin spy case.

"Anyway, here's the deal. Gray says you can work the case as a kind of consultant. If there's any good publicity, the FBI will take the credit; your name won't be mentioned. Gray says he's covering his own butt. In exchange, you'll get standard pay plus expenses. Gray said to tell you if this works out, he might send more work your way. He wants you to report to the base commander and he wants weekly reports, too. So, what do you think?"

Keys looks to Mary, who silently claps her hands, nodding her head yes.

Keys stands up from his chair. "I say yes. Let's go celebrate over an early lunch. I'm buyin'."

Chapter 2

The next morning, Keys, sitting at the little table in the kitchen, stares down at his breakfast plate. His eggs, laying sunny-side up, are draped over slices of Spam on a corn tortilla and covered with diced onions and tomatoes.

"Uh, our bacon ration's gone already, Mary?"

"Don't stick your nose up at my breakfast 'til you try it, Barry Keys. Some people have to eat Spam everyday. You get to have a nice breakfast with real eggs, tomatoes, and onions. I got the corn tortilla idea from one of the Texas gals at Marinship."

Mary watches Keys take a tentative bite. He looks up from his plate at her, shrugs, then punctures the egg yolks. Without further comment, Keys devours the rest of the color-splashed breakfast.

Keys sets down his coffee cup. "That was not bad. Actually, it was pretty good. So, what have you got planned for today?"

Mary smiles back at Keys knowingly. "I'm going to find a good phone answering service for the office this morning. It looks like it's going to be nice today so I thought I would tend to our victory garden while you're at Mare Island."

"Isn't it too early to plant?" Keys asks.

"It is, but I need to mark our plot and tend to the soil. With all the rain we've had this winter I'll bet the weeds are knee high."

Keys takes his plate to the sink, running water to rinse it. Walking past the table, he stoops to kiss the top of Mary's round-faced head, taking in the scent of her long auburn hair.

"Do you think you'll be home for dinner?" Mary asks.

"Yes, but I'll have to depend on the ferry," Keys responds.

"Without the FBI car, we don't have enough ration points for gas or tires to use the car anymore than we have to. We're lucky to live where we really don't need to drive. I could take one of Mare Island's buses. They run from here three times a day. I just like the ferry better; plus, I can walk around if I feel like it.

"It should be an easy day. I'll meet with Commander Morsey and see how he wants to handle the investigation. He'll have to authorize a credential for me so that I can wander around the

14

base. I know my way around the waterfront from the Nick Devin case, but I haven't been anywhere else.

"They have the old elephant train from the Treasure Island exhibition to transport people around the base. If I can get some ID today, I may ride it around a little to get the lay of the land. If you find the answering service you want, have them hook up to our home phone too. We can pick up messages from here or the office, okay?"

"I read you five by five," Mary says.

"Did you get that from Nick?" Keys asks.

"Yes, he said that means the message is understood. I already thought I would set up a code word for the answering service operator so we could retrieve messages from any phone we might call from."

Keys slips on his coat and hat on his way out. "I have missed you. You've always been two steps ahead of me. I'll call in later and, if I'm back early, I'll stop by the office and make notes on the day. Hey, you know there's a premiere showing of that new Barbra Stanwyck film, *Double Indemnity.* Wanta go?"

Mary stands on her tiptoes to give Keys a peck on his cheek. "You bet, big boy, she's a favorite of mine. That woman's got so much talent and confidence I really admire her. My friend Jan, from the library, says it's a must see; she's a big Edward G. Robinson fan, and he's in it too."

As Keys opens the door to leave he turns back to Mary. "Stanwyck's a beautiful woman alright but she's got nothin' on you, kid."

Keys steps lively walking to the streetcar, his mood buoyed by Mary's return and a new career path. He exits the streetcar, walks a few blocks to cross The Embarcadero and stands in line for the Vallejo ferry. Out on the bay it's a windy day: trees on Angel Island bend back and forth as if waving to the passing ferry.

After passing through Mare Island's security, Keys makes his way to Commander Morsey's office. The commander's aide, Mitch Rider, shows Keys into the office.

The Commander's appearance and demeanor have changed since Keys last saw the man. On Keys' previous visit, the commander was a man unhappy with his lot. Today's man, a smile on his face, comes around his desk to shake Keys' hand.

"Thanks for agreeing to help us sort this problem out, Mr. Keys. I want you to know first thing that I am expecting to be ordered to New London any day now to assume command of a new boat."

"Congratulations, Commander, I can see you're ready to get to it."

"Thanks, Mr. Keys, I was beginning to think I was going to be passed over for command of my own boat. The thought of not getting into the fight weighed me down. I'm going to pass you to Captain Crane. He'll take over for me while the

16

Navy decides if this will be a permanent position for him or not."

Morsey presses a lever on the intercom box on his desk. "Mitch will show you to his office. If you need anything while I'm still here, don't hesitate to let me know. Good hunting, Mr. Keys."

The commander's aide steps into the office to show Keys to Crane's office. Before Keys leaves, he shakes Morsey's hand again.

"Good hunting to you too, Commander. I hope you clean the seas of those backstabbers."

Morsey gives Keys a jaunty salute. "I'll do my best."

Mitch leads Keys down a flight of stairs to another hallway. They pass offices, some with the doors open, other doors are shut; sailors and officers busy themselves with America's war machine.

Mitch stops at an open doorway to knock on the frame; he announces Keys, then turns back down the hallway. Keys enters to see a captain seated behind a desk and another man in a chair in front of the captain's desk.

"Come in, Mr. Keys. Morsey says you're the man for this job." He motions to the man seated in front of him.

"George Booth here is a yard supervisor. He's been here for years and knows the base inside and out. I've decided to let him run this deal. I've got a lot to do before Morsey goes, as I'm sure you can understand.

"George, why don't you take Mr. Keys to your office and get him squared away? You're in good hands, Mr. Keys. George will let me know what you find."

Booth lifts his bulk from the chair, thanks the captain and turns toward Keys. George Booth stands about 5'6 and weighs around 280. His full head of black hair, greased straight back, does not complement the unevenly grown small black mustache that crosses Booth's pock-marked face.

Keys, unamused by being passed off from one office to the next, is trying hard not to take an instant dislike to yardman Booth. He follows the man downstairs and out of the Administration building to a small clapboard building.

Booth sits behind a scarred wooden desk in a small corner office devoid of windows. There are no other chairs in the room; Keys stands with his hands in his pockets looking down on the yardman. Without waiting for Booth to begin a conversation, Keys opens.

"I'll need an ID badge today. It has to be one that will let me have access to the entire yard. I want to meet with the Supply Depot people as soon as possible."

Booth's chair creaks in protest as he leans back. He looks up at Keys, smirking.

"I don't know about any ID today, we're mighty short-handed. The Supply Depot people would want time to set up a meeting…they're real busy."

Booth pauses. "Look, Keys, we really don't need you here. We can manage the little pilfering that goes on here ourselves."

Keys leans down, resting his hands on the edge of Booth's desk.

"So you're tellin' me that you have decided to ignore the commandant's orders on your own? I should go whistle Dixie 'cause you've got this handled. Is that what you want me to report to Commander Morsey?"

Booth raises his hands in surrender. "Hey, hey, hey, don't get riled up Keys. Crane said we didn't need you. I got no juice here, man; take it easy."

Booth reaches down to open a desk drawer. Keys instinctively reaches under his coat before remembering he doesn't have his gun. Booth brings a printed form out of the drawer, not realizing what his movement to the desk caused Keys to think he was up to.

Booth slaps the form on the desk. "Look, Keys, I hear you got canned from the FBI so you could probably use some dough." Booth wiggles his bushy eyebrows. "I'll tell you what, if you don't say nothin' to Morsey, I'll make it worth your while. You sign this pay form and I'll send you a check every payday. You don't even have to be here. Easy money, right? You can take a vacation if you want. How 'bout it?"

Keys leans forward on the desk, pushing his face toward Booth. "What percentage do you get?"

"Well, you know, I gotta do all the paperwork, Keys."

Keys stands back from the desk. "You do know there's a war on…right? That kinda stuff will put you away for a long time."

Turning to go out the door, Keys says, "Enjoy Alcatraz, Booth."

"Wait up, Keys. You try and make trouble for me and I'll bury you."

"Grab your shovel, Booth. I'm headed for Commander Morsey's office right now."

Keys arrives at Morsey's outer office expecting Booth to be on his heels. He stops at the aide's desk.

"Mitch, I need to see the Commander, please. Can you get me in?"

"I think so, sir," Mitch replies. "He's totally changed since he got a boat to skipper. He wants to make things right, I kinda hate to see him go now."

Mitch returns from the Commander's office. "He'll see you now, Mr. Keys."

"Back so soon, Mr. Keys? Did you round up the pilferers that fast?"

"I found one bad apple, sir," Keys replies.

"Really? Did Captain Crane take care of the bad apple for you?"

Keys sits on a chair, taking out a cigarette. "Mind if I smoke, Commander?"

"Go ahead, smoking lamp is lit. Tell me about it, Mr. Keys."

"Just call me Keys, sir. That's what I'm used to. Your captain passed me off to a yardman named Booth. He took me to his office to tell me that I'm not needed here. He said he and Captain Crane decided that they could take care of any 'little problems'."

Morsey's eyes narrow, his face takes a serious set. Before he can speak, Keys continues with his story.

"Booth tells me the supply depot people are too busy to see me and that I can't get an ID because his people are short-staffed. He says if I'll put my signature on a pay voucher I can get a paycheck every week. I can take a vacation and he'll make sure I get the check after he takes his cut.

"I thought he was right behind me. I told him I was on my way to report back to you."

Morsey's face colors as he presses a lever on his intercom.

"Mitch," he barks, "get Captain Crane and yardman Booth to my office immediately. Do not take any excuse from either of them. As a matter of fact, take a Marine with you. I want them in my office right now!"

A startled Mitch bolts out, gathering up a Marine guard at the end of the hallway.

Morsey pats his pocket, then opens his desk, searching through a drawer. Keys shakes out a cigarette and stands to offer it to the commander. Morsey unclenches his right fist to accept the cigarette as Keys flips open his Zippo to light the Chesterfield.

Morsey takes a deep draw, then forcefully expels twin streams of smoke through his nostrils.

"Thanks, Keys. I hate guys trying to steal money our government is spending to protect vermin like that. Men and women at this yard are putting every hard-earned dollar they can in war bonds. The problem now is what to do with you.

"I need to talk to the commandant. We have to find someone we can trust. When Mitch gets back, I'll have him get you an ID while I talk to Captain Crane and Booth. If you'll excuse me a minute, I'll call the commandant. You can wait in the outer office, okay?"

Waiting in the outer office, Keys fidgets, lifting his wrist to watch the second hand of his wristwatch twitch. A half-hour later Mitch enters, followed by Captain Crane who looks very small and sheepish in contrast to the huge Marine behind him. Mitch knocks on Morsey's door before entering.

As Crane waits standing by the desk, he gives Keys a hard look. Keys returns the look with a harder one of his own. "You got something you wanta say to me, Crane?" The captain looks away. A few minutes later Mitch returns to usher Captain Crane into Morsey's office.

Mitch sits behind his desk before addressing the Marine.

"Gunney, thanks for your help. If we need you, I'll come get you."

The Marine snaps a salute, turns and exits, his shoulders just clearing the door frame.

"Mr. Keys," Mitch says, "Commander Morsey would like you to wait until he's finished with Captain Crane."

Keys sits down in a chair. "I'm beginning to feel like I'm the player no one wants in this game."

"I'm sorry, Mr. Keys. I don't think you'll be in for a long wait. I know you've won over the commander again. He said you'd only been here a short time and you already found two bad apples."

Keys notes Mitch's grin. "You look like the cat that ate the canary, so give with the story."

Mitch sits forward in his chair, eager to start his tale.

"When I got to Captain Crane's office, he ordered me out, saying that he'd see the commander when he had time. He lost all that bravado when I called in the Marine gunnery sergeant. The Marine winked, and asked me if I wanted Crane handcuffed. It was all I could do to keep a straight face. 'No,' I tell him real cool like, 'that won't be necessary'. When I got to George Booth's office, it looked like he cleaned out his desk and vanished."

Chapter 3

Mitch and Keys both look up at the sound of Morsey's angry, raised voice. Minutes later, Captain Crane, eyes downcast, shoulders slumped, emerges from Morsey's office. Morsey comes to the doorway and asks Keys and Mitch to wait a little longer as he has to call the commandant back.

"Would you like a cigarette while we wait, Mr. Keys?"

"Thanks, Mitch, I would. I'm just about out of Chesterfields and the stores in the City are out of all the good brands."

"I've got a fresh pack here, Mr. Keys, and I can get you more if you want."

"Are you the local black-market man, Mitch?"

"No, sir. You may forget this is a Navy base. Our PX has a lot of stuff civilians can't get. Cigarettes, vegetables, fruits, meats, people on this yard aren't goin' hungry I can tell you. Our submariners are the best-fed fighting men in the world."

"In that case, I'll take you up on the cigarettes, Mitch, and call me Keys, my friends do."

Morsey comes to the doorway to beckon the men in.

"Take a seat, men. The commandant has worked a deal to keep me here. I don't mind telling you that I thought I'd lost my chance for a sub command. But the deal he made is that I'm going to get the next new boat that's being built here. I'll probably be in the fight even before the boat I was assigned at New London.

"The commandant wants me here to oversee your investigation, Keys. He's very concerned about the materials that are being stolen from our inventory. He wants to make sure Navy personnel are not involved. Captain Crane denies any wrongdoing. But I'm not so sure he hasn't some involvement.

"So what do you need to get going, Keys? You have my full support, and I mean every word of that. I'll be on the yard for as long as it takes to get my new boat ready."

"Thank you, sir. I'll need a credential that will allow me to access the yard, sir. I'm thinking some kind of supply inspector. I need to be able to wander the yard and inspect any freight cars and any storage buildings.

"The credential needs to be something that can't be traced back. I'll have the FBI make up a fake background for me in case anybody checks. With Booth in the wind, I'd like to take over his office. It could be very interesting to see who shows up there with their hands out."

"Good idea, Keys. Mitch can get you started. He knows all the ins-and-outs of this place. Stay in touch with him; he'll know more scuttlebutt than me about anything that happens here. As long as I'm here, I will be available to you."

Keys stands from his chair to shake hands with Morsey.

"I'll need to be able to carry a gun here, sir."

Morsey comes around his desk. He stops and rubs his chin in thought. "I don't want gun play here. I know that may sound silly with all the armed Marines here, but you're a civilian."

"I carried a gun here with the FBI sir, and I am on loan to you from the FBI as their consultant. I hate getting shot and I feel naked without it. I'll be operating on my own without any backup. That's a dangerous thing to do in my profession."

"Okay, Keys," Morsey extends his hand to shake Keys hand. "You've already proved yourself, that's why you're here. Mitch, see to it this man gets whatever he needs. Report as often as you can, Keys. I need to keep the commandant informed."

Keys gives Morsey a good-natured salute. "Captain has the word," he says.

Mitch closes the door to Morsey's office behind them.

"Let's go get your yard pass taken care of first. Do you want something from the Navy or a civilian ID? Will you want to get into the freight cars?"

Keys snaps his fingers. "Bingo, that gives me an idea. I don't want anyone to think I'm a replacement for Booth. I don't have enough information about what he was into here. If anyone asks, I was sent by the railroad as a safety inspector.

"I think a safety inspector can go anywhere there's railroad tracks, and into any freight cars, locomotives, or shops. That oughta do it for me."

"Sounds good to me," Mitch says. "We'll need to get your picture taken for a yard badge."

"Okay, let's go get that done. I want to get back to Booth's office as soon as possible and go through whatever he left behind. I need to have the lock changed on that office door, too."

Mitch smacks his forehead with the heel of his hand. "I shoulda thought of that; I'll call and have that done while we get your credentials."

Mitch stays with Keys during the registration process to make sure there are no delays. When they are done, he takes Keys to the locksmith shop to get the new keys to Booth's old office.

Mitch leads the way into the locksmith's. "Hey Smitty, did you get to the lock in 125?"

"Hiya, Mitch. Yeah, I got it, but it looked to me like I was a mite too late. Someone pulled the file drawers out and dumped the papers all over the floor."

Mitch slams his fist on the counter. "I shoulda thought about having you change the lock sooner Smitty. Thanks for getting right on it though. This is Mr. Keys, Smitty. He's the new railroad safety inspector that'll be using that office."

Smitty shakes Keys' hand over the counter and lays down two new keys.

"Pleased to meet you, Mr. Keys. Here's your new keys."

"Thanks, Smitty. Just call me Keys. Do you have keys for every building on the yard?"

"Some I do and some they don't want out, but there ain't hardly a one I can't get into," the locksmith says with a wily grin.

Mitch reaches across the counter to shake the locksmith's hand. "If you need anything I can help with, let me know, Smitty."

"Sure thing, Mitch."

Mitch leads the way back to Building 125. Walking down Railroad Avenue, they pass the huge concrete smokestack of the island's powerhouse. Keys turns to Mitch, wanting to know more about Morsey's aide.

"Seems like you know everybody on this yard, Mitch."

"No, not everyone, but I do make it my business to know the Navy officers, and the shops' foremen. If you want something done around here it pays to know who can do it and have them know me. If I need to grease the wheels, they know I'll do my best. Sometimes I can trade for something they need, to make things I need happen faster."

Keys nods knowingly. "I think you're a very valuable man to know. Are you gonna ship out with Morsey?"

Mitch stops walking. "How do you know about that?"

"Like I said, you're a very valuable man. I don't think Morsey would want to let go of you."

"You're a good thinker, Mr. Keys. The commandant doesn't want me to go, and I haven't been to submarine school. That's a good excuse, but I don't know how I'll feel if I don't get into this war."

Keys rests his hand on Mitch's shoulder. "You are in this war, Mitch. You may be more valuable here than at sea. But I know it's a big decision only you can make. If you'd like to talk about it over a beer with a non-Navy man, let me know."

Mitch cocks his head, looking at Keys, sizing him up. "You're not what I expected, Keys. I may take you up on that."

As they enter Building 125's hallway, Mitch steps aside to let Keys unlock the door.

Both men enter the office to survey the damage. The shabby 8-by-10 room was intended as a storage space for the building when the small offices were dashed up during the war's need for expansion. Exposed electrical conduit and phone wires that provide power and communication are stapled to the walls, exaggerating the room's unfinished appearance.

Gray metal file cabinets line two of the walls. They stand square-holed, the drawers pulled out, littering the floor. File folders and paperwork are scattered everywhere. The old desk drawers add to the clutter.

"I'm sorry about this, Keys." Mitch turns to the door, eyes darting down the hallway. "Gossip travels around this place at the speed of sound. The yard's probably alive with stories about you. I can call the commander and get some time to help you clean up."

"I'd rather do it myself, Mitch. I wanta look over all this paperwork; there may be something here I need to see. I'll reorganize this stuff so I can find something in the future that may be important. Someone wanted to find something here. There may be a gap in the files that will lead me to what they were after."

"Sounds like a lot of work. I always think of detectives shooting it out with the bad guys and gettin' all the great lookin' dames."

"I can do without the shoot-outs, Mitch, but I am married to the greatest lookin' dame there is.

I'll tell you, though, most of detecting is putting pieces of a puzzle together. A lot of that is pretty boring stuff: the chase is the buzz."

Mitch lifts his shoulders with a shrug. "I guess I thought it would be more like Dick Tracy. Well, okay, Keys. I'll send the rest of your ID paperwork down here when I get it. Let me know if you need anything I can help with."

Keys begins his cleanup, gathering the files and paperwork, then stacking them on the desk. He returns the drawers to the file cabinets and the desk after inspecting the drawer's bottoms and sides for any concealed papers that could be taped onto them. On the bottom of one desk drawer is an outline of sticky tape residue the size of a business envelope.

Keys gets a line out on the phone to the Sutter Street FBI office. "Frank, Keys here. We need to find a suspect from Mare Island. The guy bolted as soon as I braced him. His name is George Booth; his home address is in Richmond. Can you put someone on it?"

The FBI boss, Frank Gray, grins at his end of the phone. "You didn't waste any time, did you? So how long have you been there anyway? Oh, never mind that. Who's this Booth and what's going on?"

Keys explains his run-in with Booth and that the man bolted. "Someone searched Booth's office and I'm goin' through the stuff now. I don't know that Booth is involved in the stolen materials but he is in on the fake wages scam we've seen at other yards.

"I'll bet he's got a nice big nest egg put away somewhere. That may be what whoever searched this office was lookin' for. If you can find him, we may break this whole thing in a hurry."

"That's good work, Keys. I'll put some men on it and let you know. By the way, I'm still your boss. In the future, my title is Mr. Gray, or boss."

"Yes, sir, Frank," Keys replies, hanging up the phone.

Gray looks at the dead phone receiver in his hand. "You're a real piece of work, Keys."

Chapter 4

Keys shuffles the stacks of files to make space on the desktop. In the cramped space, Keys notes the papers he goes through, recording what they contain and where he files them. The stack of papers slowly diminishes. Most of the papers are normal work and supply requisition orders, duly signed off.

"Hey, what the hell you doin' in here with all them papers?"

Key's head snaps up. He did not hear the intruder until the man's outburst.

"I'm the new safety inspector and this is now my office. Who the hell are you?"

The intruder wears a hardhat, rakishly tilted over one ear. His face is almost hidden by a bushy mustache and the huge stub of an unlit cigar in his mouth.

"I'm askin' the questions here, buddy. Where's Booth? Me an' him's got business. I don't need no guff from no pencil pusher."

Another man enters the room. "Hey Casey, I heard you hollerin'. What's goin' on?"

Casey's cigar juts up and down as he answers. "Hiya, Biff. Looks to me like this here pencil pusher's tryin' to muscle in on Booth's business."

"That right, buddy?" Biff growls.

Keys' face colors as he pushes back from the desk to rise. "I'm gonna need to see your yard badges."

Biff rushes forward, shoving the desk across the floor toward the wall. The desk legs screech loudly, skidding across the wood floor. Keys, taken by surprise, fights to keep his chair upright. He leans forward to protect his head as he is smashed back against the wall.

Biff struggles with the desk, pushing hard to keep a thrashing Keys pinned. Turning his head, he yells at Casey. "You wanta learn this boy a lesson?"

"Yeah, I'll smack the story outta him. Okay, buddy, what's your deal? You tryin' ta move in on Booth's territory or what? Give with the dope or I'll have ta get rough."

Keys stretches his feet under the desk to brace it. He holds his hands on the desk's edge as if to keep pushing back against Biff. He grins at up Casey. "You don't look tough enough to shine my shoes."

Casey lashes out with his left hand. Keys ducks away, then grabs the man's arm, pulling him over the top of the desk. The man's Bakelite hardhat bounces off the desk to skitter across the floor. Grabbing a handful of hair, Keys slams Casey's head down on the desktop.

Casey's yells come from the side of his face that is not mashed on the desk. "Jesus, get 'im offa me, Biff."

Biff lets go of the desk to pull Casey away. Keys quickly pushes the desk away from him with his legs, knocking Biff back, who pulls Casey down with him.

"These boys givin' you any trouble, Mr. Keys?"

The big gunnery sergeant Keys saw at Morsey's office hauls the two men off the floor by the back of their collars, the men struggling to pull away.

"Stop makin' a fuss or I'll bang your heads together so hard your ears'll ring for a week," the Marine shouts.

Keys smiles up at the big Marine. "Thanks gunnery sergeant; I'm mighty glad you showed up."

The Marine shakes the two assailants like rag dolls to make them stop struggling. "Mitch told me I oughta look out for you, Mr. Keys. He gave me some papers for you."

"Well, sergeant, let's herd these bad boys up to the commander's office. I'm kinda anxious to hear what their story's gonna be."

The gunnery sergeant marches the men in front of him to Commander Morsey's office.

Keys enters the office behind the Marine. He approaches Mitch's desk as the commander's aide looks over the men with a bemused grin.

"You certainly don't waste any time do you, Mr. Keys?"

"It sorta seems like I'm a magnet for federal felons around here." Keys turns to look over the two men the Marine holds on to.

"Hey, wait a minute, we didn't do nothin' federal," Biff calls out.

"Sergeant, could you keep these boys quiet while I speak to the commander?" Keys asks.

"Yes, sir," the Marine replies. He shakes both men so hard their heads flop on their necks. "Don't say another word."

"Can I see the commander, Mitch?" Keys asks.

"Let me ask him, Mr. Keys. I'll be right back."

Mitch comes back out of the commander's office, standing at the doorway.

"The commander says you're taking up a lot of his time," Mitch grins.

Keys walks past Mitch into Morsey's office and turns to close the door behind him.

"Don't get up, commander, I'll only be a minute. These two men jumped me in Booth's office. I want to have the FBI come pick them up and take them to San Francisco. I don't want them, or the post police to know who I am or that I'm investigating here. They're pretty scared now.

If you'll rattle 'em a bit, I think they'll spill all they know to the feds."

"I'll see what I can do, Keys. It'll probably be the most fun I'm gonna have today. While you call the FBI, have Moose march 'em on in here."

"Moose is the gunnery sergeant I take it?"

Morsey looks up at Keys. "That's what they call him around here, and with some respect I might add."

Keys calls to the gunnery sergeant from Morsey's door. "Sergeant, the commander wants to see those two rats before the FBI comes for them. March 'em on in, would you?"

Keys pulls Morsey's office door shut after the sullen two men are marched past. He turns to Mitch's desk to phone FBI headquarters. He is almost to the phone when he thinks his call would be better placed in private.

"Mitch, I'll be over at my office if the commander needs me. Okay?"

"Yes, sir, Mr. Keys, I'll let the commander know."

In the commander's office, the two men stand in front of Morsey's desk. "We didn't do nothin' wrong here, man," Casey blurts out. "You can't let nobody take us. We got rights. We ain't in the Navy. I demand to see my union rep!"

"Sergeant, you will gag both of these rats if they speak again without my permission," Morsey bellows. "You two have forfeited any rights you may think you have. If I can prove you have been getting double wages, or any kind of payoffs, I'll

37

personally see you go to Alcatraz for as many years as possible.

"You are stealing from the government that is protecting you from a vicious enemy. You are stealing from your fellow workers here on the island. If I had my way I would have you both shot on the Marine's firing range today.

"Sergeant, strip their ID badges off and put them on my desk. I want to remember their names. I hope the FBI doesn't make any deals with you two. The men at Alcatraz are gonna take a dim view of two birds that sold-out America."

Staring into the two men's worried faces with a glare that would melt steel, the Marine rips the badges from their shirts.

"Lock them up downstairs, sergeant; they're stinking up my office. Find another Marine to guard them and report back to me."

The big Marine carries out Morsey's orders and returns to his office.

Morsey marks a place in the manual he is reading before he addresses the Marine. "Sergeant, I want you to look after Mr. Keys when you can. The man gets results, but he's on his own here and I don't want him getting into trouble. I'm not asking you to babysit, just do what you can when your other duties allow."

The Marine answers in the affirmative and with a smart salute leaves the commander's office. He decides to look in on Keys to get his take on what dangers he sees. As he goes out of the building he pays little attention to the power house's tall smoke stack across the street on Railroad Avenue. The pall of smoke it adds to the all ready overcast sky blunts any sunlight and reflects the noise of the busy yard. The Marine thinks he hears angry voices.

Rounding the corner of the Administration Building the sergeant sees Keys confronted by a group of yardmen in front of Keys' office building. No one in the group takes notice of the Marine as he approaches from the rear.

"I'm tellin' you," the Marine hears Keys explain, "I'm a railroad inspector. They gave me Booth's office after he left. I don't know where he went or what he was into. Two yard birds jumped me in the office and just got hauled off. If any a you guys want the same trouble, the FBI will be here later today."

A loud voice comes from the group. "You're the one we got trouble with right now. We heard you put the feds onto Casey and Biff, so you got trouble with us now."

"There won't be no trouble at all," the Marine booms. The group angrily turns to the intruder and, to a man, shrinks at the Marine's bulk. One of the yardmen turns back to Keys. "You're new here buddy, you ain't got no idea how we run this place."

"You don't run this place," Keys snarls, "the Navy runs this place. If any a you guys are into anything other than doin' the job the Navy gave you, you'll get the same treatment those other two guys are gettin'."

"You ain't seen the last of us, buddy. The Moose ain't always gonna be around. Let's go, men."

Chapter 5

"Thanks again, sergeant. You must have some kinda sixth sense for me getting' in trouble."

"I'm just doin' what the commander asked me to do, Mr. Keys."

"Come on inside, sergeant. I wanta see if they got into my office."

Keys unlocks his untouched office door. "I guess they didn't come in after all. I'd offer you a chair but I don't have another one. What do I call you other than sergeant?"

"They call me Moose, sir."

Keys pushes his desk back away from the wall. "That's okay, if that's what you want me to call you. You can call me Keys, my friends do. Barry Keys is my name."

"Larry Mazurki is my name, sir. People have called me Moose since high school. I guess I'm

41

stuck with it. I don't mind, it's better than some names I've been called."

"How 'bout I call you Larry, if you stop with the sir stuff?"

"Sounds fair s… uh, Keys."

"Let me ask you, Larry, do you know any of those guys that were here? We may have more guys that are up to no good. Part of my job is to weed 'em outta here."

"Briggs Marvin is the loud mouth. I don't think he's into anything other than runnin' his mouth. He's a guy that just wants to have people think he's tough. Some a the guys call him Jelly behind his back. From what I've seen around here is 99.9 per cent of the people on this yard are the most dedicated yard workers there are.

"These people not only pull their shifts, they stay over to make sure the next shift can go straight to work. If the next shift needs help knowing where to start or what materials they're gonna need, the previous shift helps 'em along. These are mighty good men and women here, Keys."

"That's good to hear, Larry. I'd like to believe all these people are here to win this war. How long have you been here?"

"Since last year." The big Marine reaches down to knock on his right shin. The hollow sound made by his knuckles surprises Keys; it's not wood, he can't place it.

"They made me a new lower leg after I got it blown off on Guadalcanal. The hospital here is doing great pioneering work with prosthetics. They made this leg, then trained me to use it. I hardly pay any attention to it anymore."

Keys pulls his eyes away from the Marine's leg. "You carry yourself very well, Larry. I wouldn't have known."

"It's okay. They won't let me fight Japs anymore but they didn't take the Corps away from me. The Corps is my life. Light duty here is better than bein' drummed outta the Marines."

"You're a good man to have around, Larry. The reports I've seen about Guadalcanal said there were more men lost to disease than fighting. It musta been a lousy place to be."

The big Marine shrugs. "We lost a lotta good men, but not near as many as they did."

The Marine faces Keys but no longer sees him. The expression on his face goes hard; he is back on Guadalcanal.

"Their guys were dyin' like flies; our Marines just kept on fightin' even if they were sick. I'll say one thing for the Japs, they kept makin' frontal assaults. Wave after wave that were plain murder. I guess they figured we'd fall back, or get overrun; we never did."

Chapter 6

In a rural section of Vallejo, a little over three miles away from Keys' Mare Island office, four men are plotting his demise.

Three men sit on fruit crates listening to Heinrich Roedman in an old barn off Benicia Avenue. Heinrich, or Harry Bower as he is known to the three men, is a slim man. His long face is marked by an injury that pinched in a cheek bone and left him with a crooked nose. He has little facial hair but a full head of light brown hair.

The barn sits at the far corner of the lot, away from the road, by a stand of old live oak trees. Gnarled branches rustled by wind reach out to leave fan-like impressions on it's rust-streaked tin roof. Heinrich has lived in the barn since he escaped from a Sharp Park guard where he was being detained for illegal entry into the United States.

A small wiry man bangs the hilt of his knife on the plank table the men are gathered around. "I say we slit his throat and be done with him. Booth told me the Feds sent the guy here to find us. We got a good thing here; double pay for doin' nothin' and all we can steal. I'll kill 'im tonight if he's there."

Harry jumps up from his crate, his pale face coloring.

"Shut up, Tom. That's all you want to do is kill something. We still have to get rid of Booth's body. I told you not to kill him until we found out where he hid his money."

Tom plunges the knife's blade into the plank. "And all you wanta do is blow up the damned ammo depot. That ain't gonna make us any money."

Harry pulls the knife out of the plank and lays it down in front of Tom. "Money, money, money, it's not about money. Blowing up the arsenal could seriously damage their war effort. It sends a message that these bastards are vulnerable to espionage. You know Ireland wants to be rid of the English, and my country is willing to help."

Tom picks up his knife, wipes it with a handkerchief and returns it to a sheath on his belt. "Bah, Ireland. Just cause my Ma and Pa come from there don't mean much to me. I'm in this for the dough." He looks pointedly at the faces of the other two men. "Am I right boys?"

Harry doesn't want to lose control of the men. He hurriedly interjects before the other two can join in.

"Look, we can still make this work. There's plenty of money to be made. I know you men love Ireland, and you know I love my country. We can strike a blow for both our countries and get rich doing it too. Right now, I need Alby and Rian to get to Booth's place and find where he hid his money."

"Why ain't I goin'?" Tom asks. "And what are we gonna do with the Keys guy?"

"You think you can run this deal, Tom?" Harry demands. "Where do you think the money came from to start this? I found Booth, got all of you yard badges and paid to get your cars fixed to haul out the stuff we stole. I found the black-market guys to sell our stuff to. I got our files out of Booth's office." Harry looks at the men at the table trying to gauge their reaction.

"If we kill the Federal man now, the people that sent him will flock to the yard in droves. That will certainly shut us down. We won't be able to make a move. That means no money and having to lay low until they leave, if they ever leave. Is that what you want?"

Harry stops to catch his breath. Looking the men at the table, he reaches out to his best bet. "How about you Alby, what do you think?"

Alby is the largest man of the group. His child-like face fits his slow, gentle nature. Harry relies on his physical strength for heavy work.

Alby sheepishly looks at the others then answers, "You're the boss, Harry."

The third man, Rian, is heavyset and prone to dark moods. He is the least educated man of the group, with a violent temper matched only by Tom's.

Before Rian can answer, Tom surrenders.

"Okay, Harry, you made your point. You're the boss, but why can't I go look for Booth's money?"

"Because you're going to help me get rid of Booth's body. I have to live in this rat hole so I can protect our goods and stay away from the police. I don't need Booth's corpse stinkin' up this place. Maybe you can think up a way to get him out of here while I send Alby and Rian on their way."

Harry leans on the doorsill of Alby's car. "You two watch for cops when you get to the house. If anyone reported Booth missing, the cops may have the place watched. Remember to wear gloves; don't forget your fingerprints are on file at the shipyard. Do not leave any fingerprints."

Harry sees the two men off, then returns to the barn. He stops short in the doorway. "Holy Christ, Tom! What the hell are you doing?"

Tom is poised over Booth's body. He is using a wooden hand saw to remove a leg. Bloody body parts are scattered on a canvas tarp.

Tom looks up at Harry, grinning. "I'm makin' it easy to get rid of our ol' buddy Booth. Ain't no different than butcherin' a hog. After dark, we can dump this stuff in the river."

Harry doesn't want to watch the grizzly scene and goes to his room. Shutting the door behind him, Harry looks somberly around the room. He finished the inside with materials that he and his crew stole from Mare Island. The walls and ceiling are plastered and paneled, insulating it from the outside. His floor is covered with tile and thick rugs. The bed frame is military issue but the mattress is a premium one he had Alby buy from Macy's in San Francisco.

He has all the modern amenities a room can have, but he still feels trapped. Annoyed, and depressed, the provocateur turns on his Zenith radio to drown out the sawing noise. Thinking of Tom a few yards away happily butchering Booth, reminds Harry that he views Americans as a society of mongrels. He vehemently believes in Germany's efforts to cleanse its population to produce a true Aryan race that will rule the earth.

Harry, aka Heinrich, was deported from America in 1934 for illegal entry and subversive activities. After he arrived back in Germany, the Abwehr sent him to undergo extensive training. His heavy accent hindered his earlier US activities. An Abwehr controller sent him to a voice coach who relentlessly pounded on Harry until he could speak English, embellished with American slang, like a native.

His combat and espionage training were brutal, more so than necessary. In a local rathskeller Harry foolishly decided to chat up his drill instructor's comely girlfriend. The instructor, a stodgy brute, did not see the charm in the man his girlfriend had. During a combat training session Harry was knocked cold when he missed a parry with his rifle and received his drill instructor's rifle butt in his face for the mistake.

After the bandages were removed, Harry held up a mirror to see his reflection. The mashed nose and misshapen cheek he saw shocked him. Moments later a new light came to his eyes; his mood lightened. Grinning into his reflection he realized no one in America would recognize him as Heinrich Roedman.

Harry Bower returned to America to bring the mongrel race to its knees. In early 1938 he jumped ship in San Diego and, after escaping from Sharp Park, made his way to the West Coast's most important Naval Shipyard. When he presented himself for employment, he found the Navy was crippled with government budget cuts: Mare Island wasn't hiring.

Harry knew what to do. Across the Mare Island Strait in Vallejo, old Georgia Street was lined with bars; here was where he could mine all the information he needed. The Abwehr provided him with plenty of money. Buying drinks for his newfound friends soon paid off.

A dark-haired fat man elbowed his way to Harry's side at the bar. "I hear you're lookin' for somebody to help you get a job on the Mare Island yard."

Harry looked the man over. "If you got any connections, I got some moolah."

"That's always a big motivator, my friend. George Booth's the name. Why don't we go somewhere we can talk?"

"Hey, George," one of the barflies yelled above the din. "Don't be takin' my new buddy away."

Harry throws some bills on the bar. "Next round's on me, boys."

Outside in the sun it was an unusually hot, humid day. Booth wiped his reddened face with a handkerchief.

"I know a place down the street that's cool on a day like this. We can talk there."

Harry pulled a knife out of his pocket; he unfolded the blade and scraped under his fingernail as they walked.

"I don't mind talkin' friend, but I didn't just fall off the turnip truck either."

Booth did an admirable job of looking shocked. "No, no. It's not like that. I can help you. You ain't gonna get rolled where we're goin'. Look, I know everybody at the yard that's got juice. If you've got some dough to spread around I can get you hired."

"You got my attention," Harry says.

The house was a squat old adobe. The thick walls and Spanish tile roof insulated the interior from the sun's punishing heat. Harry stood just inside the door to let his eyes adjust to the darkness. Booth had vanished into another room. Just as Harry was about to leave, Booth re-emerged with two bottles of beer.

Booth sat the sweating bottles down on a table and motioned Harry over. "Have a seat, Harry. It's nice and cool here. We can talk without anybody hearin' nothin'."

After Harry's eyes became accustomed to the dim light, he stepped down onto uneven stone floor tiles to the table and chairs. The room was small; a cabinet filled with plates and cups was the only other furniture in the room.

He took a chair against a wall where he could see the rest of the room. Booth raised his beer bottle. "Drink up, my friend. The Navy yard is a place full a opportunities for guys smart enough to find 'em."

Harry raised his bottle to his lips but did not drink.

"I'm a guy that's lookin' for opportunities, Booth. So, what's it gonna cost me? What's your take?"

"You give me a hundred bucks and I can find you a job on the yard. I take ten percent of your wages for my end. What kinda work do you do, Harry?"

Booth gulps down the rest of his beer. "You ain't drinkin', Harry."

Harry pushes his bottle toward Booth. "Nah, I've had enough today, you can have it."

His trust in Booth goes up a notch when the fat man grins at Harry, then lifts the bottle to take a deep pull.

"Ten percent's too much, Booth, but I'll tell you what. You get me on a graveyard shift in the freight yard and I'll make the deal."

"You already got something goin', Harry? You know something I should know?"

Harry smiles back at Booth. "I know where there's usually easy pickin's."

"Okay, pal, but it'll cost you another hundred."

The game of cat and mouse over, Harry sits back in his chair.

"I'll make it another fifty, Booth. Don't get too greedy. I'm sure we'll be doin' more business."

Harry was in a good mood. After leaving Booth, he decided to find someone to help him celebrate. A woman of the street plied her trade well and Harry was exhausted. When she demanded more money for what she called extra services, Harry's good mood vanished; he punched her, knocking her to the floor and left.

Some days later he found, to his dismay, the woman had a good customer who was also the local police sergeant. A police poster with a description of his face now made it dangerous for him to go out in the daytime without a disguise. A beard made his face itch, from now on he would have to use a fake one when he had to go out in public.

All the pain he went through recuperating from damaging his face was wasted. Harry grew angry for his mistake with the hooker. He thought he should have shut her up for good. The old barn would become his virtual self-imposed prison. Only Mare Island in the dark of night had any real safety for him.

Chapter 7

Rian and Alby ride in silence to Booth's house in North Richmond. Alby keeps his '36 Ford sedan in good running order because Harry demanded it upon threat of death. The cars must never be allowed to break down. Some of the materials they steal from Mare Island are transported in their cars. Rian looks over at Alby waiting to see if he is going to stop at Booth's house.

"Yeah, I see it." Alby flashes Rian a dirty look. "You ain't any smarter'n me."

The little three-room house is beside a small hill on Garden Tract Road. The whitewashed exterior, baked by the sun, has faded to a dusty brown. Weeds, glistening from the rain, grow tall around the lot. Only the driveway and a path to the front door are beaten down.

The men get out of the car taking care to walk down the pathway to try the front door. "No soap," Rian says. "Take the car down the road and park it. I'll see if I can find another way in."

Alby returns to the house to find Rian at the back door trying to force the lock. "Give me a hand, Alby. You can probably twist the damned knob off."

Alby grips the knob and twists it off in his big right hand. The door remains locked. Alby drops the knob with a smirk and takes a pace back; he charges the door, using his shoulder to hit it. The doorjamb explodes: splinters the shape of knife blades scatter in all directions. The door flies inward, hits a wall and bounces back on its hinges. Alby extends his arm using the palm of his hand to stop it with a dull thump.

Rian steps back from the house to see if the noise stirred anyone. There are no other homes close by and few cars on the road. Satisfied no one will bother them, he follows Alby into the house. The broken doorway yawns open to a tiny kitchen.

Rian catches up to Alby and barks a command. "You keep a watch on the road; I'll make a quick search."

Alby turns to face Rian, cocking his head as if he doesn't understand. "Harry said we'd both look for Booth's dough. He didn't say nothin' about you bein' boss."

"Look, Alby, we both know you ain't the brightest boy here. I was in the Army so I know how to give orders."

"You said you was throwed outta the Army for tryin' to kill some sergeant that called you a sissy. I don't see how that makes you no order giver. You search some, then you can watch and I'll search some."

Rian, shaking his head in disgust, begins to search the kitchen. Kicking away the ruined remains of the splintered door frame he looks through cabinets next to an icebox. There are a few canned goods, plates, glasses, and utensils. The icebox has several bottles of beer, a bottle of rum, and two potatoes.

Alby looks into the kitchen. "You findin' anything?"

"Jesus Alby, I just started. The guy musta ate out. There's nothin' here 'cept beer and potatoes. Go on back and check the front. It won't take long to finish here and you can take the bedroom, okay?"

Ripping away a cotton curtain under the sink, Rian rummages through cans of Ajax and rat poison to finish his search of the kitchen. He throws the cleanser can in the sink and goes to the main room.

"Okay Alby, you take the bedroom and I'll watch the front."

Alby goes into the room, his hand rubbing the back of his neck as he tries to decide where to start. The sparse room has a metal-framed, unmade bed, a scarred wood night table, and a two-door clothes cabinet. One wall has a window with a roll shade pulled halfway down. By the clothes cabinet is a pinup wall calendar.

Alby opens the clothes cabinet. One side has hanging clothes, the other side has drawers. He carefully goes through the hanging clothes, then pushes them aside to look behind them. The drawers have underclothes and socks, some shirts. One of the bottom drawers has two Navy-issue Colt .45 automatic pistols with a box of cartridges.

"Hey Rian," Alby shouts, "lookit what I found."

Rian runs into the room to see Alby holding up the two pistols.

"Big deal, I thought you found some money. Did you go through everything?"

Alby looks around thoughtfully. "I didn't get the last drawer." He points to the clothes cabinet.

Rian shoots Alby a hard look, then bends down to open the bottom drawer. He finds a small metal box with a key lock. Rian holds up the box to inspect it, then shakes it. Something in the box rattles metallically. He tries to pry it open with his fingers.

"I can do it, I can open it," Alby says.

Rian shoves the box at Alby who takes the box in both hands. He can't get his fingers under the lid to pull it apart.

"Don't take your gloves off. Harry said we can't leave no fingerprints," Rian shouts.

Taking the box to the night stand, he sets it down with the lock facing up. Alby, fist balled, cocks his arm, then smashes down on the side of the box. The lid pops open and a gold pocket watch, a man's ring, papers, and some gold coins fly out onto the bed.

Rian grabs the papers from the bed. "Nothin' but a car title and some letters. That bastard had to hide a lotta dough someplace. Put the stuff back in the box an' we'll take it with us."

Alby gathers up the articles from the bed to stuff them back into the box. Rian takes the two pistols. He checks the almost-new gun's magazines finding both full. Working the slides back, he sees both pistols have rounds chambered. Pleased with the pistols, he puts one in each of his coat pockets.

"You plannin' on keepin' both a them pistols? Maybe I outta take one a them," Alby says.

"You don't know how to use 'em, you big palooka." Rian pulls a short-barreled .32 pistol from his pants pocket, pitching it underhand to Alby. "Here you can have this one. All you gotta do is aim an' pull the trigger. Did you look under the bed?"

Alby studies the little gun in his hand, his index finger barely fitting in the trigger guard. Unhappy with the trade, Alby shoves the pistol in a pocket, grabs the bed frame and flips it over on its side. The bed crashes into the wall causing the window roll shade to unlatch and flap around noisily at the top of the window.

Startled, Rian grabs the roll shade. "Take it easy Alby, you could wake the dead. There ain't no money here, let's go."

Alby rights the bed, setting it down with a crash. "We better see if there's anything in the attic first. I'll boost you up; there's an opening above the door."

Rian pulls off his coat to step into Alby's cupped hands and is lifted to the panel in the ceiling. He slides the panel out of the way and sticks his head through the opening.

"There ain't much space up in here."

Alby pushes him further into the attic. "Go on and get a good look. Harry's gonna wanta know if we looked everywhere. Mind where you step, you gotta step on the beams or you'll fall through the ceiling."

Rian crawls on in. "I know that. It's kinda dark in here."

Alby hears the beams creak as Rian knees across them.

"Ah, hell, there's spider webs up here. I just gotta face full."

Alby chuckles. "Don't be a baby. Use your flashlight and see if there's anything up there."

"Man, there's spiders that can kill ya, you know. I don't see nothin'. Aw jeez, there's somethin' crawlin' on me."

Rian's feet and legs crash though the ceiling above the living room in clouds of plaster dust and debris. Alby dashes to him.

"I'll pull you on through. Cover your face."

"No, don't. Wait, wait." Alby yanks Rian on through. They are both showered with dust.

"Damn it, Alby you coulda ripped my face off. Them busted boards got jagged edges. I'm getting' my coat and leavin'. Harry can come look for himself."

Rian swats at the dust on his clothes and fingers the plaster out of his hair. He puts on his coat and heads for the door.

"Come on, Alby. I've had enough."

"Stop where you are! This is the FBI. Put your hands in the air."

Two men come through the kitchen, their guns pointed at Alby and Rian. From their direction, Alby momentarily blocks their view of Rian who pulls one of the .45's from his pocket and cocks the hammer back.

He pushes Alby out of the way and shoots the lead FBI man in the upper thigh; the man crumples to the floor. The second agent takes cover behind the kitchen doorway.

Rian yanks on Alby's coat pulling him out through the front door. "Go get the car. I'll cover you." Rian fires back into the house to give Alby time to get their car.

The FBI agent calls to his partner. "Are you alright, Ben?"

"Hurts like hell. I'm bleeding bad."

"Take care of your man," Rian calls out.

He fires another round into the house, then runs toward the street.

The second agent hears Rian's feet pounding; he waits a moment before checking on his partner. By the time he gets to the doorway, Rian is almost to the street, twenty-odd yards away.

The FBI man stumbles on the door step, firing blindly at Rian who is now on the street. One round ricochets off the edge of the pavement; fragments of the bullet hit Rian in the butt.

Rian jumps in the air. "Goddamn, you son of a bitch." Rian turns back toward the house, pulling the second pistol from his coat. Alby brings the car to Rian's side. "Get in the car," Alby yells.

Rian, holding his left hand on his butt cheek, starts back to the house.

"Get in the car!" Alby shouts.

"I gotta shoot that dirty bastard." Rian fires at the FBI man who is lying prone below the tall weeds, trying to reload his pistol. Alby jumps out of the car, circles his arms around Rian and drags the flailing man back to the car.

"Let me go! I gotta shoot that Fed. He shot me in the butt. Let me go or I'll shoot you."

Alby squeezes Rian from behind, pinning his arms. He continues to squeeze until Rian goes limp. Throwing Rian and his gun into the back seat of the car, Alby leaps behind the wheel and roars off. The FBI man runs to the road, firing at

the car that is too far away to hit or to get its
license tag number.

Chapter 8

Back on Mare Island at his office building, Keys stands up from behind his desk. "I gotta get the rest of these files organized, Larry. You think you could find me another chair for this room?"

"Sure thing, Keys."

"Thanks. I'd like to talk with the head federal man when he comes to pick up those two birds you've got locked up."

Keys goes back to inspecting the files. The Marine returns with another chair.

"How 'bout some lunch, Larry?"

"I can always eat," the Marine says.

They walk to the cafeteria for a late lunch. When Keys and Larry return, they find Frank Gray, Keys' former FBI boss, outside his office, pacing restlessly, waiting for him.

Gray is a big man who has a habit of hooking two fingers under his shirt collar as if it's strangling him. It's only been a month since Keys broke Gray's office window but the man looks years older. The lines in his face are deeper, his eyes puffy. "Hi ya, Frank. How's it goin'?"

Gray looks up at the Marine, then at Keys, rolling his eyes. "I need to speak with you, Keys."

Keys grins, turning to Larry. "Thanks for lunch, Larry. If I told my wife we had steak, she'd murder me for not bringing some home."

"You just gotta know the right people around here, Keys. We eat well most of the time. I've gotta check in upstairs. I'll see you later."

Keys unlocks the door to his office to usher Gray in.

"Have a seat, Frank." Keys takes a toothpick from his pocket to poke in his mouth. He waits for the effect.

Gray sits down, looking up at Keys, shaking his head. "Grow up, Keys. You're as easy to read as this week's *Look* magazine. You had steak, I got it. Enjoy it while you can."

Keys' face sours. He takes the toothpick out of his mouth. "It's good to see you, too, Frank."

"I told you, Keys, you call me boss or Mr. Gray."

"Just so people around here won't think I know you, I'll call you Mr. Gray. Larry, the Marine that was just here, tells me that there is a certain element around here who want your head. I don't want 'em to think I work with you."

"Why me, Keys?"

"Well, Mr. Gray, I think it's because you're taking their pals away. Booth was definitely into a wage scam here. I don't know how many people he had on the take. In the short time I've been here, and from before on the Devin case, I'm convinced this is one of the most dedicated shipyards in the Navy. These people are loyal to each other; they think they're all one big happy family. But something stinks."

Keys waves his hand toward the stacks of files. "I've found blank work orders in these files. I think Booth ordered materials and, instead of the materials goin' to a job, he sold 'em. He musta had others involved to move the stuff. Did you send guys to Booth's place?"

Gray gets up to thumb through one of the stacks of files. "Yeah, they had some car trouble and didn't go before I left, so I haven't heard back from them yet. Have you got any leads?"

"Not yet, but I haven't been through all the files. There's lotsa work here."

"Okay, Keys, keep at it. The commander says you want a gun to carry here. You feeling naked or just nervous?"

"I'm on my own here, Frank. There's plenty of places on this island that I could get done-in easy. There's 45,000 people employed on this yard. If you figure even less than one percent of 'em's bad apples, that's a big number."

"You want your old gun back?" Gray asks. "Maybe a howitzer?"

"Gee Frank...er I mean Mr. Gray," Keys grins boyishly, "I didn't know you had a funny bone, but no thank you. I like my own gun a lot better."

Gray shrugs his big shoulders. "I'm just lightening the mood, boyo. Suit yourself. I'll make sure the commander gets you a permit or the papers you need. Keep me posted, Keys. If you need backup, call me."

"Thanks, boss. And thanks for getting me on this case. I appreciate it."

"You could come back if you want, Barry. We've got a big case load."

Keys notes the mood change in his old boss. "No thanks, Frank. My decision to leave had nothing to do with you. The bureau has changed too much, and Mary wouldn't stand for it either. But watch your back when you're on the yard here. Booth is in the wind and I don't know who the other players are yet. Whoever these bums are, they have to know it could be the electric chair when we catch 'em. They might be very dangerous, and I'm betting they are."

After several hours, Keys has the files sorted and put away. He took notes detailing what he thinks he has found and what he hasn't. Picking up the phone, he calls Mitch.

"Hi, Mitch, I'm just getting' ready to call it a day. I need to get a map of the island so I can find my way around. Can you get one for me?"

"Can do, Keys. I'll have it for you tomorrow. Have a good night."

"You too, Mitch. Thanks for your help today."

Keys fingers the phone button down to kill the call, then dials his new office number. He hears an unfamiliar voice answer, "Keys' Detective Agency."

"Oh, hi, this Barry Keys. Is this the answering service?"

"Hello Mr. Keys. Yes, sir, your wife set everything up today. She said to tell you she would be home after five. She is going to a victory garden meeting and then to do the change of address at the DMV and pick up the new ration books."

"Thank you. Most people call me Keys, what do I call you?"

"I'm Mildred, sir. I'm on from 8 to 5. We are a 24-hour service. Our company rotates the late night and the graveyard shifts so I'm not sure who will be on then."

"Okay, thanks, Mildred. Have a good evening."

By the time Keys reaches the California Street cable car, he is looking forward to being home with Mary. Turning down Mason Street, he sees the lights are off in the office. After crossing the street, he goes up the stairs to the apartment. Mary meets him at the door with a gorgeous smile and a cold bottle of beer. Holding up the bottle she asks, "Which do you want more?"

Keys makes the right decision with a passionate kiss.

Mary pats her ruffled hair. "Whew, I almost dropped your beer. Take off your coat and stay awhile, sailor. I'll get another cold one and join you."

Keys hangs up his coat, then settles into his overstuffed chair. He takes a sip of his beer and leans back with a contented smile.

Mary comes from the kitchen, looks at Keys and asks, "You look like the cat that ate the canary. What's up?"

"Huh, I just used the cat and canary thing myself today. Must be catchin'. Actually, I was just thinking how nice it is to come home now that you're here."

Mary laughs. "Ah shucks, you sure know how to treat a girl."

"Yeah, yeah, I mean it, Mary. I look forward to coming home now that you're back. Tell you what, how 'bout we go find some dinner? It's a nice night, a little chilly but it isn't raining. We can walk down to John's Grill and see what they've got. It doesn't matter what they ration, the place's always got something good."

They walk down Powell Street, a breeze from the west bringing the scent of the sea. Keys seems distracted at dinner. Mary looks up from her plate across the table. "Is there something wrong with your fish, Barry?"

"Uh, no, sorry, Mary. I was just thinking about the office at Mare. I shoulda had a guard posted. I can't think of anyone I can call tonight to get a guard on it. It's probably nothin' but it's naggin' at me. I may go in early if I can't sleep."

Mary reaches across the table to pat Keys' hand. "I thought the place was lighted 24 hours a day, Barry. Aren't there people working around there?"

"Yeah, but my little building is dwarfed between the new administration building and a storehouse. The shadows those places cast make my area dark as a cave. Kinda like down on the docks."

Keys rubs his hands together. "Makes me think of a stake out at the old docks on a cold, foggy night. How 'bout a tot a brandy to warm us up for the walk home?"

Keys wrestles with sleep, then finally he gets out of bed slowly, trying not to wake Mary. Carefully taking out work clothes from the dresser, he goes to the living room to change. Pulling on his heavy wool long coat, Keys heads out. "Call me later, Barry. I worry about you."

Keys turns to see Mary, framed by the bedroom doorway, rubbing sleep from her eyes.

"Sorry, I was trying to be quiet. I'll call after 8. Go back to sleep, Sprite. There's plenty of Marines on Mare so there's nothing to worry about."

Mary comes to Keys and kisses him. "It seems like a lifetime ago when we were kids going to Coffee Dan's joint. That's the first time you called me Sprite. You dared me to go down the old speakeasy's slide instead of the stairs."

"If your mother knew I took you there, she'd a killed me."

Mary smiles at the thought. "I'd have been the next in line, but that was half the fun. Be careful Barry, okay?"

"Five by five, I'll call you. I love you, Sprite."

A light rain is falling; Keys pulls his coat collar up as he steps off the cable car. He paces, waiting inside for the next Mare Island ferry. Being between shifts on the yard, there are some seats to choose from on this ferry.

Keys finds a comfortable seat under one of the heating vents to ward off the early morning chill. The old paddlewheel ferry chugs past Angel Island. The clouds the ferry passes under seem to radiate their own lights. A low overcast reflects the many lights of the bay's defense plants; sounds of shipyard work echo across the water.

Keys remembers when the city and all the surrounding areas were forbidden to have any lights on at night. Everyone knew the Japanese were just offshore planning an attack. Now people of the Bay Area had a new purpose, a new strength, and were turning out thousands of war machines. With all the defense plant lights, it was as if they were daring anyone to attack.

AGENT KEYS STEPS OUT

The ferry's thumping paddle wheel pushes Keys through the islands and rocks of the Brothers and Sisters, then turns to port and on to Mare Island. Keys lifts his wrist to get light on his watch; the hands indicate 4:15 am. Rain is still light when he steps off the ferry, the sentry's wet steel helmet glistens under the floodlights.

The super-bright lights and the variety of loud noises still take some getting used to in these early morning hours. He walks past the Number One Ways and crosses Railroad Avenue. The small one-story Building 125 is indeed shaded from the bright lights by the new, tall administration building.

Stepping up on the sidewalk, Keys catches a glimpse of movement at the corner of his office building. A match flares and Keys yells out, "Who's there? Step into the light." No one answers his challenge. Keys runs up the little hill, finding some footing on the loose dirt.

At the top of the hill, he slips on the wet grass, going down hard. His chin hits the ground just as a burst of flame flares out from the building. For an instant, a man's face is frozen in the crazy dancing light. Keys can't tell if the face he sees is distorted by the flames or if the face is oddly misshapen. The man turns away and vanishes into the night.

Keys gets to his feet, pulling off his coat. Dragging the coat across the wet grass he starts beating at the flames on the building. His wet coat makes slapping sounds that echo off the nearby

71

buildings, but the flames continue to climb the wood panels, spreading toward the roof.

Steam rises off his coat as he rubs it on the wet grass to keep it wet. Sparks fly as he continues to beat on the flames. Keys sees the fire growing. He yells in frustration at the top of his lungs, "Fire, fire, come on you bastards! Someone help me put out this fire."

Chapter 9

A Marine guard skids on the wet grass rounding the corner. He awkwardly recovers to point his rifle at Keys. The detective stops beating at the fire for a moment to yell at the Marine.

"Put that rifle down and help me put out this fire. Or better yet, go find fire extinguishers and some people to help me put this out."

Keys slaps his coat up at the climbing flames; sparks and ash rain down on him. He looks over his shoulder at the confused Marine. "Get goin', damn it!" he shouts. The Marine lowers his rifle, then lifts it as the sounds of a fire alarm and pounding feet startle him.

A few men with fire extinguishers round the corner. One of the men steps in front of Keys and starts spraying the flames with an extinguisher. Keys moves out of the way as more men move in to fight the fire. He watches for a moment before dropping his smoldering coat to grab an

73

extinguisher out of a fireman's hands, then runs toward the front of the building.

Inside his smoke-filled office, the fire has just burned though the top of a corner above the file cabinets. Keys sprays the flames with the extinguisher. Two men rush in behind Keys; one, in a police uniform, has his pistol trained on Keys.

"Put the extinguisher down and raise your hands slowly," the uniformed man demands.

Keys turns to see the policeman and the fireman he took the extinguisher from. "Let me make sure the fire is out in here first."

"I said put it down," the cop shouts. "The fireman here will secure this office."

"This is my office!" Keys shouts back.

"Where's your yard badge?"

Keys pats his pockets. "It's in my coat."

"Where's your coat, buddy? Put your hands up like I said. I ain't foolin', man."

"Look, officer, I came in early because I should have put a guard on this place last night. I saw a man start this fire and I've been tryin' to get it out since then."

"I'm going to take you to the station until I can get some ID on you. You can come along peaceable like or I'll drill a coupla holes in you and drag you out."

Keys hands off the extinguisher and raises his hands. "No need for gunplay officer. You can ask Commander Morsey for my ID. You can call him from here right now."

"I'll call from the station. Let's get goin'."

Handcuffed, Keys is marched to the police station.

***

Keys looks up from the metal-framed bunk in his cell. Morsey's aide, Mitch Rider, looks back at him through the steel bars.

"Yeah, Jenkins, I'm pretty sure that's him."

"Be damned sure, Mitch," the jailer says.

"Okay, I'm sure. You can let 'im out in my custody. I'll sign whatever you need."

Keys follows Mitch out of the police station.

"What the hell did you mean you thought it was me, Mitch? Someone tried to burn down my office, man."

"Cool down, Keys. You should get a look at yourself. Anybody that sees you is gonna swear you're either rabid or the wild man from Borneo. Come on, I'll take you to my place and you can get cleaned up."

"I want to go back to the office and get my coat and hat."

Mitch shakes his head negatively. "I'll go back for your coat and hat after I drop you off at my quarters. You go back looking like you do and you'll get arrested again. I'm in an officer's duplex with my own bathroom and shower. One of the perks of being a commander's aide."

"Okay Mitch, but someone wants to make sure the files in that room are destroyed. Can you get a guard on the place until we can find a safe place for 'em?"

"I'll take care of it. Do the world a favor and take a shower. I'll get some clothes from the PX and then we'll go get some breakfast before we go back to your office. That okay, Keys?"

"Yeah, you're right, Mitch. Thanks."

At the duplex, Mitch opens the door and shows Keys to the shower. "Take a good long shower; I'll be back in a jiffy."

He hands Keys a pad of paper and a pencil.

"Write out the clothes sizes you need on this note pad. There's milk in the icebox if you want something to clear your throat."

Getting out of the shower, Keys wraps a towel around his waist. He finds a blanket on the living room sofa to pull over him, rests his head on an arm of the sofa, and is soon asleep. The sound of the front door opening snaps him awake. Mitch comes in with an armful of clothing and a duffle bag hanging from his other arm.

"Rise and shine, Keys. I've got a full change of duds and a new coat for you. The work boots are what most of the guys wear here; these've got steel toe plates. All the heavy steel parts on the yard caused a lot of injuries; so now the yard provides good steel-toed work boots at a reduced cost.

"Your old stuff's in the duffle bag," Mitch holds up the bag, pinching his nose. "You may want to throw the old stuff away after you go through the pockets. Your coat's junk and I couldn't find your hat."

"Thanks Mitch. You know I was thinkin' of billin' the Navy for my clothes that got ruined on the Devin case. Maybe this makes up for it. I always wanted a pea jacket. You guys get first class stuff."

"The Navy's a good place to be. Let's go get some breakfast, I'm starvin'. I'm not usually up so early but I had to go save our chief investigator from the dungeon."

Keys makes an elaborate bow. "You may be assured your chief investigator deeply appreciates your stalwart efforts."

Keys changes into the clothes and pulls on the pea jacket. He turns up the collar on the jacket, grins at Mitch and heads for the door.

"Now I look Navy. Let's eat."

Outside, the sun burns through the wispy fog that still clings to the hill tops.

Mitch thinks it might be good for Keys to be seen in the central cafeteria. On their way walking down Walnut Avenue to cross Alden Park, he is about to mention his idea when Keys slows his pace.

"Should we stop in at Booth's old office and make sure the files are all right?" Keys asks.

Mitch rolls his eyes. "I had a couple Marines take the files to the administration building. Commander Morsey got a small office for you; he agrees that there must be something pretty important in those files. The administration building has a 24-hour guard, so there won't be anymore arson attempts.

77

"Now can we go eat? The cafeteria is a good place for you to be seen. The more workers that see you around the yard the better. You'll find they're good folks, after they think you're one of them. Just try to blend in; I'll introduce you to people I know."

Keys sniffs the air. "Wow, I can smell coffee from here."

Mitch nods, taking a breath. "That's the coffee roasting plant. They roast mountains of it every day. The yard supplies coffee to Navy personnel all over the world."

"I can see why you like the Navy; maybe I should have thought of that before I joined the FBI. One thing you can count on in police work is lousy coffee."

The cafeteria buzzes with hungry men and women readying for their work day. Mitch picks up a Bakelite tray and leads the way past piles of eggs, bacon, sausage, and toast. The lady behind the counter spoons his selections on to his plate as he glides the tray down the line. Keys follows suit. Mitch nods to yard workers on the way to a table.

"I appreciate your help, Mitch. I'd like to find the guy that set the fire. I might be able to ID him if I saw him or an ID picture of him. Is there somebody in administration that could pull the files to help me find the guy?"

Mitch pauses his coffee mug a moment, then takes a sip before answering. "That would be a mighty tall order Keys. There's over forty thousand people working here."

"Well, how about the night shift then?"

"That's still over ten thousand. I don't think we're gonna get the security people to pull files on that many. Give me a description of the guy and let me ask around."

"Okay, that'll have to do for now. I'm gonna wander around today and get the lay of the land."

Mitch puts his empty plate and coffee mug back on his tray, readying to leave. "You know you can't go on the Ammunition Depot land. If you come to suspect trouble there, the commander will have to get you a different badge."

Keys brow lifts in surprise. "It's a good thing you told me. I coulda gotten myself in trouble. I don't think that area's the problem though. The materials that're getting out have to come from the ship building part of the yard. I'm kinda anxious to get out and about."

Mitch gets up to take his tray back. "Okay, let me introduce you to some guys on the way out."

They come to a table where a dozen men are eating. The table buzzes with conversations. Mitch rests his hands on the shoulders of a man at the head of the table. "How are you guys doin' today? I want to introduce you all to my friend, Barry Keys."

One man pipes up from the other end of the table. The rest of the people at the table watch with interest.

"Yeah, Mitch, we already heard your friend done jailed Casey an' Biff. That don't make him very friendly."

Mitch raises his voice. "You don't always hear the real story. Keys was brought in to do safety inspections for the railroad. You know we had some accidents and lost some goods to improper loading. What happened is, we gave him Booth's old office when Booth cleared out.

"Casey and Biff showed up, attacked Keys and we found out that they, along with Booth, were being paid for shifts they didn't work. That means both got wages for work they didn't do. Work that's vital to the war effort and didn't get done.

"Booth took his cut and we don't know yet who else may be involved. Those guys stole from all of us, and during wartime; I don't have to tell you they're in serious trouble. Keys didn't fold when they attacked him and Moose was there to drag 'em to Commander Morsey.

"So, like I said, Barry Keys is a friend. I hope you'll extend him every courtesy. You're all good men and Keys is here to do a job just like you. If you guys need anything, you know where to find me."

The man at the table's far end says, "Well, that's different; I didn't hear that end of the story. So I guess thanks are in order; we didn't know they was stealin'. We're all workin' hard to get this war won. You know any more guy's stealin', Mr. Keys?"

"No, I don't and it ain't my job," Keys says. "I'm here to look after the railroad. Things get slowed to a stop when goods get ruined or accidents happen. If any a you see something that could help, I'd appreciate it if you'd let me or Mitch know.

"Thanks for listening fellows," Mitch says, "We've got to go."

"Nice meeting you guys," Keys says.

Chapter 10

Outside men and women fill the streets during the shift change. Each person coming on to their shift has a place to be and, like an ant colony, are on their way with a similar determination.

Others are on their way home, some by buses on one end of the island, some by ferry. People with cars are required to share with as many riders as possible. Car loads head for the causeway's Bascule Bridge.

Standing back from the stampede, Keys looks at his watch. "I need to call home, Mitch."

"Okay, I'll show you your new office, then I'll get that map you want."

Mitch leads Keys to a door on the second floor of the Administration building. The office is in a room that is divided by a partition making it about the same size as Booth's old office. The file cabinets are there along with the same desk and chairs.

"Wow, Mitch, a window! I musta stepped up in the world. Ah sorry, that came across as more of a smart-assed remark than I meant it to be."

Keys walks over to the window to take in the view.

"I can see the corner of Booth's old office. Can you give me a hand moving these two file cabinets? I'd like to move the desk so I can watch out this window. Maybe the guy that set the fire will want to come back to see his work."

"That sounds like a long shot to me, Keys. Let me check in with my boss first; he'll want to know how this all worked out with his morning coffee. I'll bring the map back with me."

Keys nods and waits until Mitch leaves to pick up the phone. He puts the receiver to his ear, hears a dial tone and dials out. He hears Mary answer, "Keys' Detective Agency, how can I help you?"

"It's me, Mary. You have a very nice business voice."

He gives her a run down on the fire saying that he ruined his clothes and got a new Navy wardrobe for his effort. He laughs, saying that he always wanted one of those real Navy pea jackets and now he has one.

"Mitch is bringing me a map and I'm gonna take a look around this place. I won't be too long at it. I just wanta get a feel of the place, so I'll be home early.

"I'll make dinner when you get home so you can get to bed early," Mary says. "I practically had to strangle the butcher today, but I got a nice little beefsteak. I know we all have to do our part, but rationing is a pain."

Keys smiles, returning the receiver to the cradle. He briefly muses back to the days of missing Mary. There were few smiles then. Unwanted dark thoughts and bad memories would at times flood into his head. Both he and Mary found their lives lacking without one another. Keys thinks their relationship now is even better than before.

Mitch returns, waving a rolled-up map. "Here you go, Keys. Hot off the press, as they say."

Keys takes the map to his desk and begins to unroll it. As he holds one end, the other end rolls off the desk.

"How long is this thing?"

Mitch laughs. "It's like ten feet long. I brought some thumb tacks; we can put it up on the walls if you want."

After tacking up the map, which takes up one wall and most of the partition, Keys stands back to examine it.

"Wow, now that's a map. Mitch, you've outdone yourself again. This kind of detail is far more than I expected."

Mitch removes a tack to smooth down an edge before replacing it. "It just came out. It's got every building with its number and purpose listed in the legend."

Both men stand back to take in the map's detail. "Have you got any questions before I get back to work?" Mitch asks.

Keys takes a moment, eyes wandering the map. "I don't know where to start yet. I need more time to study this thing. Where do you think the best place for our bad guys to hang out would be?"

Mitch points to the map. "The entire perimeter is guarded by the Marines; but my best guess is the west side. It's the most isolated, least populated part of the yard. I haven't roamed around there at night so I don't know what the activity level would be there."

Keys steps closer to the map. "Man, that's a lot of ground to cover. Are all of the warehouses and smaller buildings open at night?"

"I don't know, Keys. I'll see what I can find out for you. You can see our problem and the big reason the commander brought you in. The yard is over 4000 acres, has almost 50,000 people in and out every day, and a thousand buildings to investigate."

Keys whistles. "Oh, no big deal, I'll have this wrapped up in no time."

Mitch deadpans his response going along with Keys' reply. "We knew the FBI's best ex-investigator wouldn't have any trouble with our little problem."

"Who told you I was the best investigator?"

"Your old boss, Mr. Gray. He was full a praise when the commandant asked for you."

"Huh, he never told me that. If you'll give me a hand movin' the file cabinets, I'll be on my way too. I'm thinkin' you're right about the west end. Knowin' the ways of bad guys, I'll bet they'll wanta do their work on the graveyard shift. I'm gonna take a quick look over there. I'll come back tomorrow and stay for that shift."

"Well, be careful, Keys. It's a different world here after dark. Don't forget to wear the hard hat I got for you. The numbers on it mean you're with the railroad. Most of the hard hats have numbers that designate the person's station. You may need yours to keep the bad guys from dropping something heavy on you."

"Thanks for the good cheer, my friend. I'll come loaded for bear tomorrow."

With his hands in the pockets of his new pea jacket, Keys heads over to the west side of the island to check it out in daylight. He tilts his hard hat rakishly, mimicking some of the other workmen. His new work boots keep his feet warm and dry crossing the wet scrub brush and puddles.

On the west side of the island beyond Cedar Avenue are the yard dumps and oil storage intersected by service roads and bordered by San Pablo Bay. Turning south is the Marine shooting range. To the north is a treeless, and now muddy, open plain. Tall radio towers and a few scattered small buildings make up the northwest section of the yard.

The detective takes mental note of the topography and the buildings. Walking along the dump road, Keys passes a sprawling scrapyard. Continuing to the oil storage area, he turns north and, after a short distance, is stopped by a Marine guard.

The Marine, unslinging the rifle from his shoulder, steps in front of Keys. "Where's your pass? What are you doing here, buddy?"

Keys points his badge. "I'm a new railroad inspector just getting' the lay a the land."

"There ain't no railroads up here past the dumps," the Marine barks.

Keys thinks a beat before answering. "Not right now, but we're thinkin' of layin' a line past the oil storage."

"My orders say no one is allowed here without the right pass. And you ain't got the right pass."

"Okay. Say, how many guys are up here with the right passes?"

The Marine studies Keys before answering. "Mostly dump guys and the fire fightin' school men. There's a truck garage, some other stuff. Say, you're mighty curious, buddy."

"Look you can take down my name and badge number if you want. If we decide to extend the line, I'll be back. I was told by the yard commander that this badge was all I needed to go anywhere on the yard except the ammunition depot."

The Marine shifts the rifle back to his shoulder. "All I know is what my sergeant tells me."

Keys makes a face, gives a wave of dismissal and turns around to head back.

Chapter 11

Rian wakes in the back of Alby's car. "What the hell Alby? I wanted to shoot that son of a bitch. My butt's got some lead and it hurts. Stop an' take a look, willya? I might be bleedin' to death."

Alby glances up at Rian's angry face in the rearview mirror. "You think killin' a FBI man's gonna do us a lotta good? I don't think you're anywhere's near as smart as you think you are. We're almost back to the barn. Harry can take a look at your butt, see if you need sewin' up or somethin'."

Alby exits his car without helping Rian out and enters the barn. Rian curses, then groans as he gets out, hobbling to the barn.

Harry stands inside the barn, hands on hips, waiting for Rian to come in. "Alby's not talking so what the hell is wrong with you? You look like an old man with a busted back."

Rian rests his hands on a chair back. "I got shot by a FBI man. I wanted to go back and shoot the guy but Alby knocked me out."

Harry stiffens. "FBI? Was this at Booth's place? Are you sure he was FBI?"

"Yeah, at Booth's. There was two of 'em. They said they was FBI. I shot one but the other ducked back. I hustled Alby out to get the car while I held 'em off."

Harry turns to Alby who is seated at the table with the box from Booth's in front of him.

"Is that what you saw, Alby?" Harry demands.

"Yeah, Harry. We just finished lookin' through the place when they showed up. I didn't want to see nobody killed so I wrestled Rian to sleep and took off. All we found was this box and some guns."

"What's in the box?" Harry asks.

Alby opens the box to shake out the contents.

Harry fingers through the items, then inspects the papers. He closely scrutinizes one of the papers, holding it up, then turning it to put light behind it. "Alby get me a candle."

Alby returns to the table with a candle. Harry lights it, waiting for the flame to prosper. He waves the candle back and forth behind the paper bringing it closer and closer to it. "Ah ha, just as I thought. It's a bank account number. I know he had accounts at that big old bank in Vallejo."

Rian and Alby peer at the paper. Harry holds the paper so they can see it as he brings the candle to it.

"Wow, that's like a real magic trick," Alby exclaims. "How'd you do that? How'd you know it was there?"

"It's an old trick. You write with lemon juice; the heat brings the words out. This letter is of no real importance, there had to be another reason for Booth to keep it locked up in a box. Was there a key in the box? Did you find a key anywhere?"

"No, we didn't find a key, boss," Alby says.

Harry puts the paper back on the table. "Did Tom show you anything he took from Booth?"

"No," Alby and Rian say in unison.

Rian utters a low moan, rubbing his behind. "Harry, my butt hurts. Can you take a look and see if I need a doctor?"

Harry takes a stern look at Rian, shaking his head. "Pull your pants down and bend over the chair."

"Can't we do it in your room, Harry?"

"You know damn well you are not allowed in my room under any circumstances. Pull your pants down if you want me look at it."

As Rian unbuckles his belt, he looks up to see Alby smirking. "Make Alby leave first."

Alby walks past them. "I'll go help Tom with that rubber stuff we're gonna ship out."

"Tom's out burying Booth," Harry says. "You can load it up in the truck and pile some sand bags over it."

As Rian and Alby return from Booth's house, Tom drives east from the barn to a slough near the Carquinez Strait where he goes duck hunting. He backs his car down an old trail as close as he dares to the bog. This is well off the beaten path where he is sure there is no one around. Tom waits for a moment by the back of the car listening: all is still.

Silently he opens the trunk, taking out his waist-high waders and a shovel. He pulls the waders on over his clothes, then hauls out the burlap bags containing Booth's body parts. Wading into the dark water the mud sucks at his boots. Slogging on to shallow water, Tom goes behind a mound that rises above the water level.

Dropping the bags he could carry, he goes back for another load. Already tired from wading with the heavy loads, he starts shoveling the muck to make a hole for the bags. It is not as easy as he thought it would be. The slimy black ooze smells of rot and collapses back into the hole as fast as he can dig.

Growing frustrated, Tom puts a bag by the place he digs, lifts out a shovel full and kicks the bag in the hole. He stamps down pushing the bag deeper only to lose his footing and falls into the muck. Cursing with rage, he scrapes off the clingy black slime, then continues to plant the other bags.

Setting the last bag by the intended hole Tom angrily stabs the shovel hard into the muck. He pushes down on the handle bending it with all his weight. The handle snaps sending him face down into the bog. Tom gets up screaming, muck flying from his mouth. He throws the broken handle as hard as he can. The handle crashes through the underbrush, raising a raft of noisy mallards.

Tom looks about nervously, his neck gone tight. He wipes his mouth, then stomps the last bag into the bog. Worn out, the muck sucking hard at his waders he struggles to get to dry land. Finally on solid ground, he walks a few hundred yards down to the water of the Carquinez Strait to wash off. Shucking off the waders he washes off his face and clothes, the muck sends an inky cloud staining the water. Tom kicks the waders into the water and watches the current carry them away.

Driving back, Tom passes the barn to go on into Vallejo. At his favorite bar on Georgia Street, he orders a beer. After several more, he decides to take a case of beer back with him. When he opens the trunk, Tom sees a burlap bag he missed at the slough. Cursing under his breath, Tom closes the trunk and drives to a vacant spot on the waterfront.

Using parked train cars as cover, Tom opens the trunk, quickly shoves a jack handle in the burlap bag and tosses the bag, underhand, into the water.

"Hey, whatta ya doin' here, buddy?" Tom practically jumps out of his skin. A man in bib overalls, with a railroad badge pinned to them, comes from behind him.

Flustered Tom takes a moment to answer. "Uh, I just stopped to pee."

"You ain't spos'd ta be here. What'd you throw in the water?"

"Just a beer bottle…sir."

The railroad man steps past Tom to peer down at the water. "Well, I oughta report you. You ain't spos'd to put nothin' in the water here. What's your name? You got some ID?"

"Look, mister, I'm sorry. I drank too much beer an' I gotta go on my shift at the yard. If you report me, I could lose my job. How bout I give you a coupl'a beers and we part friends?"

The railroad man walks away, beer bottles clinking together in his pockets.

The burlap bag, weighted with the heavy steel, sank quickly into the murky water. It thumped to the rocky bottom jolting the jack handle, causing the sharp end of the handle to tear through the coarse burlap. Booth's cold dead hand slowly emerged through the bag. The hand gently swayed in the current, fingers splayed, as if craving the light on the surface.

Chapter 12

Tom's foul mood is evident to everyone upon his arrival at the barn. Rian sits on a pillow of burlap bags at the table. Alby puts two mugs of coffee for himself and Rian on the table and sits down.

Tom reaches for Alby's mug. "I'll take yours bright boy; go get yourself another one."

Alby moves his hand to cover his mug. "Your legs ain't broke."

Tom snaps his razor-sharp knife to Alby's face. "Gimme that mug or I'll slit your throat, you pea-brained idiot."

Rian draws and cocks the pistol that comes instantly to his hand. "Back away, pig face, or I'll ventilate it."

The angry, raised voices bring Harry into the room.

"What's goin' on here? Tom, put that knife away. Rian, put your gun down. What the hell's the matter with you men? If you haven't enough to do, I can find work for you."

Rian uncocks his pistol and lays it on the table top. "Tom's pissed at the world again. He's got that goddamned knife out, boss."

Tom lays his knife on the table. "That scare you, Rian?"

"That's right, pig face, it does scare me. You come at me with that and I'll empty this pistol on you. All you wanta do is kill and butcher."

The mugs on the table bounce as Harry brings his fist down.

"Shut up, both of you. I don't know what the hell's a matter here. You men are makin' good money without havin' to work too hard at it. Plus, you're not gettin' shot at in a foxhole with mud an' snow up to your butts."

Tom slaps his hand down on the table. "I just hadda stick Booth's parts down in the slough. I got that bog shit all over me. Then I gotta put up with these idiots."

Alby watches the quarrel go back and forth. He is usually the quiet one in an argument.

"What'd you take off Booth before you cut 'im up, Tom? You didn't share nothin' with us. Where's his wallet?"

Surprised, Harry looks at Alby as if a stone spoke. "That's a good question, Alby," Harry says.

Tom's hand moves toward his knife. "Don't you guys start crowdin' me."

Harry moves around the table toward Tom. "Don't pick that up, Tom. I want to know where Booth's wallet is, and what you found in it."

Tom snatches up the knife knocking over his chair as he gets up. He crouches, holding the knife out. "I said don't crowd me and I mean it. I ain't answerin' to none a you right now."

Harry faces Tom who jabs out toward him with the wicked blade. The spymaster feints to his right. Tom twists to follow, slashing down with the knife catching Harry's shirt sleeve. Harry pulls back and kicks Tom hard between his legs. The knife wielder hits the floor doubling up. Harry steps on Tom's wrist, bending down to pull the knife away.

Harry stabs the knife into the ground, then kicks it to snap the blade. "Alby, haul Tom up and walk him around some."

Alby lifts Tom off the floor. The man's face is contorted in pain and rage. Not yet able to stand erect, he cups his damaged goods with both hands. Glaring at Harry, tears streaking his face, he spits hate. "I'll kill you if you've ruined me."

"Ah, yes," Harry says, "I need to address that. Alby, sit the killer down in a chair."

Tom groans as Alby plops him down on a chair.

Harry stands before Tom whose head hangs down, eyes cast at the floor.

"Look at me, Tom. I'm gonna tell you what happens if you try killin' me. I said look at me, Tom."

Harry grabs Tom's hair, lifts his face and smacks him hard with an open hand. Blood and spittle fly off Tom's face. His eyes flare with hatred. As Harry cocks his hand back, a new look of fear clouds Tom's glare.

Harry's eyes shine with a look of satisfaction that spreads to his face. He braces his hands on the table, then looks at each man eye to eye.

"Let me tell all of you what happens if I am not successful in my mission. Each of you submitted to me the names and addresses of your family and friends as was necessary to obtain your yard badges. I have passed that information on to my Gestapo friends in Mexico. Should I be killed by one of you, all of you and your families will be hunted down and killed by them.

"I can, and will, order your deaths at any time I deem necessary. I hope I have impressed that on all of you. Now, Tom, I want to know what you took off Booth's body, and I want his wallet."

Tom's head hangs to his chest. "Alby, get him up and walk him around until he's able to talk. Rian, go search his car. Find Booth's wallet."

Alby unceremoniously hauls Tom up from the chair. Supporting Tom's weight with his arm around him, he parades the painfully groaning, stumbling man about the room.

Rian returns. "I didn't find nothin' boss. He's got a case a beer with a few bottles missin' from it in the trunk but I don't see Booth's wallet."

Harry shoots a dark look at Tom. "You looked in the all hidden compartments?"

Rian sits at the table. "Yes, sir. He's got a bunch a knives wrapped in a blanket in the one under the rear seat."

"Alby, bring him over here. Hold him up straight."

As Tom sags back against Alby, Harry goes through his pants pockets. He takes keys, change, two pocket knives, and a straight razor, tossing them on the table. The rear pockets have two wallets. Harry places one on the table. The other wallet is considerably thicker with a clear outline of a key.

Harry quickly unfolds the wallet to dig for the key. He holds the key up for all to see.

"This is Booth's. I'm hoping we'll find more than money: he could have files on his shipyard contacts, security badges and clues to some of the other schemes he had. He was on the yard for a long time, and a very greedy man."

Harry counts the money in the wallet and divides it into three piles.

"Alby, see if Tom can stand by himself."

Tom grasps a chair back to remain upright.

"You and Rian can each take a share and I'll take mine; I'll assume Tom already got his. I'm going to keep the wallet and go through the rest of it later. If there's anything worth money, I'll let you know."

Tom scowls, gently lowering himself into the chair.

"I oughta get all the money. I killed 'im, butchered 'im and planted 'im."

Harry puts Booth's wallet in his pocket then pivots around to face Tom.

"That's reason enough for you to get nothin': I told you not to kill him. You don't want to take orders and you don't want to share. I'm not sure you've got a place here anymore, Tom."

Startled, Tom sits up in the chair. "Are you plannin' on kickin' me out, Harry?"

"You don't get kicked out Tom; you know that. Nobody gets kicked out. If you don't have a place here, you don't have a place on this earth."

"Look, Harry, I'm sorry, but Booth was getting' scared. He coulda ratted us all out—I done what needed doin'. I know you're the boss, I just learned my lesson. I'll do whatever you want. I'll pledge allegiance to your Nazi flag if that's what you want."

"I'll give high marks for a fast turnaround, Tom, but that doesn't really earn my trust. You're a lone wolf; you don't want to take orders or share the spoils. I don't believe you care if I do have your family killed. But I do know you well enough to know that you fear for yourself.

"You will be watched from now on. You will obey my orders to the letter. If you fail, you will pay with your life, and—the Gestapo likes to play with their meat before they kill it."

Tom reaches out from his chair offering his hand. "I'm with you, Harry, one hundred percent."

Harry ignores Tom's hand. "We'll see, Tom, we'll see."

Chapter 13

Entering the Mason Street apartment, Keys takes in the rich smell of beef drifting out from the kitchen. The hint of garlic makes his mouth water. Mary, wearing an apron and wiping her hands on a dish towel, peeks around the kitchen door. She comes to him, standing on her tiptoes, to kiss his cheek.

"My, you do look rather dashing in that pea coat. Nick would be proud of you. We got another letter from him today."

Keys wraps his arms around Mary in a gentle bear hug. "You smell almost as good as that beef you're cookin'."

Mary untangles from Keys' hug. "Well, that's a fine hello. You like beef better than me?"

Keys chuckles. "I like beef but I do dearly love you, Sprite. So, what did our hero submariner have to say?"

Mary hands Keys the letter. "Have a look. There's some censoring, but he does say they're sinking a lot of enemy shipping. Take your coat off and stay awhile, sailor; I'll get you a beer while you read the letter."

Keys hangs his coat in the closet and sits down to read Nick's letter. Mary brings a bottle of beer.

Raising the bottle, Keys says, "Thanks, Sprite, here's to Tojo's demise."

He finishes reading the letter, then goes into the kitchen to hug Mary around her waist while she tosses the salad.

"Come on, stand back, you big bear, you'll make me spill the salad."

Grinning, Keys heads to the kitchen table. "Okay, don't get riled. You know I can't stay away from you."

Mary brings the salad to the table to serve on their plates. "What did you think about Nick's letter?"

Swallowing a forkful of salad Keys answers. "He likes his captain and crew, that's for sure. The captain's the youngest he's sailed with and, I get the impression, the most aggressive. They're a brave bunch a men; I almost wish I was with 'em."

"You've done your part, Barry; and Nick wouldn't be on that boat if you hadn't broken that spy ring. Nick said nobody but you believed him when he told the police he was kidnapped. I'm

103

glad we got to know him. He told me I had to come back to you."

Keys chews his first bite of beef. "This little steak is the best ever, Sprite. You know I'll always be grateful to the kid for that even if he did get me shot again."

Mary gives Keys a stern look, then laughs. "That's not the way Nick tells it. What time are you going in tomorrow?"

"I should go in early. I've got a lotta files to go through. I'd like to see if I can get somebody in security to pull some ID pictures of men on the graveyard shift. I'm plannin' on stayin' for the graveyard shift so it'll be a long day."

"You went in early today, Barry. You need to get some sleep if you're going to stay up for the graveyard shift. I wish I could help with your files."

"That would great, Mary, but I can't take anything off the island."

"Well, maybe I could help out in the security office if you could fix it. We don't have a lot of business right now in our office."

"That's a damn good idea," Keys beams. "Brains and beauty, that's just more of what I love about you. I'll call Mitch right now and see if there's some way Morsey can swing it."

"Finish your dinner first, Barry," Mary admonishes, "we don't get meat like this very often, and I have dessert."

Keys, still clutching his fork, gives a mock salute. "Captain has the word."

After dessert Keys phones Mitch.

"I was just about to call you, Keys," Mitch says into his phone. "The commandant wants to know if you can do something to keep the FBI from over-running the yard."

Keys squeezes the phone receiver to his ear. "What's goin' on Mitch? Gray hasn't said anything to me about sendin' more men out."

"Your FBI boss called the commandant to tell him one of his men was shot at Booth's house. He thinks it's likely someone on the yard did it, and he wants to send men out to try to identify the shooter."

"Who was shot, Mitch? I know most of those guys."

"I don't know, Keys. The commandant just told me to call you. He said he'd authorize anything you need to placate your boss so you can get on with your investigation."

Keys looks over to Mary who is standing with her hands extended palms up in a 'what's going on' gesture.

"What I need is your security people to pull ID's so I can find the guy that tried to burn Booth's office. We find him and we find the people responsible for the yard losses and probably the shooting.

"My wife, Mary, would be a real help if she could go to work in security to pull the ID's. She has government clearance from her work at

Marinship. That would be the best way I can think of to get a faster result. She can blend in with the security people instead of the FBI demanding an office takeover.

"That's the best way to put an end to this faster. But listen Mitch, I'm not gonna sell out 'cause the commandant wants a fast end to this. It won't work if we don't really catch these guys. They have to be stopped. If they're dumb enough to shoot FBI men and then get away with it, it will just be the start of more trouble."

"Okay, Keys. I'll call the commandant and give him your message. I'm sure he doesn't want this to just go away. The thing is we've got a huge number of ships with battle damage to repair and many more new ships on order. No one on the yard will say we can't do it all, only that we will get it done.

"That's what the commandant has on his mind. We've got to get these ships out. If the FBI comes out in force, our work will be slowed, and we can't afford to be slowed down. We can't put more men and women on because there aren't any more and nowhere to house them anyway.

"We need everyone we have on the job and not being interrogated by the FBI. Come see me when you get here and I should have word from the commandant by then."

Keys hangs up the phone as Mary comes to his side.

"Mitch says he's gonna ask the commandant about you helping me. He may have an answer for us when I get to the yard. I'll give you a call as soon as I know something."

"It sounds really exciting, Barry, and I'll be on a case with you for the first time."

"Yep, Sprite, you're gonna get to see how really boring some a this stuff is. I gotta call Jerry."

Chapter 14

At the Vallejo barn, Harry is frustrated with the men's squabbling. Wanting peace and quiet to scheme, the men have to go. With the dead man's wallet in hand, Harry sends his minions out of the barn. He is bent on formulating a plan to get into Booth's bank box, and sits at the table fidgeting with a pencil. With the big money from what he is sure Booth's account will bring, the German provocateur stares at the wall, dreaming of blowing up the Mare Island ammunition depot.

Tom, relieved to be able to get out of the barn alive, slouches in the bathtub at his tiny Vallejo apartment with his pants still on. His fists clench when he thinks of begging for his life before Harry; his dark mood eats away at him.

He hates that Alby and Rian both witnessed his shame; he feels like the world is closing in on him. There is no place to hide from this gnawing humiliation. Plotting some ruthless revenge is the only option.

Tom knew Harry was right, his threat of the Gestapo murdering his family is not a big concern for him. His death at the Gestapo's hands is. He does not want to run and lose the easy money at Mare Island. He's always been good at getting Rian and Alby to do the heavy lifting at the yard. He makes some deliveries of the stolen goods, but shirks any work he can.

No, the problem, he thinks, *is how to get rid of Harry, so he can take over the whole operation.* His devious mind tumbles into gear. An idea sparks him to sit up in the tub. Maybe he could engineer an accident on the job. It would be written up in the yard's newspaper, *The Grapevine*. Just like when the men were killed falling into the dry docks, or the gas blew up in the pipe shop. The Gestapo could think it was just an unfortunate accident.

With a plan of revenge beginning to emerge, the pain in Tom's groin subsides. He gets out of his wet pants, dries off, dresses, and heads for a Georgia Street bar. Swaggering into the bar, Tom pounds on the polished wood and yells at the barkeep to serve him a boilermaker.

A man next to Tom at the bar grabs his beer mug. "Hey Tom, take it easy. You damn near made me spill my beer."

Tom slaps his hand down on the bar. "You better hold on to it, bud. I ain't in a mood to be fooled with."

"Ya know, Tom, I ain't ever seen you in any other kinda mood."

Tom delivers his bar mate a narrow-eyed sneer. "Come on, barkeep, get the lead outta your ass."

The bartender puts a full shot glass and a beer mug down in front of Tom.

"Mind your manners, buddy. The Navy'll shut this place down if we have any more trouble here."

Tom, not bothering with putting the shot in the beer mug, knocks the whiskey back. "Bah, they ain't got nobody big enough ta fool with me."

The bartender's lips go tight; he shrugs, then moves on down the busy bar.

Tom's bar mate turns to him, beer mug in hand.

"The Navy's got some big ones. How 'bout that Marine, Moose? I hear he dragged Casey an' Biff out ta the feds like two rag dolls. We all know you're a big shot; some of us are tryin' ta raise some money for their wives an' kids. How 'bout helpin' out? You always got a wad a cash."

"That slob messes with me, I'll filet 'im before he knows what happened. I ain't got no money ta throw away. Now get outta my way, bud. I got drinkin' to do."

Tom hunches over the bar oblivious to the din. Drinking and planning Harry's demise is all he needs. "Shame an' pain," Tom mumbles into his mug. "Yeah. Shame an' pain, that's what I wanta see." Hatred, and at the same time fear, eat at his gut.

Some time and liquor passes before the man at the bar breaks into Tom's reverie.

"Hey Tom, look who just walked in. It's the Moose. Let's see how tough you really are, man. Where's that big knife you're always talkin' about?"

Tom turns from the bar to see Moose moving around the tables headed for the bar. Men reach out to shake his hand or pat his back. Larry "Moose" Mazurki glances toward the bar to see a small round dark-haired man staring at him, seething with hatred. The Marine smiles, then heads for the end of the bar where some other yard men are holding out a beer for him.

"You ain't so tough now, huh, Tom?" Tom's antagonist prods.

Tom downs his whiskey shot, slams the glass down, and moves to cut off the Marine.

"I hear you been draggin' yardmen off ta the feds, you big ugly slob."

Larry smiles down at the angry man. "Looks to me like you've had too much to drink, my friend. I don't want any trouble here. Why don't you go home and sleep it off?"

"Whatta' ya, yellow? You big slobs 'er all the same. You ain't got no fight in ya."

Moose's hands ball into fists. "Buddy, you need to get outta my way an' go home. I don't wanta have ta kick your butt."

The knife appears as if by magic. The long blade catches the overhead light, the matte black handle molded to Tom's hand.

The bar goes quiet: men move away, forming a ragged circle, no one wanting to miss the action.

Tom is acutely aware of the men watching: he can't be shamed again. He crouches, legs spread. Taking in the faces, he looks up at the Marine and makes a show of shifting the knife hand to hand.

"Come on slob, come an' get it. I'm gonna cut you down to size."

Moose stands, fists on hips, watching the knife. "I've come to have a beer with friends. Let's just agree you're a real tough guy and call it good."

"I knew you was yellow." Tom lunges forward, lashing out with the blade.

Moose pulls his hands away and sucks in his stomach as the wicked blade passes, slashing his shirt. The knife came within a fraction of an inch of slicing into him.

Tom puffs up, beaming at the crowd. He goes back into the crouch, passing the knife hand to hand.

Larry, no longer amused, studies the timing of Tom's knife juggling. He advances, plants a foot, and lashes out with his leg, knocking the knife from Tom's hand. Tom watches helplessly as the knife arcs through the air, never seeing the Marine's fist smash into his face.

Someone pours water on Tom; he comes to, sputtering. The Marine reaches down to grab Tom's shirt front, pulling him to his feet. Larry bends his head down until he is nose to nose with his no longer arrogant assailant. His eyes bore into Tom's.

"Get the hell outta here now. I don't wanta see you again, anywhere, anytime. You got that, man?"

Tom tries to pull away from the Marine.

Larry glowers down at Tom. "I said, you got that, man?"

Tom hesitates, swallowing his humiliation. "Yeah," he mumbles.

He pulls loose from the Marine, looking down at the floor for his knife as he heads toward the exit.

"Leave the blade," Larry growls. "You pick it up and I'll make you eat it. Now get the hell outta here!"

A cheer goes up from the crowd as the thoroughly humiliated Tom vanishes.

Someone in the crowd calls out. "Hey Moose, I'm buyin' the beer."

Chapter 15

In the city by the bay, Keys gulps some air, a little winded after bounding down the stairs of the apartment. He had gone across the street to make some notes, then back up to the apartment to give Mary the mail. On the street, he pats his stomach with both hands, momentarily distracted by the bulge. Mary's home cooking and regular meals are beginning to take a toll on his waistline. Cars flash by on Bush Street, busy as ever, even with the tire and gas rationing. The war is limiting auto supplies as is evident by the battered and rundown taxicabs he sees.

Mary urged him to sleep in a little later with the promise of a good home-cooked breakfast. He planned on not returning home until after he nosed around the Navy yard during the graveyard shift. He'd be some twenty hours or more on the job; it reminded him of his early FBI days.

AGENT KEYS STEPS OUT

The sun is out; its warmth feels good on his face as he heads down the hill toward the ferry. Arms swinging by his sides, striding along the sidewalk, Keys muses that opening the detective agency is like starting all over again. He enjoys the freedom and the anticipation of what a new day will bring. The detective takes in the fresh-scented morning on the bay while riding the ferry to Mare Island. His first stop at the yard is to see Mitch in Morsey's office.

"Mornin', Mitch. You hear anything from the commandant?"

"Hi ya, Keys. Yeah, he said if you can call off the FBI dogs, he'll bring your wife in on special assignment to his office. With his letter, she'll be able to bring you the files you need and I'm to smooth things over. I'll give you a pass to get her on the yard. I'll need her to bring me her security information when she gets here."

"Thanks, Mitch, that sounds good to me. I'll call Frank Gray as soon as I get to my office. I'd appreciate it if you'd not let on Mary's my wife. I don't want her in any danger here. I think it'd be better if she could deliver any files to the commandant's office and then have them brought to me. Maybe you could get the gunnery sergeant assigned to me. I trust Larry and I think we'd work well together. He could be the go-between from the commandant's office.

"By the way, I called my old FBI partner about the Booth house shoot-out. He said one a the guys packs two .45's and likes shooting 'em.

So these guys have stepped up a notch from petty thieves. Could be one a them isn't scared to set a yard building on fire either."

Keys' first call at his office is to Frank Gray.

"Hi Frank, er I mean boss, how's it goin'?"

Before Gray can get a word in, Keys continues.

"I've got things workin' good here and the commandant will let me bring Mary in to pull the yard's security files so I can ID the guy that burned my old office. In turn, I've got to guarantee him that you'll hold off sendin' in the troops."

"Look Keys, one of my new guys got shot at Booth's house. He damned near bled out before we got to him. Whatever's going on out there is escalating. I need to get a handle on it. Washington's gonna want to know what I'm doing and telling them you're on the job isn't gonna make me any points."

"Frank, you can't close this place down to make your investigation. These guys have got too many ships to repair and a bunch a new subs due the next few months.

Can you give me some time to try and get the bad guys? I just got things movin' here. If your agents march in demanding answers, ships ain't gonna sail and the war department's gonna want to know why.

"Maybe you could report that you've got undercover agents in place. I need time to identify the guys. I'm pretty sure it's a small group. Like I told you I got a look at the guy that torched Booth's office. All I need is to see his picture on his security file."

"I'll give you a week, Keys. If Washington thinks this is a big deal, they'll send in the cavalry. If you have the commandant's ear, you might want to mention that Roosevelt's an old Navy man. That might buy you more time."

"Thanks, boss. I'm staying on the yard tonight to find out what goes on during the graveyard shift. My bet is the rats are busy after dark. I'll keep you posted."

"Okay. Take care, Keys. Try not to collect any more lead, will you? You know as a consultant there's no medical."

"Uh, thanks, boss…I think."

Keys hangs up, then calls the commandant's office to pass along Gray's comment about Roosevelt and get an okay to bring Mary in. With an affirmative from the commandant, he calls Mary.

"You're in, Sprite. I'll have Larry, the Marine I told you about, meet you at the ferry slip tomorrow morning."

"Wow, Barry, I'm really excited. Are we going to share an office?"

"No Mary, definitely not. I don't want anyone to know we're related. I can't do my job if I'm worried about your safety."

"Oh come on, Barry, aren't you being a little over dramatic?"

"Over dramatic!" Keys thunders. He stops talking momentarily to take a breath and release the pressure of the phone against his ear.

"Mary, my love, these people we're after are growing more desperate. They tried to burn down a Navy building; the fire could have spread through the yard. I believe, as does Gray, that the same gang shot an FBI agent at Booth's house.

"If they succeed in damaging more Navy property, or in murdering someone in the process, they're gonna fry for it. We have them for stealing government property now in a time of war. These rats wouldn't think twice about using you to keep me from lockin' 'em up. I don't want them sending me your ears to make me back off."

Mary's hand instinctively flies up to touch her ear. She feels her other ear tingle against the phone receiver. "Good grief, Barry, can things like that really happen on a Navy yard?"

"Mary, I was being nice. It doesn't matter that it's a Navy yard. Think of the worst things men are capable of. You know what happens when you corner a rat. There are guys that enjoy inflicting pain and grief. That could easily happen. We can collaborate when we're at home. We can write up the reports to Gray together."

Keys rebuke stings a little. Mary feels scolded. "You mean I can type them up for you."

"You've got faster finger's than I have, Sprite. Don't be cross; I can't help worrying about you. Hold on a minute, will you? Mitch just came in waving a paper around. I better call you back. Bye, Mary."

"What's up, Mitch?"

"One of the men up at the North Ways found an arm floating in the water. The yard police took it to the hospital. A doctor pulled some kinda miracle and got a thumb print. It's George Booth's."

"I'll be damned. I just told Mary that if the gang we're after committed murder, they'd fry. This is gonna up the ante. Was it just his arm, no other parts?"

Mitch drops the Photostat on Keys desk. "That's all for now. This is worse than I thought. I didn't think pcople would get killed over some stuff stolen off the yard. You better watch your step, Keys. I've cleared Moose to be at your disposal. Morsey's concerned, too. He says you can have whatever you need to run these guys down."

"Can we keep this under our hat for a while, Mitch? I just got Gray to back off. If he gets wind of this, I may not be able to keep the FBI from storming the place."

"I'll keep shut, but word travels fast around here. I'll tell the commander you want to keep a lid on this for now. He can talk to the yard police. It's probably time to bring them in on this anyway."

Keys rubs his face, then answers. "It's okay by me as long as I still have a free hand to run these guys down. I don't want the local cops tyin' my hands. Can Morsey swing that?"

"He's a pretty tough customer when he needs to be, and he's in your corner. He'd make it work. The yard cops'll jump to his tune."

"Okay, Mitch, let's go see what we've gotta do to make this work. I'm glad I have the commander's confidence. Time is short so I need to get goin' and root these guys out.

"After we get squared away with the yard cops, I wanta take another good look at the northwest corner of the yard in the daylight to get the lay of the land. I'll bet it's still muddy after all the rain we've had. I don't want any surprises in the dark and I'm sure our bad guys know every hidey hole out there."

Mitch turns for the door. "I'll get Moose and meet you at the office."

The meeting in Morsey's office goes as Mitch said it would. The commander is sharp and self-confident. He introduces Keys to the yard's civilian police chief, asking that the chief give Keys full assistance and anything he asks for.

Chapter 16

Alby bursts into the barn. Harry angrily snatches the plans he's been working on off the table. "I told you I don't want to be disturbed."

Alby pulls the cloth cap from his head, rolling it up in his big hands. "Sorry, boss, but I got news." He fidgets with his hat, looking to Harry for a sign to continue. Harry shoots Alby an exasperated nod.

"Jeff Newcome found a arm floatin' on the water up by Way 8. I heard tell it's Booth's. I went to tell Tom an' the guys at the tavern says he tried to stick the Moose with his knife. Moose knocked him out an' throwed him outta the place. He's gonna be mighty angry an' me an' Rian don't want no part of 'im. Rian says he's gonna shoot 'im before Tom tries to knife us."

"You go tell Rian I'll take care of Tom."

"Are you gonna shoot 'im, Harry?"

"No, Alby, I'm not gonna shoot him. I told all of you to stay out of sight, to keep a low profile. I told you I don't want anyone to know what we do on the yard. Now everyone will know Booth was murdered. If we get caught now, we'll all hang. Stay away from Tom. If you see him, tell him I need to see him, and don't say anything about Booth's arm being found. Do you understand me, Alby?"

Alby unwinds his hat preparing to leave. "Yes, sir, boss. I understand real good."

"Okay, I'll see you and Rian on the yard tonight."

After Alby exits the barn, Harry tears up the plans he had drawn up, then pounds his fist on the table. Sitting down, he shakes his head. "Tom, you incredibly stupid son of a bitch," he says out loud. "Now I've got to find a way to get rid of you for good."

Tom wakes up unsure of where he is. Raising his head brings sparks of light behind his eyeballs and terrible pain. He lies back down on the rough fabric of the rug on his Vallejo apartment's floor. When he opens his eyes again, he realizes the view is an unfamiliar one of his own apartment. His mouth is impossibly dry, even though the side of his face is wet from drool.

An almost empty whiskey bottle lying on its side is spilled close to his face. The smell makes him want to retch. He smacks the bottle, sending it rolling across the floor. Up on an elbow he thinks back, trying to remember how he got home. Through the blurred pain, the shame of his encounter with Moose hits him like a brick. "Oh Jesus, if I had a gun I'd kill myself." His head thumps back to the floor.

Tom wakes some time later to the shrill of his phone eating a hole in his brain. Holding his head, he staggers to the horrible sound.

"Yeah, who's callin'? No, I ain't comin' ta work. I'm sick. If I gotta hangover it's my business, Harry. No, I don't care if I'm makin' things tough for you. Go ta hell, Harry." Tom bangs down the phone. It begins to ring again almost immediately.

Tom yanks the phone cord from the wall. Plaster flies, the cord's receptacle leaves a gapping hole in the wall. Tom holds his head in both hands. "I gotta kill that asshole."

Chapter 17

Key's fingers trace a path over the map on the wall when Gunnery Sergeant Mazurki knocks on the door frame.

"Hey, Larry, come on in."

The big Marine hesitates a moment. "You know, I've been called Moose for so long it's kinda confusin' to hear Larry."

Keys chuckles. "Well, okay, if there's any kinda panic, I'll yell Moose."

"That might be best," Larry answers. "Mitch sent me over, said I was assigned to you for as long as you need me."

"Yeah, Morsey, okay'd it and I'm glad to have you. My wife, Mary, is comin' tomorrow to pull files on the graveyard shift. I don't want anyone to know she's my wife. I want you to collect what she gets and bring it to me. I'm worried about her because someone found George Booth's arm floatin' in the river.

"That probably means the guys we're lookin' for are not opposed to murder. They may have killed him for his money or to keep him quiet. I don't want my wife to be in any danger, and we need to keep quiet about Booth's arm. I'm tryin' to keep the FBI from overrunnin' the yard."

"I won't let nothin' happen to your wife, Keys."

Keys reaches out to squeeze the Marine's arm. "I'm gonna count on that, my friend."

Larry shrugs; protecting people is what he does. "Why do you think the graveyard shift is bad?"

"I'm not sayin' the whole shift is bad, but in my experience rats always play at night."

"That's good, Keys. Like one a them detective novels." Larry lowers the pitch of his voice, "rats always play at night."

Keys is surprised at the Marine's levity. "Who's that spos'd to be, Cagney?"

A grin spreads across Larry's face. "I kinda think that's what Marlowe would talk like. Anyway, I kinda like how it sounds. I ran across a graveyard shift rat last night; little punk tried to knife me."

Keys goes serious. "What, here on the yard?"

"Naw, in a bar on Georgia Street."

"You know this guy's on the graveyard shift?" Keys asks.

"Yeah, I've seen him around. His name is Tom; I don't know his last name. But mostly, before he goes to work, he's at a bar drinkin' an' pissin' people off. He's not well-liked. Last night he was juiced to the gills an' lookin' for a fight."

Keys sits down at his desk and pulls out his notebook. "What's this guy do on the yard?"

"I don't know," Larry answers, "but I can find out."

Keys jots 'Tom' down in his notebook and underlines it.

"It's important we find out everything you can on this guy. He may know something about the guys we're after. I could haul him in for assault and grill 'im for information. When you talk to people, if Booth's arm comes up, say you heard it's just scuttlebutt, okay?"

"I got it, Keys."

"I'd like you to meet Mary at the ferry tomorrow, and take her to the commandant's office, okay?"

"Sure, Keys."

"Thanks, Larry. I'm gonna have a look around the yard in a little while. Tonight, I'm gonna visit the graveyard shift."

"I better go with you, Keys." Larry puts on a serious face and lowers his voice. "I know rats when I see 'em."

Keys chuckles, realizing Larry is becoming more relaxed, less formal; the big Marine has a welcome sense of humor.

"Okay, Marlowe, see what you can find out about your Tom character. There are a coupla buildings I wanta check out in the daylight. Then I plan on a nap for a coupla hours. If you don't have plans, I'll meet you back here at 22 hundred and we can have some dinner before we do the graveyard tour."

"Should I get me one a them notebooks like you got? I see you writin' in it all the time."

Keys goes to his desk. "Here's one for you. What bein' a cop, then an FBI agent taught me is to keep notes. You've got your own record of people and places that you can refer to long after you can't remember if something's important."

Larry takes the notebook. "How do I know what's important?"

Keys hands Larry a Parker pencil. "Well, the more notes the better. As you make the notes and use 'em, you'll get a feelin' of what's important and what's not. Sometimes it's helpful to jot down what you're thinkin' at the time, or what you see and even smell.

"Let's say we meet a guy tonight and he's not answering all our questions. You might note what questions he ducked or why you think he did. You'd want to know his name and where you found 'im. You might need to come back to 'im later. If the guy blinks, or looks away, gets nervous, or takes too much time to answer you'd make note a that.

"If you know he's not givin' you the straight dope, you can nail 'im with his evasiveness.

You'd check your notes and say to the guy, 'don't look away when I ask you a question.' Or you're blinkin' or shufflin' your feet or whatever you see. Then you say 'I know you're lyin', I can tell every time you lie to me.'

"That can get you answers sometimes, if the guy thinks he can't lie to you. The notes can help you, you can't remember everything. It's a tool, it's like the log books the Navy makes every ship captain keep."

"Thanks, Keys. Your line a work is kinda interestin', maybe I'll learn something. The Corps wants every Marine to be sharp; there's lots a stuff we've gotta remember."

"You're plenty sharp for my money, Marine. Let's get a move on. I want ta check out a coupla buildings out by the dumps before it gets dark. Don't forget to bring a good flashlight with you tonight."

Keys checks the items in his pouch before slinging it over his shoulder. He walks between the buildings down the pathway to Railroad Avenue on his way to see Smitty the locksmith.

"Anybody home?" Keys raps on the counter of the locksmith's shop. A man emerges from the dark depths of the shop, past shelves full of locks, hinges, machinery, and piles of ironworks. Some of the locks are old green-hued brass; there are huge keys as long as a man's forearm.

Keys sees Smitty, wiping his hands on a rag, coming out into the light.

"Hi yer, Mr. Keys."

"Hi Smitty. I'm glad you remember me."

"Kinda hard to forget Keys, if you know what I mean."

Keys smiles up at the man. "Good one, Smitty. I'm lookin' for small shops that aren't bein' used. The railroad manager tells me that some of the company's tools and switch boxes are missin'. I'm thinkin' maybe they just got misplaced, so Mitch gave me a big map and I'd like to take a look at buildings 701 and 709. Can you tell me if those places are locked and if I can get keys to get in 'em?"

Smitty nods knowingly.

"I wouldn't be surprised if somebody walked off with one a your trains. Some a these guys'll take anything that ain't nailed down. They put a fluoroscope at the gates ta keep 'em from pilferin' tools. Let me take a look at my books.

"The building numbers don't mean nothin'. I mean they ain't in any kinda order. 701's on the northwest side as I remember but like 702's way down the other end a the island by 15th street."

Smitty pulls a large weathered-gray bound book from under the counter. Opening the book, he turns the grease-stained pages to run his finger down the entries.

"Yeah, 701 and 709 are up by the HF radio station. They're both small shops an' not used much. I'll get my tool box an' take you up there."

"Thanks Smitty, but if you're busy I can take the keys an' check 'em out."

"I'd bet if someone's been usin' those shops, he ain't usin' the same locks I got keys for. It's a nice day, it ain't rainin' for a change an' I could do with some sunshine. Meet me around back an' I'll drive us up there."

Smitty yells to someone that he's going out as Keys exits the shop. At the back of the building Keys finds Smitty backing a Jeep out of the shop. Keys stands back while Smitty turns the little odd-looking vehicle around.

"Jump in, Keys."

The detective takes a minute to look over the Jeep before stepping through the door-less cutout to settle on the hard-padded seat.

"I've never seen one a these things up close before."

Smitty grins at Keys before pulling the floor shift gear lever into low gear.

"I got one a the only nonmilitary ones on the yard. This is one helluva of a car. I gotta keep it locked up in the shop so's nobody takes it. This thing'll go anywhere. It's got a ton a pullin' power. Hell, I've pulled them big trucks outta the mud with this thing.

"If I gotta go to one'a the pump houses up in the hills through the mud, this little doodlebug zips me right up there. Hang on to your hat after we pass Cedar Avenue, I'm takin' the levee road. I love blastin' this thing through them mud puddles."

The sun is getting low in the sky. Keys pulls his hat down to shade his eyes. After they stop for traffic on Cedar Avenue, Keys does have to hold onto his hard hat. Smitty accelerates through first gear, snaps the lever up to second. Muddy water flies; coming out of a deep puddle, all four wheels leave the ground.

Keys quickly tucks his shoulder pouch under one arm so he can hold onto his hat while gripping the seat's rail to keep from being thrown out. He glances over at his demon-eyed driver who has a huge grin plastered on his face.

Smitty comes to a gravel-spitting stop past the radio station in front of a small group of buildings. He bounds out of the Jeep and goes to the back to get his tool box. Untying the rope holding the box to the Jeep's bed, he calls to Keys.

"701's the little one here. I don't think anyone uses 'em. There ain't many building's on the yard that ain't in use. How'd you find 'em?"

"Mitch gave me a map that just came out. 701's marked as unoccupied. 709's marked as storage but looks to me like it's too far away from anything to be used."

Smitty examines the padlock on the metal door of 701.

"Well, that's just what I thought. Whoever's been here changed the lock."

"Can you pick it?" Keys asks.

"Oh yeah, I got just the tool." Smitty opens his tool box pulls out a two-handle bolt-cutting tool and snaps through the padlock's shackle.

"Best lock pickin' tool I got." Smitty holds the cutters up, grinning proudly.

"Well, that's wonderful, Smitty, except I didn't want anyone to know we were here."

"Sorry, Keys. It's a cheap lock. I can replace it with another that'll take the same key if you want."

"Let's see what's in the place first," Keys says.

Smitty opens the door, looks inside, then returns to the Jeep to get a flashlight. Keys quickly steps back to give way to the fast-moving locksmith.

"Oops, sorry, Keys, can't see a damn thing, it's dark as a cave in there. Guess I'm kinda anxious ta see what's in there."

Keys extends his arm, hand palm-up. "Lead on, I'll try to keep pace."

Smitty enters the building, pointing the cone of light from his flashlight to the floor before him, then to the walls looking for a light switch. He finds the switch, flipping it up to illuminate the interior.

Keys enters beside Smitty. "Well, well, well, the rats have been busy."

The small room is cluttered with tires, 55-gallon steel drums, yard-made 5-gallon paint cans, batteries, red-painted yard bicycles and bags of coffee beans.

Smitty lets out a low whistle. "Whew, this stuff's worth a fortune. It ain't railroad property so whatta ya gonna do, Keys?"

"I'm gonna take some pictures, and a quick inventory of this stuff, and give it to the yard police. Let's see what's in the 55-gallon drums. Have you got some pliers we can unscrew the caps with?"

Keys is jotting down items in his notebook when Smitty returns with pliers.

Smitty hands Keys the pliers. "You wanta do the honors?"

"Sure," Keys replies.

Keys rolls tires and bicycles out of his way to get to the drums. He unscrews the cap on one and bends down to sniff. "Gas in this one." He screws the cap back on and climbs over some boxes to open another drum. "Oil in this one," he says.

"Lets get down to 709, Smitty, but don't bust the lock. I don't want whoever's stealin' this stuff to know we found that one, too."

Smitty examines the padlock on the door of the 709 building. Using a ring of keys, he selects one that fits the lock. Slowly moving the key into the lock, he feels the lock's tumblers while gently holding turning pressure on the key. After several minutes, the hasp springs open.

"Ain't lost my touch," Smitty beams.

Sliding the big door back on its tracks, the first thing that catches both men's eyes is a

133

recently-painted torpedo sitting on a heavy wood cradle.

"Holy Ka-rist, Keys! What the hell do they want with that? You sure as hell ain't gonna sell that on the blackmarket."

"Don't touch anything, Smitty. I'm gonna take a quick look around and take some pictures, then we'll get out of here."

Smitty closes the door and snaps the lock shut. "You ain't really a railroad dick, are you, Keys?"

"What I am, Smitty, is concerned. Can I trust you to keep quiet about this?"

"I been on this yard twenty-eight years, Keys. I got secrets that'd fill a book. I won't say nothin' if you say so," Smitty answers indignantly.

"Okay, Smitty, thanks for the help. Let's get back to your shop. I'd like to get a key for that lock."

Chapter 18

Tom stays in his apartment the next day, nursing his hangover. With his hand shielding his eyes, his head throbbing, he struggles to yank a window curtain on the murderous sunlight. It is early afternoon before he remembers the almost-empty whiskey bottle he shoved away the previous night. Tom grunts, getting down on his hands and knees searching to find the bottle that rolled under a chair.

The first sniff of the whiskey makes his stomach churn. He sits on the chair and pulls the bottle to his mouth. The cheap liquor burns its way down his throat. He hesitates to see if he can keep it down, then empties the rest with a determined gulp.

After sleeping restlessly until evening, Tom feels somewhat better. He drives to Mare Island early to go to one of the worker cafeterias. After filling his tray with soup, potatoes, and bread, he sits by himself noisily slurping the soup, hoping the food will soak up the rest of the booze in his system.

Tom pulls the lever punching his time card, then heads for the scrapyard. The yard's huge lights seem to bleach out any color; the heavy shadows are like black holes. He scowls when he sees Harry waiting for him. Shrugging, his hands ball into fists in his pockets. *"Be calm,"* he tells himself, *"don't let on you're gonna kill 'im."*

Harry steps in front of Tom, pulling him away from the harsh light.

"You are a big disappointment to me, Tom. You seem set on exposing yourself and the rest of us until you have all of us hanged. I called you because Booth's arm was found. I want to know how that could happen. Is the rest of him going to pop up somewhere?"

Tom pulls away from Harry's grasp. "I ain't tryin' ta get us caught. I buried Booth's parts as deep in the damned muck as I could. Maybe some animal got the arm, or some bird dragged it off…hell, I don't know."

Harry grabs the front of Tom's coat pulling him close. "Get out to the place you buried Booth tomorrow and make sure nothing else surfaces. Alby and Rian need help loading the railroad cars. I expect you to do your job and stay away from that Marine, Moose. Do you understand me?"

Tom swats Harry's arms away and steps back. "Don't go layin' your hands on me no more.

I ain't somebody you can push around. I'll…I'll…"

Harry grimaces, pushing his face close to Tom's. "What, Tom? You'll kill me. I told you what will happen if you try that. Don't be stupid. Get up there and help the boys. If you try any rough stuff on them, I'll crack your head."

A group of yardmen pass by the two men; someone whistles, another says, "Hey, lover boys, get a room."

Harry turns away into the darkness. "Aw, shut up, ya bunch'a assholes," Tom shouts, and stalks away.

Harry heads to a modest wood-framed building off the Dump Road that serves as a sawmill shed. He climbs up a ladder to a small windowless office he made for himself in the eaves. Settling into a chair behind a wood plank resting on saw horses, he opens the hardbound journal he keeps with him.

The journal pages contain his black-market connections, the items he sells to each, and monies taken in. His success at black-marketing has been outstanding. Aligning himself with the late George Booth has been a boon financially to both men. Booth's long service at the yard gained Harry entrance to many of Booth's scams.

Booth's influence also granted Harry his position of authority on the graveyard shift. During Harry's Abwehr training, he had been instructed to look for night shift work as the security was usually the most relaxed during that period. After some weeks on the graveyard shift, Harry discovered train cars of goods for the yard were uncoupled from the locomotives in a railyard outside of Vallejo. Then the Navy yard's own locomotives would pick up the cars and bring them into Mare Island.

Harry immediately saw his opportunity. With Booth's help, he was assigned the job of overseeing the unloading and loading of the railroad cars at Mare Island's scrapyard. The rest was simplicity itself. He would have his handpicked men unload the cars, then reload the empty cars with his black-market goods.

After the yard's locomotive took the chalk-marked cars to Vallejo, Harry or one of his men would enter the railyard with forged papers and unload their booty. Some of the materials they stole would be trucked to their black-market customers. Smaller loads went in their cars modified with secret compartments. The operation was kept as simple as possible with very few people involved and payoffs only going to the Vallejo end of the operation.

All of this meant that Harry's operation paid for itself and thus did not require aid from his Abwehr masters. His radio traffic to them was held to a minimum. While this was appreciated by his masters, his lack of sabotage was not. The Abwehr wanted results. Mare Island's phenomenal success rate of ship repair and building was ruinous to their Japanese allies' war efforts.

After a long struggle with faulty torpedoes, America's submarines were decimating Japan's shipping. Japan had gold and uranium Germany wanted. Both countries wanted America's West Coast ship building and repair stopped. Sabotage had not been successful; Germany's attempts at landing saboteurs on the East Coast were met with arrests and hangings.

The Nazi's ludicrously-devised plan to blow up Hoover Dam came to nothing. The Abwehr wanted some results. Harry fed them a story of the fire he set on the yard, telling of the great destruction he wrought. However, there was no slowdown seen in Mare Island's output.

Harry spent months planning his assault on Mare Island. Each plan reached some obstacle he could not overcome until he found what he hoped was one crippling vulnerability. On the south side of the yard was the Naval Ammunition Pier. On a return trip from Vallejo, Harry observed, from across the Mare Island Strait, huge transport ships being loaded with munitions.

His first plan was to fill a boat with explosives and ram it into the pier when there were stacks of bombs and boxes of ammunition being loaded on a ship. He abandoned the idea when he could not think of a way to do it without getting himself killed.

One night he walked down to the waterfront to watch a new submarine being loaded for trials.

Perched up on a stationary crane he saw a group of sailors winching a yellow-headed practice torpedo into the boat. Harry almost clapped his hands. A torpedo! He thought, *"what an idea; pure genius."*

The next day at the Vallejo barn, he excitedly explained his plan to Tom, Rian, and Alby. He did not get the enthusiastic reaction he wanted from them.

When Harry turned away from them to get his cigarettes, the three men slowly caught the eye of each other. Genius, their arched eyebrows queried, or madness? None of the three wanted to see the south end of the island destroyed.

Hundreds of personnel would be murdered. Making a lot of money from black-marketing was one thing. It was the main thing they wanted. But this would mean the end of their time on the yard and maybe a long time on the run. They would certainly have to leave before the FBI swarmed in to investigate.

Harry was acutely aware that his men were growing tired of each other and of any thoughts of sabotage. He was disgusted by their lack of conviction. They had no loyalty to him, themselves, or their country, as he saw it. Tom was a loose cannon he had to get rid of very soon.

With Rian and Alby, he thought he could still coerce them to do his bidding. He had to get his hands on a torpedo. He knew the electric model torpedo would not leave a wake in the water. The gangs loading ordnance would never know what hit them. An explosion of that magnitude could never be hidden. The ammunition depot and the south end of the island would be out of commission for a long time.

Harry dreamed of the day he would receive a hero's welcome in Berlin. The Führer himself would place medals on Harry, now Heinrich Roedman again, and an adoring crowd would cheer him. The huge red and black Nazi banners would wave on a gentle breeze, the sun bright in the crystal blue sky.

Heroes of the war would be lined up, resplendent in crisp Nazi uniforms, waiting for their medals. Fighter planes would form waves, buzzing over a crowd of tens of thousands of Germans waving swastikas and cheering their gallant idols. Goebbels would make grand speeches. Harry had to have that torpedo!

Chapter 19

Keys waits while Smitty makes a key for 709. He thanks the locksmith and returns to his office. Sitting at his desk, he makes notes about the discovery in the northwest shops, then picks up the phone to call Mitch.

"Hi, Mitch, Keys here. I've got a coupla questions for you. First, I need to have some film developed that I don't want seen by anyone we don't trust. Next, I need a Jeep to use on the yard. And last, but not least, I need to report to commander Morsey that I've found a torpedo in building 709."

Mitch, startled, holds out the receiver to look at his phone. "What! Say again."

"I found a torpedo in building 709."

Mitch quickly flips open a book with building numbers and locations. Running his finger quickly down the 700-number page, he asks Keys, "Isn't 709 up by the HF radio station?"

"That's the one," Keys answers.

"What the hell's a torpedo doin' there?" Mitch asks. "Ah, never mind. I'll get to work on the film and Jeep for you. You better make your report to the commander yourself; he's gonna want all the details. Hold the wire a minute and I'll get him for you."

The first words Morsey thunders into the phone are, "A torpedo! What the hell's a torpedo doin' in 709, Keys? What model is it?"

"I don't know sir. I took some pictures of it."

"Get them to me as soon as you can get here, Keys. I need to know what we're dealing with."

"The pictures aren't developed, sir," Keys replies.

"Just get the film to me, Keys. I'll take care of gettin' it processed. I'd like a report while you're here. How'd you find the thing in the first place?"

"I'm just downstairs, sir. I'll be right up."

Keys reports to Morsey while Mitch rushes the film off to be processed.

Sitting in front of Morsey's desk, Keys opens his notebook.

"I looked up the buildings on the northwest of the yard because the list you gave me of materials stolen would have mostly come from that end of the island. I found two small buildings, 701 and 709, that were listed as storehouses but were not in use.

143

"That seemed odd to me because the war work keeps every building I've seen full up and busy. I walked up the Dump Road the other day and was stopped by a sentry. He wouldn't let me go any farther even after I showed him my badge. So that, coupled with empty store rooms, made me suspicious."

Morsey leans forward, anxious to hear the rest.

"Remind me of that sentry later, Keys. How'd you get in the storerooms?"

"I got Smitty, the locksmith, and we went up to see what was in those buildings. The first building we went in was 701 and it's filled with stolen goods. I took a quick inventory, some pictures and we went to 709. The torpedo was sittin' right in the middle of the room. We locked the place up after I took pictures because I don't want the guys that got it to know we've been there.

"As soon as possible, I'd like to have guards posted who could keep a 24-hour watch on the place and identify anyone going into 709. Whoever it is may know we went into 701 because Smitty had to cut that lock. But he jimmied 709's lock. I hope they think the torpedo is safe."

His hands clenched together atop his desk, Morsey listens intently to Keys' report.

"I'll tell you, Keys, the FBI were fools to let you go. You get right to it, man."

"Thanks, sir, but, believe me, I've just been lucky. Cases rarely go like this, and I haven't found the guys that are responsible for this job yet."

"Have you got any more of those Chesterfield's, Keys?"

Keys shakes out two cigarettes and hands one to Morsey.

After lighting up, Morsey snorts out twin streams of smoke like a mad dragon.

"What's your take on this torpedo, Keys?"

"I think two things are possible sir. One, someone is stealing secret information for the enemy. Two, someone is planning to sabotage a ship or the yard. I don't know what kind of explosives a torpedo has or how big an explosion it could make."

"I've got a number of problems with this, Keys. I gotta know how the hell someone got a torpedo in the first place and what they plan on doin' with it. I can't see how they'd launch one without a firing tube but the warhead has 600 pounds of high explosives. That will make one hell of a mess I can tell you. What color was the head of the torpedo?"

"It was bright yellow," Keys answers.

"Well, thank God for that. Yellow is an exercise head. That means it's used for practice and filled with water instead of explosives. After it's fired, compressed air pushes out the water and the torpedo floats to the surface. We use them on new boat trials before they head out for war patrols."

"We need to get guards posted on that building as soon as possible, sir!" Keys exclaims.

"Okay, I got that, Keys. I want to go see that building myself but first I want to see the pictures and get a torpedo expert to have a look at 'em. We'll have those pictures you took pretty soon. I'll get the torpedo shop to send a man here pronto."

It is growing dark as Morsey opens a window to let out the cigarette smoke that is filling his office. He has two torpedo shop men, a photo expert, Keys and Mitch all bent over his desk inspecting the stack of 8x10 photos.

"It's a Mark 18 all right," says one of the torpedo men. "I can't tell if it's complete or just parts. We need to see it up close."

Morsey walks back to his desk; the ferocity of his frown sets the men on edge. "How the hell did somebody get that outta your shop?"

"I don't know sir; we sent some out for the new boats. All of them shoulda been accounted for, but I haven't any explanation at this point."

"Commander, can we get some people on the building now?" Keys asks.

Morsey, obviously annoyed, stabs out his cigarette. "Okay, okay, let's get up there and have look at this thing. Sorry, Keys, I just don't know how a three-thousand-pound, twenty-foot long torpedo goes missing without anyone noticing."

All of the men begin to file out of the office. Keys stops at the door. "Commander, it will be best if just you and I go to 709 first. Whoever stole the torpedo is liable to have someone watching the place. I'm hoping that just the two of us won't be noticed. I have my camera and can take more pictures of what everyone wants to see."

Keys drives with Morsey to see the torpedo and directs the commander to park by the cars at the radio station.

"Let me take a quick look around sir. I'll be right back."

Staying in shadows, he looks into the radio station entrance, then at the cluster of buildings alongside. He does not see any obvious lookouts and goes back to the car.

"I can't spot anyone, sir. Let's go on down to the building. Try to stay in the shadows."

The light above 709's door is out. Keys cups his flashlight to shield the light. The small circle of light finds the door's hasp open without the padlock. He unholsters his gun and motions Morsey to stay behind him.

Cautiously sliding back the big door, he narrows his eyes trying to discern any sign of movement in the pitch black interior. Moving to the light switch, Keys turns to face the room, his gun held in front of him, before turning on the lights.

His eyes quickly take in every facet of the room he can see from his vantage point.

147

"Aw, son of a bitch," Keys moans.
The torpedo and its cradle are gone.

Chapter 20

Morsey enters the building, then stands with his hands on his hips, remembering the interior from the photographs Keys took.

"I guess I shoulda put guards on this place when you asked me to, Keys."

"No sense in cryin' over spilt milk, sir. I coulda called the yard police, too, but I don't know who to trust yet. I'm gonna take a look around. From what I can tell, they only took the torpedo. The rest of the stuff looks like its still here; I'd have to check the photos to be sure."

Keys walks through the neatly stacked stolen goods looking for shoe prints or marks on the concrete floor. At the back of the building, he finds a man-door. Trying the door, he finds it locked from the outside. He goes back past Morsey, who is studying the ground.

Outside at the front of the building, Keys plays his light over the muddy ground. Where there should have been footprints and tire marks, the ground is marked with what looks like rake furrows that go back up the road.

"Aren't we clever?" Keys mutters, holstering his gun.

Turning back, he goes inside the building and finds Morsey down on one knee, looking at something in his hand.

"Find something, sir?"

Morsey turns to Keys, looking pleased with himself.

"Yeah, Keys, I was tryin' to figure out what the marks on the floor are. Somebody mopped the place and some mud is still streaked here and there. They musta been in a hurry. I found a coupla torpedo ring bolts they knocked over here with the mop. That's how they're movin' the torpedo; they're disassembling it."

"Good goin', sir, they don't seem to miss much. Who ever this bunch is they're not the run a the mill dummies. From the two buildings, we know what they're stealin', but not who they are or how they're getting' the stuff outta the yard."

Keys rubs his jaw. "I'm thinkin' the bigger worry at this point may be what they're plannin' to do with the torpedo. How do you fire one of those things off? Do you have to have a gun barrel of some kind?"

Morsey hands the bolts to Keys.

"It could be possible, I suppose, to put a Mark 18 in the water and set it off. You'd have to know how to aim it and get all the settings right. It is not something just anyone could do; it takes a fair amount of education.

"If they're plannin' on doin' any damage, they'd have to fill the warhead with explosive and come up with a detonator. The Mark 18 has an electric motor; it's quiet and doesn't leave a wake. It can be set for depth and direction. If it's fired successfully, it would be undetectable until it hits something."

Keys jiggles the bolts in his hand. He looks up from the bolts to Morsey.

"I'd like to get a guard in the radio station to keep an eye on this place. I doubt our bad guys will be back, but you never know. You may want to get your torpedo experts to look for ways that the torpedo could be used, and for vulnerable targets. I'd like to get back; I'm gonna meet Larry for dinner and then we're gonna stake out the graveyard shift."

Morsey taps Keys' shoulder.

"Good man, Keys. Don't wear yourself out burnin' it at both ends. I've seen the toll it takes when submariners go into fights for 30-odd hours at a time. When you find these guys, I'm betting on fireworks; stay sharp, be careful. I'll go on up to the radio station and call for a guard."

Keys goes back to his office in the administration building to write up a report to send to his FBI boss, Frank Gray. After finishing the report, he rubs his face, his eyes feeling gritty.

He lies down on a cot Mitch got for him, thinking of resting for a moment before Larry shows up. Keys eyes pop open after being shaken by the big Marine.

"Jeez Keys, I thought you were dead. I knocked on the door earlier and peeked in; you were sawin' logs, man. I went down to the cafeteria had some coffee to give you some more time to sleep. Here, I got a cup for you."

Keys lifts his wrist, looking at his watch. Getting his feet on the floor he stretches arching his back, then reaches for the paper coffee cup. "Thanks, Larry, I thought I'd just doze for a minute. I'm glad you got me up. Let's go get some dinner."

After dinner, the two men walk up 5th Street to Cedar Avenue. The cafeteria with hundreds of people coming on shift was too noisy to hold a conversation.

"Let's just go easy tonight, Larry. I wanta get an idea of what goes on with this shift. My FBI people tell me that security on this yard is pretty lax. My old boss says everyone here seems to think they're just one big happy family. He may be right or not.

"Maybe it's easy to get contraband outta here. So, the plan for tonight is to keep a low profile and watch what goes on. If you see someone you know, you could ask about that Tom guy. Keep it easy, you're just makin' conversation, okay?"

"Yes, sir," Larry replies. " I'll be like Ace Drummond, Secret Agent. Real smooth, but I'll get the dope."

"Watch a lotta movies, do you, Larry?"

"That's all I had ta do while they were fixin' my leg. It took my mind offa maybe gettin' drummed outta the Corps."

"I forgot all about that, Larry. You gonna be all right walkin' around with all the mud an' water?"

Larry kicks out with his prosthetic leg. "I'll bet I can walk twice as far as you, Keys."

Keys grins, turning his head to the big man. "That's a bet I wouldn't take, Marine."

Λ crossing signal sounds; the men stop to wait for a yard locomotive to pull its boxcars across Cedar Avenue.

Keys points across the street. "I wanta go by the scrapyard office. Some a the stuff I saw in 701 and 709 looked like surplus goods. Let's just stay in the shadows for a while and watch what goes on."

Keys and Larry lean back against the front of a large storage building that gives them a view of the entire well-lighted scrapyard complex. Yard locomotives are busy along Cedar Avenue, clattering back and forth, delivering war materials.

Occasionally, a locomotive pulls into the scrapyard with two or three box cars that have scrap metal and damaged parts that were replaced on repaired ships.

153

Scrapyard workers materialize to quickly unload the materials and then load them into long, covered bins on both sides of the railroad tracks. The yard men move with practiced deliberation unloading the cars and stowing the parts and metals in the appropriate bins.

Keys speaks to Larry in low tones as they watch.

"I wonder who keeps track of all this stuff. Some a the trains that have gone by us in the past coupla hours have twenty, thirty cars, and I'm told we're on the slow part a the yard. Its gotta be a hell of a job figuring where all these trains go.

"There's hundreds of buildings on this yard with train tracks goin' in and out of 'em. Every pier, every ship building way, the Ammo Depot, all have train tracks. Its gotta be a nightmare figuring what goes where."

Keys takes his notebook out of his pocket to scribble notes.

Larry watches Keys write in the notebook. Keys puts the notebook away and winks at Larry. "I need to talk to the people that run the trains. Let's hike on down to the lumber yard; I wanta see how easy it is to get in and outta there. We'll call it a night after that and get some sack time. Don't forget to meet Mary in the morning, okay?"

Larry brandishes his notebook, shaking it in his hand. "I got it written down right here."

Chapter 21

Weeks before Keys made his discovery at the 709 building, German spy Heinrich Roedman, aka Harry Bower, lurks outside of the torpedo workshop in the early morning hours. Harry painted his hard hat with numbers indicating a waterfront ship outfitter to blend in. He watches for several mornings to find an opening. The entire waterfront is busy 24 hours a day and, even in the early morning graveyard shift hours, the activity is daunting.

He first thinks that with all of the activity he will have no chance of gaining entrance to the torpedo shop without being discovered. After pondering on the problem, he remembers an Abwehr instructor's lesson to act as if you belong. If you present an air of confidence in your manner, you can often go anywhere unchallenged.

The instructor further imparted a prop was very useful. A uniform, briefcase, badge, notebook, clipboard, or even wearing a gun, if used in an authoritative manner, would do the job.

So, instead of worrying about all the activity, Harry decides he will use it to his advantage. At 4 a.m. two men file out of the torpedo workshop on their way to the cafeteria. Harry walks to the shop's door with a clipboard under his arm. His lock pick tools are secreted inside the lining of his coat.

Trying the doorknob first, he isn't surprised to find the door unlocked. Entering the shop, he takes a brief look around to make sure no one else is there, then heads to a side office off the work floor.

On the way to the office, Harry runs his hand down the side of a cool-to-the-touch torpedo that sits on a wood-framed cradle. At the office door, he fingers the pockets of his coat, he has all the tools he needs to work on any locks. His plan is to find a torpedo manual to copy.

In the office, he sees a row of locked file cabinets. As he advances, studying the locks on the cabinets, a light blue bound book lying on a desk catches his attention. It has US Navy Torpedo in large black letters printed on the face. In smaller print under the title is "*Mark 18 (ELECTRIC)*". Luck is with him. He quickly takes a tiny Minox camera from a pocket. Moving the book under a desk lamp, he begins photographing.

While turning pages and photographing, Harry takes a moment to glance up at on the clock hanging on the wall. He can hardly believe how much time has passed. From watching on previous mornings, he knows the men will be back very soon. Rushing through the final pages, the Nazi spy puts the book and lamp back in the same positions he found them on the desk.

He quickly checks to make sure all is as he found it, then wipes cold sweat from his forehead. Taking a deep breath and squaring his shoulders, Harry relaxes his composure. He snatches up his clipboard and just makes it back to the shop floor when the men come into the shop.

It takes some moments before the two torpedo shop workmen realize Harry's presence. One of the men, in grease-stained bib overalls straining at his stomach, steps forward.

"What the hell are you doin' in here, fella?"

"Hi," Harry says holding up his clipboard. "I'm checking unattended shops for the Yard Commander. I knocked on your door before I came in just now. The commander said no shop was supposed to be left unlocked if no one was working in the shop."

The two torpedo men exchange a look before bib-overall-man speaks. "Uh, we just went out for a smoke." The other man nods his head agreeing.

Harry takes a pencil from his pocket. "I'll have to mark it down on this form the commander gave me. He said he's gonna be real tough on shops that aren't locking up."

"Hey, we just stepped out for a smoke. We can't smoke in here; I don't know how we missed you knockin' on the door. Are you new here? I haven't seen you before; maybe you don't know how things work around here."

Harry smiles pleasantly at the men, then adds, "Yeah, I'm new to this shift. I just started the graveyard shift 'cause it gives me more time with my wife and kids. Look fellas, I don't wanta make trouble for you. Maybe I can just give you a warning, okay?"

"Yeah, thanks. We've got enough to do without the commander comin' down on us."

Harry runs his hand over the nose of the torpedo he's standing by.

"Man, these torpedoes are much bigger than I thought. You guys must be some kinda geniuses to make 'em work. Close up they look real complicated."

The man in bib overalls picks up an odd-shaped wrench from a workbench and goes to the back end of the torpedo. Fitting the wrench to the propeller shaft, he looks up from the work to answer Harry.

"These things are complicated. They're made to exacting specifications and tolerances. The maintenance is crucial and demanding. It doesn't take much to have a failure. We've overcome most of the problems with 'em and this Mark 18 Electric is easier to work on."

The second torpedo workman, who has been silent so far, pipes in.

"The electric's better but still gives us headaches. We've got one comin' back tomorrow."

"Yeah," says the first man. "Somebody screwed up and shorted the batteries; I hear it's a big mess. Damn near choked those submariners to death before they found the short. It's comin' back in pieces, a real big mess. Anyway we gotta get back to work here, friend. Are we good with you?"

Harry makes a show of putting his pencil away. "Sure, sure, I don't wanta cause trouble; I can see you guys have your hands full. If you remember to lock up when you leave, you'll never see me again, okay?"

A rare smile settles on Harry's face as he turns to walk up C Street. He can hardly believe how easy it was to get the torpedo manual. He walks up the road, hands in his pockets, his mind spinning with thoughts of stealing a torpedo. After checking that his three co-conspirators are doing the jobs he gave them, he leaves the yard.

Back in the Vallejo barn, Harry climbs the stairs to his workshop. In the darkroom, he measures out the film developing chemicals to process his torpedo manual photographs. Finished with processing the film, Harry allows himself a beer. After going down to his room on the ground floor, he turns on the radio to listen to a classical music station. He leans back in an upholstered chair, sipping the beer, enjoying the music.

Rubbing his chin in thought, he picks up a notebook and begins to scribble notes.

Ideas are written down only to be crossed out. Harry stands up from the chair to pace the room, head down, concentrating on making a viable plan. His head goes up and Harry goes back to the notebook. Making more notes, he seizes on a plan he thinks will work.

The Nazi spy returns upstairs to ink the rollers, then set the type on his Kelsey Table Top Platen Press. Another smile spreads on his face as he looks over the completed form. Harry stares into the wet sheen of the press's ink disc that reflects his image. "You are a very clever man Heinrich," he mutters to himself. "Yes, very clever indeed."

Harry slept very little so when the photos dried, he read the torpedo manual with great interest. The manual explained every facet of the Mark 18 explicitly. Pictures of the actual inner working of the Mark 18 left nothing to the imagination.

The next day he outlines his plans to Rian and Tom. He has Alby return to the yard to watch for the arrival of the submarine returning with the damaged Mark 18. Alby calls in at four thirty that afternoon. Harry listens to his report.

"They're tyin' her up by the freight shed, boss. She's gonna be unloadin' pretty soon. It's rainin' here pretty good, too."

"Excellent," Harry exclaims, thrusting out his fist triumphantly, "it'll be the shift change soon, perfect timing. We're on our way; stay on watch till we get there."

Tom gets out of his chair, headed for the door. "I'll meet you guys there."

"No! You'll both go with me," Harry commands. "Grab some rope and wood planks we can secure the torpedo with, put 'em in the back of my truck."

"Them things is heavy if you didn't know it," Tom complains.

"I know exactly what each component of the Mark 18 torpedo weighs. They have to get it off the sub with a crane and they can put it in back of my truck with the same crane. All we have to do is be there when they offload it, act like we were sent to get it and be gone before anyone gets wise.

"Quit bellyaching, Tom, and get going. If anything goes wrong with the torpedo, you'll hang for killin' Booth or I'll kill you myself."

The three men squeeze into Harry's faded-blue 1934 Dodge pickup truck. Harry crunches into first gear, dumps the clutch, fish-tailing on the wet dirt as he hurries to get his prize. When they arrive at the waterfront just off the causeway, Alby, who has been nervously pacing, motions Harry to park by the freight shed.

Harry parks the truck and rolls down the window as Alby approaches. The rain comes in waves, heavy a few minutes, then very light.

"The sub sailors unloaded the torpedo on the wharf in pieces, boss. I asked one of 'em what they was doin'; he said the damned thing almost killed 'em and they took it apart to get rid a the batteries."

"Do you know where the batteries are, Alby?"

"Yeah. The guy said they deep-sixed 'em."

Harry turns his wrist to see the hands of his watch tick by. At five o'clock, the whistles sound, marking the end of shift. Men and women swarm out of the buildings.

"All right, we'll go get the parts and put them in the truck. I'll take the clipboard and have a sailor sign the form I made so he'll think it's okay.

Harry gets out of the truck, pulls his rain slicker's collar up to hide his face and heads to the wharf. Dodging a throng of people on their way home, he sees a sailor near the torpedo and calls out to him.

"Hey, sailor, we're here to pick up the bum torpedo."

The sailor also dodges workers, some of whom give him a cheerful clap on his shoulder on their way past. Looking wet and somewhat peeved, he points to the pile of rain-slicked parts and shouts over the din, "That's the pile a junk right there, Mac."

Harry jostles through the crowd, holding out his clip board toward the sailor.

"Hey! what's goin' on down there, sailor?" an officer from the sub yells from the bridge. Harry cringes, tugging down the brim of his hat.

"This guy wants somebody to sign for the busted torpedo, sir."

"Yeah, well, good riddance to bad rubbish. Sign the damned form, sailor; I ain't comin' down there. God knows that's all we do when we get in; sign forms so's somebody can cover their ass."

Harry realizes he's been holding his breath. Without looking up, he gives a backhanded wave to the officer while the sailor signs the form.

Harry loops a rope around the torpedo's tail section. With the batteries gone, this is the heaviest part of the torpedo. He runs a steel pole through the rope, ties it off and the four men strain to lift the tail section. With the throng of people thinning, the men make their way to the truck. No one takes any undue notice of them.

With the two other sections quickly loaded, Harry throws a tarp over his ultimate weapon.

"I'll drop you guys off at the car park."

Alby climbs into the truck's bed. "Don't you want help unloadin' boss?"

"I've got it from here, Alby. I'll see you all tonight in the shed before our shift starts."

Harry drives away as the three co-conspirators head to their cars.

"That guy's nuts," Tom says. "What's he gonna do with that pile a junk?"

"He's a pretty bright guy," Rian replies. "It wouldn't surprise me none if he blows the whole place up."

Tom spits on the ground, then shakes his finger at Rian.

"If he does, they'll hang us all."

Harry drives up I Street past the radio station and turns down to the 709 building. He opens the sliding door and backs the truck into the building. After closing the door, he rolls a mobile A-frame with a block and tackle to the truck.

After gently unloading the torpedo sections to the floor, Harry bends down to inspect each section of his prize. He rubs his hands together. "Good planning, none of those fools even noticed. They'll never know what hit 'em."

He wants to keep the torpedo near the yard's source of parts before taking it to the Vallejo barn for final assembly and testing. He knows his major problem will be batteries. The stolen manual has the exact specifications for the batteries, all 1215 pounds of them.

He hopes to get away with the damaged torpedo without raising much concern from the Navy. He is sure, however, that stealing the very special batteries the Mark 18 requires would indeed cause an intensive investigation.

Harry goes to a stack of 4 by 4 planks and, with a handsaw, begins cutting the wood to build a cradle like he saw in the torpedo shop.

"Batteries," Harry mutters. Sawing the heavy planks, he does the mathematics in his head. "2.12 volts a cell," he says out loud. "170 volts needed, that's what? Maybe 80 cells minimum. Hmm, that would be almost 30 6-volt car batteries."

Chapter 22

Mary Keys is excited as she jostles into the crowd on the ferry. This is new for her; at Marinship she could walk to work. On this ferry, men and women of different races and colors sit and stand, some speaking different languages.

Most of them are in lighthearted conversation, a few alone with their thoughts. The hard hats many wear are in various colors with large numbers painted on them. Mary feels the buzz: these people are making the difference, they are winning the war, and she is proud to be part of it again.

Mary files out of the ferry in the throng. She watches nervously as Marine guards check the worker's badges as they pass through an iron gate. She stands apart from the line, then sees a huge Marine step around the line coming toward her.

"Ah, I hope you're Larry. I don't have a badge yet."

"It's all right, Mrs. Keys. I'm Larry. I have your pass and when we get through the gate, I'll take you to the administration building to get you squared away."

Once through the gate, the Marine walks beside Mary in the mass of workers. At Railroad Avenue the workers disperse in all directions. The Marine holds the door to the administration building open for her.

Larry points to the stairway. "We're goin' up to the third floor to Captain Morsey's office. Mitch's got your badge. He'll take you to get your picture taken and get you settled."

"Is Barry in this building too?" she asks.

"You mean Keys? Everybody just calls 'im Keys here."

"Then Keys he is, Larry. But I've been on a first name basis with the man for a long time."

"Yes ma'am. Mitch can take you to him I guess. He told me to protect you; he's scared somebody might wanta hurt you. You need anything, ma'am, I'll take care of it for you. Keys trusts me and I won't let nothin' bad happen to you."

"Thank you, Larry. I would appreciate it if you'd look after Barry. He's the one that always seems to find trouble."

"I'll look after both a you, ma'am."

When Larry ushers Mary into the office, Mitch comes around his desk to greet her.

"Thank you for volunteering, Mrs. Keys. We're very happy you could join us. The commandant has directed me to give you any assistance you may need. Let's get your badge taken care of first. I'll call Keys. We can meet with Captain Morsey to start the ball rolling."

"I'll go get Keys," Larry says.

Mitch is setting up chairs in Morsey's office when Keys and Larry enter.

"Hiya, Mitch. Where's Mary?" Keys asks.

"She's gettin' her picture takin' for the yard badge. She'll be here shortly. The captain is down grillin' the men at torpedo repair. As soon as he gets back we can round-table a plan of attack. I'm sure he took time to pass by his new boat."

Mary enters with a temporary yard badge pinned to her blouse. She smiles, goes to Keys and kisses his cheek. Running the back of her hand over his cheek ,she says, "You must have just shaved. Is that a new cologne?"

Looking down into his wife's eyes, Keys replies, "I took time to shave and brush my teeth. The cologne I borrowed from an officer with a ton a gold braid on his shirt. I thought it must be pretty good stuff."

Mary holds her fingers to her nose. "It is different, I'll say that."

"All for you, my sweet."

Morsey enters taking command. "Please take a seat everyone. First, let me thank Mrs. Keys for volunteering. Did you find anything interesting last night, Keys?"

"Larry and I checked out the northwest side, sir. The guy's we're lookin' for are most likely thereabouts. That whole area is a bee hive of activity even in the early morning hours.

"The scrapyard would be a prime target for 'em. There are so many trains and trucks goin' in an' outta there, it would be easy to lift a few items from a load if you were smart about it. Trains, trucks, or personal transportation has to be the way they're getting' the stuff outta here. Larry and I are gonna keep an eye out there. I need to talk to the railroad guys. That's the best bet I see for gettin' loot out. Did you get anything from the torpedo guys, sir?"

"Mitch, are you getting all this down?" Morsey asks.

"Yes, sir," Mitch replies.

"Okay. The guys at torpedo repair tell me that a damaged torpedo was supposed to be returned to them a few weeks ago. The boat it was on reported that the Mark 18 had shorted the batteries and caused damage to the torpedo room and sent men to the sick bay.

"The captain of the boat was anxious to get back on war patrol and reported that his men threw the batteries overboard. The torpedo shop took it for granted when the torpedo never came back that the captain deep sixed the whole shebang.

Morsey holds up his hand. "Before you ask, Keys, I ordered a 24-hour guard on the battery shop. I did learn my lesson."

"Can the torpedo be powered by any battery, sir?" Keys asks.

"I've got the torpedo men working on that, Keys. At first, they said no way. But one of the old guys chimed in saying that if a guy was bright enough he could find a way.

"The motor that powers the Mark 18 is a direct current one. Which means with enough voltage you can spin the propellers. It then depends on what the target is and how fast the torpedo needs to go. The other problem for the guys that stole it will be explosives for the warhead."

"I'm bettin' that means whatever target our bad guys have in mind is stationary," Keys says.

"How so?" Morsey asks.

"From the little I know about torpedoes, sir, they have an intricate aiming system and a gun barrel of some kind they're normally fired from. The men we're after don't have a firing barrel and if they want a sure hit they'd have to just aim it straight on.

"I can't see they'd wanta try to get fancy an' try a moving target. I see a ship that's tied up at the waterfront or maybe the ammo pier. I looked at some pictures of the ammo pier but I'm not allowed there so I don't know if it's possible to get a shot at it."

"I like your thinking, Keys, makes good sense. I'll alert the Ammunition Depot. The Mine Wharf would be another good target. I'm going to recommend that we step up the patrol craft out there.

"What do you want Mrs. Keys to do?"

Keys smiles at Mary, then replies to Morsey. "I'd like to start with personnel records for the graveyard shift, sir. I've given her a description of the man I'm lookin' for. She'll know him if his picture's on record.

"It's important that Mary be allowed to concentrate on this single effort. As soon as we can identify this guy, I'll wanta watch 'im and make sure we get the whole gang and the torpedo. Up until now we were after thieves, but they've escalated to saboteurs. I guess they could be tryin' to sell the torpedo to the enemy; in any case, we need to nail 'em asap.

"I talked with Mitch about Larry being the go-between for Mary and me on the yard. I am concerned that her work could put her in jeopardy if the bad guys learn she's married to me. If that's good with you, Captain, I would appreciate it."

"It's fine with me, Keys. What's next for you?"

"I'm gonna talk to the yard's railroad men to see if they know of a way the cars could be exploited. Larry and I'll be going out again tomorrow night to see what we can find."

"Keys says rats play at night, sir," Larry adds.

Morsey, surprised at Larry's comment, grins. "Is that right, gunney? Sounds profound to me. You get that from Hammet, or Chandler, Keys?"

"Comedians," Keys smirks. "Well, at least you guys read the pulps. Before I forget again, sir, I need to remind you of that sentry up by the yard dumps."

"Right, Keys. Mitch, ask the Marine commander if he would question his sentries. Tell him the commandant isn't happy about having his letter disregarded. I'd like to have the sentry in question report to me."

"Yes, sir, captain. I'll get right on it," Mitch replies.

"Any other business, Keys?"

"No, sir. I'll keep you posted, sir."

Morsey stands and reaches across his desk to shake Keys' hand. "Good luck. Let Mitch know if you need anything. Thanks for coming, Mrs. Keys. Mitch will help with anything you need and I am available to you and Keys anytime."

Mary comes to Keys' side to shake Morsey's hand.

"Thank you, Captain. Please call me Mary. I am delighted to be here and excited to be working with the war effort again."

"Let me caution you, Mary," Morsey says. "This is like a small town; everyone knows, or thinks they know, everyone's business. It's a regular gossip factory: if they can't get the story from you they'll make something up. Keys is right in wanting to conceal your relationship.

"I'm going to put you in a small office and your story will be that you've been brought in to study war photographs. Mitch will gather the files and Moose will bring them to you. I believe that's the best way to keep you safe."

Keys nods his head. "Thank you, Captain. I appreciate it."

In the hallway, Mitch is ready to take Mary to her office.

Keys gently squeezes Mary's arm before going to his office. "I'll see you at home tonight."

"Aren't you going home with me tonight?" Mary asks.

"No, I can't. I've gotta get to the railroad guys and be ready for tomorrow. Get settled in here; I won't be late. We'll go out for dinner, okay?"

Mary leans in closer to Keys. "Gosh, Barry, all these men are so young. I would never have thought Morsey could be a captain."

Keys chuckles. "He's one of the older ones, Sprite. He thought he was too old to get a submarine command.

It's a young man's war. It always is. My Dad lost two brothers in the last war. He said war always takes the best of the young. Go on home on the day shift ferry and I'll be there before six."

That evening Keys locks up his office and waits outside the administration building for Mary to leave. Earlier, at the yard's used clothing store, he found a tan overcoat and a faded-red rancher's cap complete with ear flaps. Now he pulls the ear flaps down and follows Mary down to the ferry slip.

She quickly moves to the front of the ferry to a seat by a window. Keeping well back from his wife, he finds a corner he can watch from. He observes her having a brief conversation with another woman, after which she watches the bay's features wobble by through the salt-stained glass.

When the ferry lands in San Francisco, the people standing rush to the exit. Mary waits until most have off-loaded to make her way onshore. Keys hangs back after exiting. He gets out of the crowd while watching Mary make her way to the street. There are too many people going the same way to see if anyone is following her.

When Mary exits the cable car on California Street, four men and two other women also exit. Keys leaps off the back as the car starts moving. Keeping to the other side of the street from Mary, he watches as she turns down Powell Street. Two men follow down Powell. One is fast-paced and passes by her. The second man hangs back, keeping pace with her. Mary turns to her right, on Bush Street, and the man behind does also. Keys hustles across Powell to fall in behind them. Mary turns left on Mason Street and walks down to stop at the detective agency window. The man behind stops a few yards behind her.

Mary looks for traffic before crossing the street to the apartment building. Keys grabs the man from behind to shove him into the agency entranceway.

"Hey, I ain't got nothin' worth stealin', man."

Keys holds the frightened man against the door with his left hand.

"You got some ID man? Whatta ya doin' followin' my wife?"

"Jesus Christ, you some kinda nut? I'm just goin' home, mindin' my business, man."

"Let me see some ID."

The man struggles against Key's weight. "Who the hell are you anyway? I don't gotta show you nothin'."

Keys brushes back his coat with his right hand. "If I have to pull my gun, I intend to use it. Get some ID out now!"

"Okay, okay, let me get my wallet out, will ya?"

"Use one hand and give it to me," Keys orders.

Keys opens the wallet, looking at the driver's license.

"Sheldon Worst. Who do you work for, Shelly?"

"I work for the cable car company. I'm on my way home."

"Why were you followin' my wife, Shelly, an' don't tell me you weren't? I been watchin' you since you got off on California. You fell in behind her and when she stopped here, you stopped instead a goin' on by. So why is that, Shelly?"

"Aw, hell, man, I got nothin' better ta do. I'm just on my way home to nothin'. I guess I just liked the way she looks, I don't mean no harm. Just let me go on my way. I don't mean no harm, I promise."

Keys drops the wallet to the ground. "Okay, Shelly, but I see you followin' her around again an' you're gonna find the wrong end a this gun. You got that, Shell?"

"Yes, sir! I don't mean no harm."

Key stands aside to let Sheldon pick up his wallet, then watches him scramble away down Mason Street. After the man goes out of sight, Keys turns back to Bush Street. He winces seeing his reflection in an office window. Feeling asinine, he yanks the rancher cap from his head, stuffing it in a pocket. Instead of going home early, he decides to make a report in person to his old FBI boss at the Sutter Street FBI offices.

Chapter 23

Keys sees new faces in the FBI office. Glancing at the duty board he sees his old partner Jerry Walsh is out on a case. Keys asks to see the boss, Frank Gray. He enters the office and takes a seat in front of Gray's desk. The boss takes off his glasses and does the two-fingered tug at his shirt collar.

"You know, Frank, I always wanted to know why you don't buy shirts with bigger collars?"

"Is that why you came in today, Keys? If it's any of your business, I buy my shirts off the shelf. They ain't custom-made. So, if I get 'em with collars that fit my neck, the shirt's like a tent. Have you got a report for me or is that the extent of your detecting for the week?"

"Sorry ta rile you, Frank. I feel stupid enough all ready. I just came in 'cause I was close by and thought I'd see the old place and give you my report."

"So why are you feelin' stupid, Keys? Did something go bad at the yard?"

"Naw, I think we're gettin' close at the yard. I told you Mary was comin' in to pull employee files for me. I've been worried that the guys we're after might target her to get at me. Her first day was today an' I decided to follow her home to see if anyone from the yard followed her. With the way this case is goin', I might not get another chance. I see a guy get off her cable car at California and follow her. When they get to Mason, Mary stops to look in our office window an' the guy stops a few yards back watchin' her. I wait till she goes across the street an' brace the guy.

"Turns out the guy's some cluck that works for the cable car company an's moonstruck watchin' Mary walk. She's got better lookin' legs than Betty Grable so I can see how that might happen. Anyway, I felt pretty damned stupid bracin' the guy.

"Did the guy come from the yard? Was he on the ferry with her?" Gray asks.

"I couldn't tell, there were too many people crammed on the ferry to know, but I'm pretty sure he just saw her on the cable car. I did make a note of his name and address."

"I think you're getting overprotective in your old age, Keys. Give me his information and I'll have one of the men run it down. So, what have you got to report? You'll still have to give me a typed report you know."

Gray does not interrupt as Keys finishes his report.

"You're still sure we shouldn't send some men in?"

"No, Frank, please don't. I think that would just slow things down. I'm close on this. Whoever took the torpedo just upped the stakes. I've got full backing from the top yard guys. He may have the torpedo but he's got nothin' to power the motor and no warhead.

"Morsey put out 24-hour patrol boats and Mitch said he reamed the torpedo guys a new one. I'm sure the bad guys have gotta be usin' the railroad to get stuff out, and I saw the head guys there yesterday. The commandant gave me a letter that says I've got his full support.

"The railroad guys are goin' to increase their inspections, and that's no small feat. They gotta have hundreds of cars a day in an' out of that place. We're tightenin' the noose, Frank. I'm gonna get a good night's sleep tonight; tomorrow I'm back to the graveyard shift."

"Take care, Keys. Let me know if you want me to call in the cavalry, and make sure Mary has my emergency number if she needs it."

"Thanks, Boss, I'll keep you posted."

"Yes, you will, daily," Gray says.

Feeling somewhat less mortified, Keys heads back to his Mason Street apartment.

Mary is putting her coat on when Keys enters the apartment. "Oh, good, I was hoping you wouldn't be late, I'm starved."

"Whatta you got in mind?" Keys asks.

"How about Chinese? I've been thinking of food since I got home. I think going back to work has spurred my appetite."

They walk up the hill on Grant Avenue through a throng of military men to a small place squeezed between busy shops.

Keys gives up on the chopsticks to dig into the noodles. Mary has no such trouble selecting various vegetables to eat.

"Do you really think we're in some danger at Mare Island?" Mary asks.

Keys studies Mary's face before answering. "I know we are. You know rats will fight when they're cornered, and when they find out we're on their tails, something's gonna pop."

Mary smiles back at Keys. "You've got rats on the brain, Barry."

"That's the way I see 'em. We're in a war that could end the world's freedoms and some guys see it as a way ta make money. I can see a foreign saboteur wantin' to slow down our war efforts, and I hate the thought of Americans helpin' 'em.

"You need to be alert and be safe, Mary. I don't want you to be afraid of goin' to Mare, but you do have to be careful."

"I had a feeling that I was being watched on the way home tonight. Do you think I'm just being silly?" Mary says.

Keys wipes his face with a napkin taking a moment to gather his thoughts.

"I think a woman as good lookin' as you would be followed all the time. I know I like watchin' you walk."

"Come on, Barry, you know what I mean."

"I do know what you mean. If you have a feeling like that take precautions. Get to a place you feel safe. A public place, a police station, fire station, like that. If you're in the city and I'm not, call Frank Gray."

Keys gets his notebook out, flips the pages to Gray's emergency number to write it down. He tears off the sheet and hands it to Mary.

"I talked to Gray today. He asked me to give you his emergency number in case I was outta town and you needed help. I know he'd move heaven and earth to help if you needed it. Keep this in your purse. At Mare, or the yard, as the Navy guys say, Larry or Mitch will help you if I'm not handy. I don't think anybody's gonna mess with the Moose."

Mary tucks the note away in her purse. "Okay, Barry, I feel better. Who's going to protect you? I don't want you getting shot up anymore. And for God's sake if you should get shot, go to a real doctor. Jerry told me about taking you to his veterinarian to fix the gunshot on your leg."

"Jerry talks too much. The guy did a good job."

Mary puts down her chopsticks, her brow furrowed, no longer amused.

"Barry, your leg has a scar that looks like the hind end of a Christmas turkey."

"Okay, okay, I can see you're getting upset. I'll take every precaution, and Larry'll be with me on the graveyard shifts. There's nothing more I want to do than to share a long life with you. Christmas turkey, jeez."

"Just be safe, Barry, you're not the Lone Ranger."

"Yes ma'am. I'd rather be John R. Hughes anyway."

"That's just what I mean, Barry. The Lone Star Ranger. I think that's your favorite book, too. But didn't he say 'nerve without judgment's no good'?"

"He did indeed, or something close. I'll be sure to follow his tradition. He's still alive today you know."

"Are you going in with me tomorrow?" Mary asks.

"No, I'm doin' the graveyard shift again and I wanta talk to the mechanics at the FBI garage in the morning. The guys that took the torpedo will have to get batteries if they're gonna power it up. Morsey told me how much power it takes to run one a those things an' I wanta find out if car batteries would work. Those mechanics'll know."

"Sleep in, Barry. I'll be quiet leaving in the morning."

"Don't worry, Mary, Mitch got me a cot for my office. I can nap when I want. If I'm up anyway, I'll make us breakfast."

"I love your breakfasts, except for that chorizo-jalapeños wake-up omelet you make. And before you say it, I don't need hair on my chest."

Chapter 24

Harry studies the torpedo manual for days, trying to find a way around the problem of fitting automotive batteries into the confines of the torpedo's interior. So far, he has no answer to the problem. His frustration intensifies after lurking around the yard's battery shop.

A Marine guard, armed with a rifle, spots Harry. "Hey you! Whatta you lookin" at? This here's off limits unless you gotta battery shop badge. You wanta get over here an' show me your badge?"

"No, sir," Harry says. "I ain't never seen a guard here before."

"Well, you see one now, and I ain't a sir. Move along mister."

Curious, Harry goes directly to the torpedo shop. He peeks around the corner of an adjacent building where he sees armed guards patrolling there also. Wary of being identified by the guards if challenged again, he reluctantly skulks back to his shed by the scrapyard.

Harry throws his pencil across the cramped room.

"Damn it to hell, there's no way to get that much voltage with car batteries. Less than twenty inches in diameter, batteries are nine inches wide by seven inches deep. How the hell am I going to get batteries?"

Alby peeks around a crate, Harry catches the movement. "What the hell do you want, Alby?"

"Uh, sorry, boss. I heard yellin', I thought there might be some trouble."

"Yeah, Alby, I got troubles but there's nothin' you can do about it. I need batteries for my torpedo."

"I thought you were gonna use some car batteries," Alby says.

"They won't fit, Alby. The diameter of the torpedo is too small."

Alby puzzles with this for a moment, then brightens.

"Well, why don't we make the battery section bigger?"

Harry stares at Alby, his eyes growing wider. "Mein Gott im Himmel! Alby, you're a genius; why not make the battery section bigger indeed?

"No, I mean it, boss. Rian knows how ta weld stuff; he can make most anything."

"I'm agreeing with you, Alby. You have a good idea. It's so simple, and I was trying to make

185

it so complex. Yes, yes, we will make that work. We need to take one of those steel tubes from the scrapyard for the battery section and I'll need to design a new warhead.

"Go get Rian for me, Alby."

"Do you want Tom too, boss?"

"No, we'll leave Tom out of this. I'll make sure he's doing his work later."

***

"Hi, Harry," Rian says, "Alby said you wanted me."

Harry looks up from the sketch he is drawing. "Yes, I need you to get me a twelve-foot length of twenty-four-inch diameter steel tubing from the scrapyard. Put it in my truck and I'll take it to the barn later."

"Okay, Harry, anything else?"

"Yes, how many 6-volt car batteries have we on hand?"

Rian eyes roam around the room in thought. "I'm not sure; I think most, if not all, the batteries we had were in the shop that got raided."

"Damn it, that's what I thought," Harry says. "I'll have to call that pirate in Stockton. After you get the tubing, we need to get another load on the railcar for shipment. Maybe I can trade for the batteries. I'll get Tom to help you."

"I'd just as soon you let me and Alby do it ourselves, Harry. All Tom wants to do is grouse an' play with his goddamned knives. I'm gonna have to shoot 'im one a these days…but not on the yard."

"Go on then, I'll take care of Tom."

Harry goes back to his drawing, then stops, puts the pencil down and balls his fists. Scratching his whiskers, he mutters, "Tom, the sooner I get rid of you, the better."

Rian returns to the shed somewhat shaken. "Harry, there's guards at the scrapyard. I can't get nothin' outta there. The office guy says you gotta have a receipt to get anything outta the gates now, too. He says they got double guards on the gates."

"Calm down, Rian, we've seen them do this before. Here's ten dollars. Go buy the tubing. Tell 'em you need it to put in a gutter under your driveway at home. Get a receipt and give it to me. I'll drive it out the gate later."

Rian, relieved to be out of the guards' scrutiny, returns with a receipt.

"Those guards are lookin' for something, Harry."

"Stop worrying, Rian. After you get the railcar loaded, go over to the Vallejo railyard and pick up that other load with the big truck. Our customers want the paint and coffee I promised, and we need the money."

Harry scans the receipt. Satisfied with the steel tube's diameter, he takes a new sheet of paper and begins to design a battery rack system for the torpedo. After making a preliminary sketch, he gets down to calculating actual dimensions.

Harry looks up from his work when Rian returns even more agitated than before.

Harry lays his ruler down, glances at his watch, then studies Rian's face.

"You couldn't have gotten that load delivered all ready. Why are you back here?"

"Our railyard man wouldn't let me in, Harry. He stopped me at the gate and told me to get away fast. The police and a bunch a Marines are inspectin' all the railcars. I'm tellin' you, Harry, somethin's happenin'. I've never seen 'em lookin' at the cars over there."

"Okay, take it easy, Rian. Give me time to find out what's going on. Get your car packed with as much as you can. We'll have to make do for now."

"I ain't too sure that's a good idea, Harry."

"We need the money," Harry says.

"You need the money for your torpedo. Money ain't gonna do me no good if I'm in prison. Like you said, Harry, if they find out Tom killed Booth, we'll all swing."

"Rian, damn it, you're letting your imagination run away with you. Go get your car, bring it to the back door. I'll turn out the lights back there and help you load."

Rian brings his car from the parking lot. When he turns off the road to the back of the shed, he shuts off the headlights. Cutting the engine, he coasts silently up to the shed. Harry opens the shed's door to bring out a five-gallon paint can.

Rian removes the rear seat cushion to place the can in a hidden compartment.

The men go back for more cans. Rian loads while Harry goes for more contraband.

***

"Hey whatcha loadin' in that car!" Startled, Rian jerks around to see a Marine guard with a rifle.

"I, uh, just got some cans to, uh, take back to the paint shop," Rian stammers.

The Marine rests his rifle butt on the ground. "I seen you turn your headlights off and coast in. That don't look to me like you're spos'd to be here. Back away from the car so's I can see what you've got in there."

Harry rushes out of the shed to lock his arms around the Marine's neck. The Marine drops his rifle struggling to pull Harry's arms away.

"Get the rifle!" Harry hisses.

Rian stands transfixed, then picks up the rifle. Harry tightens his arms, strangling the Marine. The soldier's face goes red, fighting for the air his lungs scream to receive. Kicking his leg back, clawing with his hands, trying everything to fight back, the Marine begins to fade.

Harry dodges the soldier's defenses, feeling the power ebb out of the man. After the violent struggle ends, Harry drops the Marine to the ground. Shaking his arms to get blood circulating, he turns to Rian.

"Hurry up, Rian. Get the rest of the stuff in the car."

189

Rian looks down at the Marine before following Harry into the shed.

Harry piles coffee bags by the car.

"Pack it in, Rian. Come on, hurry up. I'll help you get the soldier in and you can dump him in a slough on your way to the delivery."

"How am I gonna get past the gate guards, Harry? What happens when the guy goes missin'? They're gonna be all over the yard lookin' for the man."

"It won't be the first time a soldier went missing from here," Harry says. "They do desert; there's a list of 'em at the post office. We'll put him in the trunk and throw a blanket over him. Just act natural and they won't look in the trunk; they never do."

"I don't like it, Harry."

"You don't have to. Get moving, Rian."

Chapter 25

Keys sleeps late; Mary has gone by the time he gets out of bed. He makes breakfast, then walks to the FBI garage. While talking with the FBI mechanics, he makes notes of their battery information before leaving on the ferry to Mare Island. The day goes by quickly. He meets with Commander Morsey in the afternoon. Morsey tells Keys that he gave orders to patrol the Battery and Torpedo shops 24 hours a day as Keys wanted.

"Have they reported any suspicious activity?" Keys asks.

Morsey looks away from Keys for a moment. "Not that I'm aware of. I didn't specifically order them to report. I just wanted to make sure no one gets away with batteries that could power a torpedo."

Keys sits forward in his chair. "If I can, sir, I'd like to have the guards report anything suspicious and take ID's. We may be able to get our guys that way."

"Okay, Keys, I'll get on that right away."

Keys closes Morsey's door and turns to Mitch.

"How's it goin'? Anything new on the commander's boat?"

Mitch walks to the hallway with Keys. "He's down there every day, makin' sure his boat's got the latest stuff.

"He's got two 5-inch guns mounted on her; one forward, one aft. All the advanced electronics are onboard; they're drillin' holes in the superstructure for faster submerging. He's havin' his crew change the pitch on the bow diving plane to get the boat down quicker.

"All the tricks veteran boat captains are havin' done when they return from war patrols, Morsey's gettin' done to his boat. He's workin' with the new men on the crew to get 'em up to speed. They seem to like him and most are eager to fight. There's no doubt he intends to fight."

Keys grins at Mitch's enthusiasm. "So, have you made up your mind about joining Morsey's greatest adventure?"

"You said I could talk to you about it sometime. I'd like to buy you a beer and get your opinion. I've been talkin' to myself a lot; it'd be good to talk out loud."

"Anytime, Mitch."

"Your wife is hard at it, Keys. I had Moose take her a mess a personnel files this morning. She's already gotten through them and called me to get more."

"You'll find she's a good worker, Mitch. She only left Marinship because I got down on my knees an' begged her a thousand times. She wants to do her part for the war effort an' she's excellent at details. I'm countin' on you an' Moose to keep her safe."

"Will do, Keys. Anything I can do for you?"

"I still need that jeep we talked about."

Mitch grins, pointing his finger toward the outside. "I've got it parked out front. It's got stars on the bumpers meaning it belongs to a heavy hitter. You probably outta keep it at Smitty's. Some prankster's liable to run off with it."

"You're a good man, Mitch, thanks."

Keys hurries down the stairs and outside. The only jeep with stars is in a space alongside the administration building. Keys gets in the jeep, flicks the ignition switch and pushes the floor mounted starter button. His new toy fires up, then settles to a satisfying purr.

The day is gray with dark clouds gathering, but Keys gets out of the jeep, unhooking the canvas top to stow it in the back. He remembers Smitty's jeep and folds the windshield down.

Mitch, standing by an upstairs window looks down, chuckling to himself. "Kids and their toys," he says, watching Keys.

Back in the jeep, Keys drives south past Chapel Park to Club Drive; at the golf course, he turns back to Cedar Avenue. He finds a short stretch of Cedar to floorboard the throttle before having to slow at the north ship barracks. Fat rain drops begin to pelt his face; he reluctantly turns back to Smitty's.

He finds shelter for his new prize behind the locksmith's building under the roof overhang, then goes around to the front door.

"Hey, Smitty, you here?" Keys calls out, knuckling the front countertop.

"Hold yer horses, I'll be there in a minute," Smitty replies from the shop's depths.

Smitty emerges from the darkness. "Hey, there's our mystery man. What's up Keys?"

"Mitch got me a jeep an' I'm concerned about how easy it is to take if somebody wants it. I need to keep it handy. If I need it in a hurry I don't wanta have ta go find some sailor off on a lark."

"Is it here?" Smitty asks.

"Yeah, out back. I was hopin' you could replace the toggle ignition switch with a keyed one."

Smitty wipes his hands with a rag. "Leave it with me; I'll fix it up for you. I like workin' on 'em, you know. Ain't nothin' to 'em; they made 'em real simple. Come on back in a coupla hours."

"Thanks, Smitty, I'm gonna need it tonight. I'll bring you a beer when I come to pick it up."

"Make it bottle a Wild Bird an' I'll give you the deluxe package."

"I'll see what I kin' do."

Keys phones Mary from his office.

"I hear you've got a new toy," Mary says.

"Mitch been givin' you the latest?"

"I called him about these files. Some of the people have worked here over thirty years. It does thin the pile some; but I've been cross-checking with pay records. In some cases, I haven't been able to find personnel files that match pay records."

"That's it, Mary. You're on to them. I think Booth set some guys up to get double pay. He may have set up the pay, then destroyed their files. We may be lookin' for guys with no personnel files. Is there anyway we can run 'em down with the pay records?"

Mary turns through another file folder using the eraser on her pencil.

"I'm doing that now."

"I shoulda known," Keys says. "It's getting' close to quittin' time. If you find anything, give it to Larry before you go, okay?"

"Will do, boss. You be careful tonight. All day, all night does not make you very alert."

"I'm gonna take a nap before Larry and I go to eat. I've got a feelin' we're closin' in on 'em. If you find those pay records and we get identities, it won't take long to round 'em up, and we can go home."

Larry enters Keys' office and presents him with the bottle of bourbon Mitch asked him to give to Keys.

"Mitch said this is the best he could do today."

Keys takes the bottle to look at the label.

"It'll be fine for now. I need it to get our jeep back from Smitty. He's doin' some work on it for me. We'll have it tonight to make our rounds a little easier. We can cover a lot more ground."

Larry sits in a chair, tilting his cap back on his head.

"You think we'll find 'em just drivin' around?"

"I think we've got 'em cornered, Larry. I got the railroad people's attention. It's gonna be real hard for the bad guys to get anything out a here on train cars. I don't know how or where they're loadin' the cars, but the railroad inspectors promised that no car will go uninspected. I asked that the gate guards report anything unusual.

"I'm hoping with the train cars buttoned up, they're gonna try to move the goods out by car or truck. When they do, we've got 'em red-handed, so we gotta keep a sharp-eye out. They're gonna show themselves and when they do, we're gonna get 'em."

"I'm ready for anything, Keys. It's been much too long for me just shufflin' around the yard. A Marine is built for action."

Chapter 26

Keys and Larry head out to the locksmith's to pick up the jeep. The night is warm but with diffused light. A heavy overcast reflects the yard's lights to an almost day-like quality. By the time they reach Smitty's, a light rain is falling.

Smitty is munching on a sandwich at the counter when the men enter.

"You're just in time, Keys. I could use a little pick-me-up. I ain't usually here this late, you know."

Keys holds up the bottle. "I hope this'll do."

"Well, it ain't what I asked for, but any port in a storm I always say."

Keys brings the bottle to the counter, holding it just above the countertop. "How's my jeep doin'? Did you get it done?"

"I hope you ain't gonna hold on to that bottle, Keys. A course I got it done."

Smitty unscrews the bottle top, takes a hit, then wipes his mouth on his shirt sleeve.

"Yeah, the pause that refreshes. Come on back, fellas." The Navy grey jeep, with the windshield and top back up, sits next to Smitty's jeep.

"I painted over the stars so's some smart aleck don't decide to haul it off. I don't know why those guys think it's funny ta heist a brass's jeep. I put a battery disconnect switch under the seat. If somebody tries ta start it, they'll think the battery's dead."

Keys looks under the driver's seat. "That's a good idea, Smitty, thanks. I'll leave it here when I'm not usin' it, if that's okay with you."

"Sure, that's fine. There's always somebody here, I'll leave word with 'em. Good to see you got some help, Keys. I don't think anybody's gonna take on both you and Moose. See you guys later, I'm headin' out."

"Okay, Larry, climb aboard. We're gonna go over to the railyard in Vallejo. I wanta see if they've found anything."

***

Keys shows his ID at the railyard gate. "Nobody's allowed inside, buddy," the gatekeeper says.

Keys gets out of the jeep. "Here's a letter from the yard's commandant—buddy. You sure you wanta play this game?"

The gatekeeper reads the letter and hands it back.

"I don't want no trouble, sir. Go on in."

A light mist in the air halos the flood lights mounted on tall poles that illuminate the railyard.

Keys gets back in the jeep, then points to the railyard. "Larry, get this guy's ID, will you? I'm gonna go to where those guys are searchin' that railcar back there."

"Will do, Keys, meet you there."

"Who's in charge here?" Keys asks at the railcar.

A Marine sergeant hands off a clip board before confronting Keys. "I'm Sergeant Willard. What can I do for you, civilian?"

Keys hands the sergeant his letter. "I'm the man who asked that you search these cars, sergeant. What've you found?"

"Yes, sir," the sergeant responds, handing the letter back. "We got a car here full a contraband. It's loaded with paint cans, coffee, some tires, and lumber."

Keys looks into the railcar. "How the hell is anybody gettin' the stuff outta these cars?"

"Your guess is as good as mine, sir," the Marine answers.

"Yeah, yeah, Marine. I was talkin' to myself more than anyone. Were there any serial numbers on the stuff?"

"We got numbers stenciled on the paint cans and the coffee, sir," the Marine answers.

"Okay, excellent, sergeant. Is everything still in the car?" Keys asks.

"Yes sir. We just moved some stuff around to take inventory."

Keys climbs into the railcar.

Larry sees Keys climb into the car as he walks up from taking the gate guard's ID. The flood lights reveal a very light rain is still falling. Slick, uneven gravel makes walking difficult with Larry's prosthetic foot; his progress is somewhat unsteady.

"Hey, Willy, what's going on here?" Larry asks the Marine sergeant.

"Hiya, Moose. I gotta big shot civilian talkin' to himself is all. Whata you doin' here?"

"I'm with the big shot, and if he's talkin' to himself that's cause he's the only intelligent guy around to talk to, pal."

"Very funny, Moose. I didn't know you was a comic."

"You're all wet, Willy, and I mean you're all wet. Make sure you give Keys anything he wants. We're after a bad bunch."

"Sure thing, Moose."

Keys climbs back out of the railcar.

"Did you get the gatekeeper's ID, Larry?"

"Here," Larry hands Keys the ID, "he's pretty shook up."

Keys brushes off the back of his pants. "Yeah, he should be. He's gotta be the guy that's lettin' the bad guys in here. We better get 'im before he lights out."

"Should I have grabbed him? Can we arrest people?" Larry asks.

"I shoulda thought a that before I raced in here, Larry. Get the number of this railcar and ask the sergeant if he's completed the inventory on it. Find out if he's checked all the other cars, too. I'm gonna go back to the guard shack to get the guy and make some phone calls."

In the empty guard shack, Keys calls the FBI office to leave a message for Frank Gray asking him to be on the look out for the gate guard. After he relays the gatekeeper's ID information, he phones the Navy yard's railroad office. He tells the railroad man he wants a yard locomotive to pick up the railcar in Vallejo as soon as possible. After he is assured the railroad man is going to comply, he heads back to the contraband-filled railcar.

"Larry, can you drive?"

"Sure, Keys. I've been drivin' since I was a pup."

"Take the jeep and go back to the locksmith's. I want two of their best padlocks to secure this car. The Navy's gonna send a locomotive to take it back to the yard. I'm gonna stay here an' nose around some. Don't be gone long, okay?"

"Aye aye, Keys. Back in a flash."

Keys turns to the Marine sergeant who is in charge of the railcar inspection. "Sergeant, how long have your men been on duty here?"

"Since 1800, sir."

"I need you to keep two men here to patrol this yard and a man to guard the gate. Your men should be armed and allow no one in. The Navy is sendin' a locomotive to pick up this car. I'll stay until the locomotive leaves. You can change the guard as you see fit, but this will be 24-7 from now on."

"I'll need an order from my captain, sir."

"You'll have it as soon as I get back to the yard. Until then you're under my orders by the commandant's authority I showed you. If you're gonna make trouble, do it now."

"No trouble, sir. I just don't want my captain chewin' my hide over this."

"I'll speak to your captain in the morning, sergeant."

Larry returns to present Keys with two huge brass padlocks.

"Wow, those are locks all right. Is this a joke?" Keys asks.

"The locks guy said it'd take a bomb ta break 'em," Larry replies.

Keys whistles, taking the locks' weight in his hands. "I'll go lock up the railcar. If the locomotive isn't here soon, I'll call those guys again. I wanta get back to the yard."

Keys looks at his watch as the Navy locomotive pulls out of the railyard headed for Mare Island.

"Let's go, Larry, it's past 2:00 am and I wanta see what's cookin' at Mare. Our bad guys have gotta know they're in trouble by now."

There is little traffic on the road as Keys ignores the presidential mandate of 40 miles an hour. Passing through the Mare Island causeway gate, Keys heads for the scrapyard.

Keys and Larry stay in the jeep out of the wet, watching the activity of the scrapyard. After a while Keys turns on the ignition switch starting the jeep. "Let's take a little tour. We'll come back here later."

On Cedar Avenue, they see a Pontiac coming toward them. The big sedan bounds over the railroad tracks that cross the street, its headlights nearly blind them as the car jounces up and down. Keys makes a U turn at 5th Street, then accelerates hard to follow the Pontiac.

"I'm gonna close up on that car, Larry. Write down the license number. As soon as you get it, I'll back off."

"What's up, Keys?" Larry asks.

"Did you see the way that car jumped at the railroad tracks? It's jacked way up off the ground. When I was back east, we used to see moonshiner's cars like that. It's got heavy springs to take a lotta weight. I wanta see where he's headed."

Before Keys can catch up to the car, a train pulling boxcars from the scrapyard crosses Cedar in front of the jeep. Keys brakes to a halt.

"Damn it." Keys pounds the steering wheel. He turns to Larry, his face wrinkled in anger. "Did you get the license?"

"No, we didn't get close enough."

Keys' fingers drum on the steering wheel, waiting for the train to go through. When the train passes, he bolts over the tracks.

"Watch to your right, Larry. I'll watch the left side."

They motor slowly, craning their necks searching for the Pontiac. Stopping at the sentry house, Keys gets out of the jeep to ask the guard if he's seen the Pontiac. He climbs back in the jeep.

"The sentry says nobody in a Pontiac has been through in the last half hour. Let's just keep going around a Cedar-to-Railroad Avenue loop, maybe we'll get lucky."

With each loop they travel the length of the busy shipyard; it takes 20 to 30 minutes every loop. After their third tour Keys begins to think about breakfast. He turns on Cedar from 7th Street, letting his mind wander.

"Hey, Keys, ain't that the car?"

Keys' head snaps straight ahead to see the Pontiac now settled low on its springs.

Keys shouts to the Marine. "See how low the car is now? He's carrying a load."

The Pontiac's tail lights are disappearing down Cedar toward the sentry gate.

Keys stomps down on the gas pedal. "He's not gettin' away again."

Keys pulls up behind the Pontiac and flashes his headlights. The Pontiac responds with a cloud of dark smoke from the tailpipe. It pulls away from the jeep, running through the sentry post without stopping.

At the jeep's approach, the sentry draws his .45; Keys slows to shout at the sentry to call the police. Rian, hunched over the Pontiac's steering wheel looks up to see the jeep fade in his rearview mirror. Coming up fast to Sears Point Road, Rian slows to make the turn only to see a Mare Island bus stopped at the parking lot blocking the road.

He hesitates momentarily, then turns left heading west. The heavily laden Pontiac won't respond, the front wheels slide on the rain-slicked road forcing him wide, almost off the road. Rian fights the car almost to a stop before regaining control.

Now pointed west, he is going away from the safety of nearby Vallejo to a long stretch of narrow road. The rain-gorged San Pablo Bay laps at the road on one side; the other side has a series of marshes and sloughs. He angrily stomps down the throttle pedal, knowing he has committed a huge mistake. The only way back to Vallejo is to go through Sonoma, many miles out of the way.

The rear wheels of the Pontiac won't get traction spinning on the wet road. Rian lifts off the throttle, cursing as he looks in the rearview mirror to see the jeep gaining on him. He gently feeds the 100-horsepower of the flathead 8 to the Pontiac. The tires find traction and the car speeds away. Once again, the jeep fades.

Sears Point Road is relatively straight but in bad repair with many undulations and puddles. The Pontiac's hidden compartment rubs on the driveshaft when the heavy car bottoms coming down after a dip in the road. Every time Rian slows to avoid bottoming, the jeep gets larger in his mirror. He jams down on the gas, desperate to get away. The next dip is deeper yet, the car bottoms so hard his teeth smash together. The steel compartment crashes into the driveshaft slightly bending it.

The bent driveshaft vibrates horribly. The faster Rian goes, the more the vibration intensifies. In some puddles on the road, standing water is so deep it almost stops the car. Rian fights to regain control. The four-wheel-drive jeep is not having any problems: it gains big chunks of distance each time Rian lifts his foot off the gas pedal.

Sweat pours off Rian's forehead, stinging his eyes. He wipes his eyes with his coat sleeve, then checks the mirror again. The jeep is almost on him. He jams the gas down again, ignoring the vibration. His face, bloody from broken teeth, turns to a fierce grin as he watches the jeep fade a bit. The car flies over another hump in the road, pulling his eyes away from the mirror.

In the dark ahead, he sees tail lights: this two-lane road is famous for fatal car crashes. He knows passing is difficult, and wants to maintain his speed and not get caught behind a slow-moving vehicle. The jeep's headlights are flashing on and off, taking his attention away from the road ahead.

Now, at close to 70 miles an hour, Rian sees more red tail lights in the distance. Closing fast on the traffic, Rian makes up his mind to blow by the vehicles ahead as fast as he can. The Pontiac jounces over another hump. Too late, Rian realizes the traffic is a line of military trucks that are waiting to turn on to Skaggs Island Road.

He yanks the wheel hard left; the Pontiac immediately loses traction and slews to the tall berm on the road's edge, then rockets off the road, soaring out into San Pablo Bay. Crashing down nose first into the water, the impact sends Rian's head smashing into the steering wheel. Bloody and disoriented, he frantically struggles against the Bay's water pressure in a losing battle to get the door open.

Freezing water pours in from the smashed hidden compartments, quickly climbing up his body. Completely panicked, Rian pushes himself up to gulp a bubble of air. The black water swirls past his chin, cold darkness envelopes him. Screaming, he claws at the headliner to find another bubble.

Keys' jeep screeches to a halt: he and Larry jump out to stand at edge of the road. They can hear Rian's muffled scream as the car goes under water. The Pontiac's lights glow eerily in the murky water before fading from view.

Larry stands by Keys in the cold rain watching the Bay's water consume the Pontiac. "I got the license number, Keys."

Keys, surprised at the comment, studies Larry's face, then slaps his shoulder. "Good job! We can still use it to identify the guy. He's not gonna need it anymore. Take the jeep back to the yard and find some cops. I'll stay here to mark the spot."

"I can hear sirens, Keys. Let's get outta the rain till they get here."

Chapter 27

Tom and Alby sit on crates in the Vallejo barn waiting for Harry. Rain beats on the tin roof as water drips into the buckets set out to catch it. Tom smirks at Alby who is hunched over, his eyes wet with tears.

Tom raises his voice to be heard over the din. "Quit ballin', you big baby. We don't even know if it was Rian."

"Shut up, Tom. I saw him tearin' down Cedar with a jeep on his tail. You don't care about anyone but yourself anyway. Rian was a good friend."

"Ta hell with you, Alby. Go blubber someplace else."

Harry enters from the back of the barn. "What are you grousing about now, Tom?"

"I can't stand Alby's blubberin'. Where the hell was Rian goin' anyway? Wasn't he spos'd ta go ta Richmond? The yard birds told me the car was headed west for Christ's sake."

"We don't know what happened," Harry says. "Alby's sure it was Rian. All we know right now is that he crashed into the bay and they haven't found him or the car yet. With all this rain, the water's deep and whatever currents are out there could have carried the car away."

"Well, I think that fed that's on the yard was chasin' Rian," Tom says. "I told you we shoulda gotten rid a that guy."

Harry shakes his head. "And I told you that would have brought a lot more trouble. I need you two to help me get the steel tube out of my truck. Alby, where's the inventory you've been keeping on the goods in the barn?"

"I got it on that clip board you gave me. Want me to get it?"

"Yes, I want you and Tom to load your cars with the goods I've promised and deliver them today. I'll give you the list. We're late gettin' them out now. I want you to go to Rian's house as soon as you make your delivery. Tom's delivery will take more time, so you get to Rian's and make sure there's nothing there to implicate us. Remember to get his bankbook, Alby."

"Don't you think it's too soon to be makin' deliveries?" Tom asks.

"You're leaving from here, not the yard. We need to deliver; our customers want the goods. They've got money and we have enough here to keep us goin' for a while. This will all blow over and we can go back to business. We just need to be smarter about what we take."

"I don't think it's a good idea, Harry," Tom says. "Those federal guys are gonna be all over the yard like bees outta a busted hive."

"Tom, I just drove through the sentry gate with that 12-foot long tube sticking outta the back of my truck. I showed the guard my receipt and that was it. I could have stuffed that tube with anything, they never looked. It'll all blow over and we'll be back in business. Right now, we need to keep our customers happy."

"Come on, Harry. This is all about you gettin' dough for that torpedo, ain't it?"

"Tom, why the hell is it you can't do your job without being angry or butting into my business. I'm tired of your stupid attitude. I'm gonna explain this to you one more time; I don't want any more questions from you.

"If we stop delivering the goods our customers want, they'll go somewhere else. If word gets out there's a federal investigation at Mare Island, they might be scared off. So, we need to deliver as if nothing has changed.

"With Rian gone it means you're gonna have to work more. The upside of that means you make more money because your split is bigger. I expect you to work with Alby, and I mean work with him. Don't think you're gonna have Alby do all the work."

Tom wrestles a moment with his thoughts, but can't hold his tongue. "You mean we're just gonna carry on as if nothin' happened? What about goin' back to the yard? You think we gotta go back on our shift tonight?"

"Tom, if we don't go back we'd look like we were hiding. So, that's it exactly; we go to the yard tonight as if nothing has happened. Just be smart and keep your eyes open. Now get to work."

Alby is up and on his way to load his car. Tom shakes his head, then gets up to follow. He mutters under his breath. "Yeah, go ta work. One a these days I'll cut your damn eyes out."

"What did you say, Tom?" Harry demands. "You have something more to say, turn around and face me."

"I just said I gotta keep my eyes out, boss."

Harry glares after Tom. "You won't have much time to do it, Tom," he mutters to himself.

Harry climbs the stairs to modify his plans for the torpedo build. He knows that his time at the yard is running out fast. It is time to finalize the plan to blow up Mare Island's ammunition pier. His mind wanders. Harry's German nationalistic beliefs, and his Nazi brethren, are dependent on bringing damage to America's war machine.

No Nazi saboteur has been able to slow the vast machine. He knows it must be slowed. Americans must see terror on their homeland. The Führer promises wonder weapons that will wipe out all of Germany's enemies. They need time to produce them and Harry has to make a difference. He knows his future, and Germany's, depends on somehow slowing America's mighty industries.

Harry's head spins, imagining huge explosions and crippling destruction. He sees parades in his honor, fame and fortune bestowed on him by his Führer. With some difficulty, Harry brings himself to the present. He sits at his desk, planning Mare Island's glorious demise.

Chapter 28

The small boats called in to locate Rian's sunken car scramble to shelter after blindingly bright lightening strikes blaze near them. Mare Island's tall radio towers vibrate with the air's electricity. Another brilliant flash, sparks fly from a tower struck. Ground-shaking thunder claps are so loud men at the roadside cover their ears.

"Let's get outta here," Keys shouts to Larry. Rain drums on the jeep's canvas top, wind and water lash through the uncovered sides of the jeep, soaking the men. They drive back to Keys' office in the administration building.

"Man!" Keys exclaims, shaking water from his coat, "I haven't seen a storm like that since I was back east. The bay looked like water boiling. Why don't we call it a night, Larry? We can get a coupla hours of sleep. I don't think anything's gonna happen till this storm breaks anyway. When

Mary gets here, I'll have her run down the license number of the Pontiac."

"You want me to ask her about it in the morning?" Larry asks. "I planned to meet her at the ferry gate."

"No, I'll call her, Larry, but thanks for lookin' out for her."

"She's a real nice lady, Keys."

"Yeah, she is, Larry. She's the best thing that ever happened to me. I'll see you later."

Keys stretches out on the cot; he quickly goes to sleep for some time, then stirs fitfully. The cot is too small to allow him to toss about; he blinks awake, his mind full of questions. *What would be the target of the gang's torpedo? It had to be a gang of men. It was surely the work of more than one or two men to be able to steal all those goods he'd found.*

How could they inflict the most damage to the yard? Was that even the objective? There could be some other target. The entire San Francisco Bay was full of targets that would be important. Keys rubs his face. Swinging his feet over the edge of the cot, he stands, gathering his shaving kit, and heads off to the bathroom. His face in the mirror looks tired as he scrapes away at his beard.

Finding the gang and the torpedo are paramount. Keys wrestles with a plan to find them. The razor nicks his chin, bringing blood. Annoyed, he dabs at the nick thinking to himself that he needs to concentrate on what he is doing.

Rinsing his face, his mood lightens. Breakfasts on the yard were festive in comparison to wartime rationing. There was plenty of food to choose from: stick-to-your-ribs-type food that kept the workforce at their peak of performance. After breakfast, Mary will be on the yard; he can call her and enjoy listening to her voice. With Mary's help, he is sure they can find the would-be saboteurs before they can bring any damage to the yard.

Getting identification on who drove the Pontiac will be a big step toward breaking the gang. Together they can stop whatever the gang is up to. Buoyed by new plans, Keys grins at the mirror, dabs the red nick on his chin again and sets off with a spring in his step.

After breakfast, Keys returns to his office to call Mary.

"Hi, Sprite, did Larry give you the license number of the Pontiac?"

"Hi to you too, Barry. You sound chipper this morning."

"That's because you're here and the sun's out. I ate too much breakfast so I'm hopin' you can get a lead on our bad guys. I need to work off some a this food."

"Larry just went to get me the vehicle registrations. I'll be able to find the number pretty quick I think. I'm anxious to see if the personnel records will match up."

Keys smiles, knowing Mary won't rest until she has something.

"If you can get me a name, then I've something concrete to go on," he says. "I'm gonna have to be on the yard again tonight. We can't let the bad guys catch a breath, we need to keep forcin' 'em into making mistakes."

"Just make sure the bad guys are ones making the mistakes, Barry. I'll call you as soon as I get an ID. We need some at-home time together. I don't like sleeping alone."

"That goes double for me, Sprite, but I'm sure the guys we're after are all on the graveyard shift. I'd love to get enough information on 'em to be able to get 'em during the day. If we find out where they live off the yard, Gray's guys can watch 'em, and I can come home."

"I know you, Barry. You're not going to hand the bad guys over to Gray."

"Mary, if I were smart that's exactly what I'd do. The case would be his to close and I'd make points with you, him, and the yard."

"I hope you're that smart, honey. Larry's back, I'll call you, bye."

Keys goes to the Mare Island ten-foot-long map that covers his office walls. On the south end of the island is a ring of ammunition bunkers. His finger traces the building numbers. In the building number legend, he sees the words 'storehouse'. On the waterfront below the Mine Wharf, two piers where munitions are loaded onto warships would also be vulnerable.

A short distance from the piers, the ammunition plants scatter over a wide area near the water's edge. These plants contain great quantities of explosives. Men and women load 5-inch gun shells and millions of .50 caliber rounds. If there were any way to set all of these storehouses, wharfs, piers, and plants to detonate in a chain reaction, the entire island and miles beyond would be destroyed.

Keys picks up his phone to call Morsey's aide.

"Hiya, Mitch, Keys here. I gotta question for you. Is there anyway that an explosion on the south end of the island could set off all the storehouses and plants?"

"I can answer that for you, Keys. The commandant wanted the same information. Each storehouse and plant is built to be self-contained. If an explosion happened in one of them, it cannot spread. We have had explosions in the past and have learned from them. The most dangerous storehouses have earthen banks around them.

"Powder in the plants is kept to a minimum; the loading of shells is very closely watched. The workforce is well trained and well aware of the dangers. An explosion in one of the plants would be devastating to that plant; however, that would come from within.

"A direct hit from an aerial bomb could blow up a storehouse or a plant. But, again, it would not set off a chain reaction. You know we're not even putting barrage balloons up now because the Japs aren't able to get aircraft here anymore. Does that answer your question?"

"Thanks, Mitch. Yes, it does, and that relieves some anxiety for me. I'm tryin' to think of a target our torpedo thieves could be thinkin' of."

Mitch stairs at ceiling, going over the island in his mind's eye.

"If you could make one go without a torpedo tube and be able to aim the thing, I'd shoot for a ship being loaded at the ammunition pier. That would take out the ship, the pier, and all the men loading. That's the most damage I can think of. I didn't think that stolen torpedo had an active war head."

"No, Morsey said it had an exercise head," Keys says.

"You know, Keys, whoever's got that thing's gonna have to be pretty sharp to get it to run. If they get that to happen, they have to make a warhead that'll explode. I don't see that happening."

"I hope you're right, Mitch, but I don't think we can take the chance. I've seen some astonishing stuff in my day. Like guys you'd think were dolts that came up with ingenious ways to make money or make trouble. I don't think we wanta underestimate these guys. Mare Island may not even be the target, who knows?"

As Keys sets the phone back in the cradle it vibrates in his hand, ringing.

"Barry," Mary says. "The Pontiac is registered to Rian Murphy on Virginia Street in Crockett. I haven't found his personnel file yet but I thought you'd probably want to get out there as soon as possible."

"That's great work, Mary. I'm gonna hustle right over there."

"Do you want me to have Larry meet you?"

"No thanks, Sprite, I'm in a hurry."

Keys grabs a folded-up road map from his desk and does a quick march over to Smitty's to pick up his jeep. The day is warm and sunny. When Keys gets to the jeep he can't resist folding back the canvas top. While crossing the Carquinez Bridge, wind whistling through his hair, he takes in the panorama.

The hills are emerald green, the water below sparkles in the brilliant sunshine. He wishes Mary was with him. They could drive on the road that snakes along the crest of the hills marveling at the views afforded by the open jeep. Back to the job at hand, he stops in Crockett to unfold his map. The address he's looking for is on a narrow winding road heading up a steep hill.

The houses are mostly small clapboard affairs with a few adobes sprinkled in the heavy foliage. Live oaks and ivy grow down to the road's edge. Climbing up the hill there are some spots where the land drops away to his right allowing Keys another grand view of the busy Carquinez Strait.

Driving slowly, he finds the house completely hidden from the road by trees and thick vegetation. A weathered mail box by wooden stairs bears the just-legible numbers of the address he's seeking. There are no other cars parked on the road. Keys backs the jeep against the dirt berm, setting the hand brake and leaving it in gear to keep it from rolling down the steep hill.

Climbing from the jeep, he adjusts his holster, moving it forward on his hip. The stairs are narrow and steep but the old gray wood seems to be in good shape. There is a thin galvanized-pipe handrail, dotted with white bird droppings, on one side of the stairs.

Ducking under low branches, Keys makes his way up the stairs. A tin roof shack is at the top of the stairs nestled under vines of wisteria. There is a screen door on the front with a yellow Nehi door push bar. Keys opens the screen door to knock on the wood door behind it. He waits a moment, then knocks again listening for any movement inside.

The door knob rotates easily in his hand; he pushes the door inward. It scrapes on the floor announcing his entrance. It appears to be a three-room place. A main room, and to his right, a small open kitchen. Off the main room is a closed door to what must be the bedroom. The main room has a nice leather sofa, a low table and two arm chairs.

Sunlight floods the main room from high windows; the walls have bright porcelain advertising signs nailed up. Glass penny gumball machines flank the sofa. A Home Run pinball machine is on a table against a wall next to a very expensive Philco radio phonograph console.

"This guy lived high on the hog," Keys mutters. He turns his attention to the kitchen, noting that all of the nice cabinet doors are opened. Some of the drawers are out. The stove and icebox are new, clean, and expensive. Flour, spilled from an open bag lying on the counter by the sink, dusts the bright linoleum floor.

Keys turns away from the kitchen to the closed bedroom door. He stops at the door to listen for any movement. Turning the doorknob, he opens the door to enter. The door violently slams back at him, knocking him to the floor. A big man rushes by; Keys grabs at the man's legs. The man stumbles, then kicks at Keys, grazing the side of his head.

The blow stuns him. Keys takes a moment trying to get to his knees. He reaches for his gun with his right hand and falls to his side. Pushing up from the floor with both hands, Keys wobbles to the front door. The big man is hunched over going down the stairs, almost hidden by the foliage. Keys yells, "Stop or I'll shoot! Stop!" He pulls his pistol and fires a warning shot at the ground. "Halt! Halt!"

By the time Keys gets to the street, the man is gone. There is no sign of him on the street below and he does not hear a car. Keys does not believe the man ran up the hill, he didn't have time. He must have gone over the edge and down to a street below. Keys waits to see any sign of movement or to hear a car.

Rubbing the side of his head, he looks at the hand red with blood. "Son of a bitch!" He has to hold on the handrail to steady himself on the way back up the stairs. Reentering the shack, he heads to the bedroom. There he sees a big double bed with a beautifully carved headboard. A polished wood bureau with a full-length mirror is on the other side of the room. A large frameless window looks out on an enclosed courtyard.

Keys hurries to the rear door, snatching it open when he sees smoke drifting from an outdoor brick oven. Whatever paperwork was used to feed the fire is ash now. Keys uses a metal poker to shift though the ashes. There is nothing left of any use.

He walks around the perimeter of the walled-in deck, testing the floor boards for looseness. Finding nothing, he goes back into the shack—that is really only a shack on the exterior— to do a thorough search.

Chapter 29

In the safety of the Vallejo barn, the blue flame of Harry's cutting torch melts away the metal of the steel tube sending showers of bright red sparks and molten metal to the ground. He pushes up the dark goggles to inspect his work. Wiping away sweat with a cloth, he can feel the intense heat that has reddened his face.

Looking at his work both pleases and excites him. The small pie-slice wedges he cut into the ends of the tube are to allow him to bend the ends down to meet the smaller diameter of the original warhead and motor sections. He picks up a heavy electric grinder. Holding it tight with both hands he switches it on; the torque of the motor tries to wrench the big machine free of his hands.

Harry works the grinder's sanding disc over the burn-scarred tube ends. Carefully guiding the sander, he cleans the ugly ends to a bright luster.

He uses the torch again to heat the metal, gently bending the wedges to the proper diameter.

The next part of the operation is to cut off the joint rings from the original battery tube section and weld them to his new tube. He takes up the grinder again to finish the work smoothing out the beads of weld. Each weld must be perfect to be sure his new tube is watertight.

Any water collecting in the battery section will lead to electrical shorts and disaster. Everything must be perfect. He will need full power from the batteries to smash the torpedo into the pier and set off an explosion that will detonate the ordnance. The tons of bombs, huge gun shells and powder men are loading will cause a massive explosion.

If successful, Harry can count on much of the south end of Mare Island being out of business for months. The explosion will be too great to be hidden from the press. He hopes the loss of life and the terror of a successful act of sabotage will make world-wide news.

After days of labor, Harry stands back to enjoy the finished product. He can't resist the urge and paints a skull and crossbones on both sides of his masterpiece.

There is still plenty of work to be done. The next phase of his plan is testing the torpedo in an abandoned stone quarry in the eastern hills. The winter rains have swollen the quarry to capacity.

It is a perfect place to test and retrieve his package of terror.

Alby enters the work room; stares at the torpedo, then studies Harry's face. "You did it, boss, you did it! It's beautiful."

"Don't touch it Alby, the paint's still wet."

"I didn't know you could do all that stuff, boss. It's really gonna work, ain't it?"

"I've been well-trained, Alby; of course it will work. Did you get the money from the delivery and take care of Rian's place?"

Alby pulls a wad of bills from his pocket, holding them out to Harry.

"Here's the money, boss. I burned all the papers I could find at Rian's. The same guy that chased Rian came to the house while I was there. I knocked him down and ran out. He shot at me but I got away clean."

Harry stiffens. "How do you know it was the same man?"

"I saw the jeep parked in front a Rian's when I ran out. It's got stars painted over just like the one that chased Rian."

"Damn it! I don't have time to deal with him and get my torpedo finished. Are you sure you got all the paperwork destroyed? Did you find his bankbook?"

"There wasn't no bankbook I could find. I think Rian had it with 'im when he went in the bay. But I burned every piece of paper in the house, boss. I had plenty of time before the guy got there."

"Okay, good job, Alby. Go get some rest. When Tom gets here, we'll plan tonight's work at the yard. We have to be careful and stay out of sight. We're not going to steal anything for a while. We'll have to use up our inventory here to make up the orders we have.

"You and Rian banked at the same place, didn't you?"

"Yeah, we did, but I think Rian kept most a his money in his car. You told us not to deposit any big amounts in the bank. I did like you said an' just made small ones. I keep most of it at home."

"Well, it's too bad about Rian. I could use that money. Where do you hide your money at home, Alby?"

"I keep it under my mattress, boss."

Harry turns away from Alby, rolling his eyes. "Okay, Alby, get some rest. I don't want any foul ups at the yard. You and Tom are going to stay out of trouble. We're close to bringing my plan to fruition; anybody getting in my way is going to die. You understand, Alby?"

"Yes, sir, boss."

Chapter 30

In his search of Rian's place Keys does not find any papers or links to the identity of any of the other gang members. He is just pushing the bed back in place after looking under it when he hears rain drumming on the tin roof. He moves quickly outside and down the stairway to pull up the jeep's canvas top.

Back in Rian's place, Keys calls Frank Gray at the FBI office.

"Hi, boss. Mary found the address of the guy that went in the drink. I'm at his place on Virginia Street in Crockett now. Someone was here and burned papers in a fireplace. I haven't found anything to lead us to the rest of the gang. You may wanta send a man out to watch the place. I'll put a X on the mail box; it's almost at the top of the hill. The place looks like a shack from the outside but it's nice, with high buck stuff inside. The guy had dough to spend."

Gray pulls at his shirt collar. "Did they find his car yet?"

"I don't know. I left as soon as Mary found the address. After that storm last night, I don't think it's gonna be easy to find it. It's raining again here, so the water's probably still stirred up. If it gets rainin' harder, they'll probably call it off till it clears up. I'll check as soon as I get back to the yard an' call you."

"Okay, Keys. Ah, damnit," Gray snorts.

"Whatsa matter, boss?"

"I just popped another collar button."

"Why don't you just leave your collar unbuttoned anyway, Frank?"

"'Cause I like to look professional, Keys. People expect the head of an FBI office to look professional. It's what sets us apart from the guys we chase. I can't go around lookin' like you, Keys."

"Jeez, Frank, that's a low blow. I always dressed snappy just like the Bureau wanted. I kinda set an example for the other guys."

"You always give me a headache, Keys. Get back to Mare Island and get this case solved, will you? I just remembered how peaceful this office is with you gone."

"Okay, Frank, but I'll have to tell Mary how you hurt my feelings."

"Oh, shut up, Keys, and call me 'boss' or 'Mr. Gray' like I've told you a million times. I'd tell you not to call unless you say 'boss', but it'd just give you an excuse not to call. I'll send a man who knows what he's doing out to search the place. Go find our bad guys before they blow up the whole damned yard out from under you."

Keys chuckles as he hangs up the phone. He makes another tour of the house and grounds before he is satisfied there's nothing more Gray's man might find.

The rain comes in squalls as Keys drives back to Mare Island. Over the Carquinez Bridge, the sun bursts though the clouds only to be driven away by rainfall so hard Keys has to slow the jeep down to be able to see the road. Back on the yard at Smitty's, he calls the police chief to get an update on the search for Rian's car.

The police chief tells Keys the boats went out at first light. Using chains and grappling hooks they dragged a few sections of the bay and did not find anything but old tires and junk. When the storm hit, the boats called it a day.

Keys calls Gray to tell him the search found nothing. He has to leave a message as Gray is out of his office. "Probably had to go buy another shirt," Keys muses. On his way to his office he stops in the bathroom. As he washes his hands, he looks in the mirror. The welt over his eye is an ugly purple. "Good thing Mary won't see me tonight," he mutters.

Getting into his office he is surprised that it is after six o'clock. He calls Mary's phone, hoping she will still be there.

"Hi, Barry. I stayed to let you know there's no personnel records for Rian Murphy. Frank Gray called to say you didn't give him an address for Murphy's place so I asked him to see if they have anything on the guy."

"Thanks for stayin', Mary. I told him I'd put a X on the mail box. It's easier than tryin' ta find the numbers. I'm not surprised about the records. It's like we thought: Booth probably destroyed the personnel records so nobody'd get wise to the double pay scam. Do me a favor and take the ferry home. The roads are a mess with all this rain. I practically had to slow to a crawl drivin' the jeep back."

"Okay, Barry. I was thinking of taking a bus over to see my girlfriends at Marinship but this rain is too much. I'll be warm and snug in our apartment tonight, but I'll be lonely, too."

"Chin up, Mary. That's what the Brits say. I really miss you; I'd like to come down there an' give you a big hug. This investigation won't last much longer, and we'll get more work out of it, too. It's you an' me, kid; we'll have more fun an' adventure than a barrel a monkeys."

"Ha, ha, Barry, you're such a sweet talker. It's no wonder you swept me off my feet. I must have fallen and hit my head."

"I love you, Mary. I'll make this up to you, I promise."

"Ease up, Barry. I'm only kidding you. We make a great team. I don't know about your barrel a monkeys but we're a team always. It's you and me, Keys. Be careful tonight. Larry's looking forward to your graveyard shift; you're all he talks about."

"That's funny, you're all he talks about to me, Sprite; I've been gettin' kinda jealous. Stay warm tonight. I'll be thinkin' of you."

Chapter 31

That night Harry forces himself to stop work on his torpedo to drive to Mare Island. He cools on the thought of killing Tom; he still needs him. Money is a problem: he spent large amounts buying the Vallejo barn property, and setting up his gang. He fronted the men money to buy cars and the costs to modify them to haul loads.

Bribes, trucks, supplies, his own luxuries, and now a fortune spent in batteries for his torpedo. Harry needs money. He needs help with the torpedo. Weighing over three thousand pounds, it is too much for one man. Rian was the real mechanic, he could also fabricate and weld. Now it is all up to Harry. He likes the challenge of making the torpedo work, he does not like the heavy lifting.

Waiting for Alby and Tom in the sawmill shed, Harry draws up plans for a portable crane he can attach to his big truck for lifting the torpedo. Alby is the first man in; he and Harry wait for Tom.

"Maybe his car broke down, boss. He don't take care of it much."

"Maybe he just don't care about anything but himself, Alby. Do you know anything about why he killed Booth? Were Tom and Booth friendly? I've got to wonder why we never found Booth's bankbook."

"Me an' Rian never had nothin' to do with Tom, boss. He's a mean drunk—always gettin' in bar fights. The way he tells it, Booth told you ta hire 'im. We didn't find any bankbook at Booth's house, but he coulda hid it anywhere, I 'spose."

Harry scratches at his chin. "Yeah, Booth did say Tom would be a good man to have around. I've always wondered why. There's more to this and Tom will have to answer for it."

"Me an' Rian was sure glad you hired us, boss. Us fixin' that old broke down car a yours was real good luck."

"It was fortunate you and Rian came along when you did, Alby. Let's get to work. For the next few days I want you to just blend in with the scrapyard men. They all know you so when they need a hand, just help out. You can tell them we're being reassigned and you were told to help out at the scrapyard for now. It looks like Tom isn't going to show up tonight."

Harry goes back to his design work on the crane. He plans to pack up all of his paper work here and take it to the barn. He no longer feels it is safe to leave anything on the yard that will lead back to him. The federal man is closing in. Harry will have to deal with the man soon; nothing can stand in the way of his plans.The would-be saboteur carries his papers to his pickup truck to tuck them under the seat. Harry takes a clipboard and heads to the scrapyard to pick out the materials he needs for the crane. With tall boots on, he slogs through the mud and water.

***

Keys rises from his nap to meet Larry for a late dinner. Although the rain has finally abated, the gutters still run with currents of water. The night is warm, but both men wear coats unbuttoned to ward off the dampness.

Larry piles a mountain of potatoes onto his already full plate as he slides the brown Bakelite tray down the rails. Keys trails behind, stopping only for a sausage sandwich and a piece of apple pie. Both men fill their cups with coffee at the end of the line. Keys pays for the meals, then leads the way to an empty table by a window.

Keys hangs his hardhat up before sitting down.

"How'd you get that knot on your head, Keys? You're not eatin'; you sure you're okay?" Larry asks.

"I ran into one of our bad guys today and I ate too much breakfast this mornin'; it's still sittin' on my stomach."

"Too bad, this liver an' onions is the best."

"It looks like you got plenty of it, Larry; you need to be alert tonight. We're closin' in on our bad guys."

"Yeah, my eyes are bigger'n my stomach sometimes. I'll lay off some a these spuds. Have the cops had any luck findin' the guy we chased into the bay?"

"Not yet. Mary probably told you I went over to Mister Pontiac's house in Crockett. The guy lived well. His place looked like a shack from the outside and a palace inside. He had an enclosed deck on the back of the place that had more square footage than the house. I'd like to have a place like that for Mary an' me someday. That's where I ran into trouble." Keys points to his head. "I'm glad Mary can't see this."

"She's a real nice lady, Keys."

"She is Larry, an' she's mine."

The Marine stops his fork to look up from his plate. "I'm just sayin' you're a lucky man, Keys."

"Okay, sorry Larry, maybe I'm too wound up. The plan for tonight is we'll run the jeep over to the scrapyard parking lot so we'll have wheels if we need 'em. The men we're after gotta know we're close, so we need to be careful.We'll split up to cover more ground. You take the east side; if you get in trouble fire a round from your .45 an' I'll come runnin'."

"There's no trouble I can't take care of, Keys."

"Larry, we don't know how many guys there are. Lots a these guys carry guns and knives. I know you can take care of yourself, just don't rush into anything. I'll meet you by Building 679 at 0400. We'll plan our next moves from there. Be sharp, Marine. I got this knot on my head from not bein' careful enough."

"I outta be takin' care a you, Keys."

Keys shakes his head walking away. "Ah, to be young and immortal."

***

Harry is looking through the pipe and bar shop on the northeast section of the scrapyard. He checks his crane drawing on the clip board against the materials, trying to find parts as close to his drawing as possible. The steel tube is heavy; the lengths here are very long. They are too long for loading or hauling in his truck.

He wants shorter lengths so he can load them himself and get them out in his pickup truck. Harry does not want to draw attention to himself or have any undo trouble at the sentry gate. He decides to plod through another lot where random lengths of pipe are lying in the muddy ground.

Tom stayed at a Georgia Street bar long enough to miss the meeting Harry ordered. He prided himself on drinking just enough whiskey to get righteous. He was going to kill Harry—the Nazi bastard—tonight.

He drives to the far end of the scrapyard parking lot so no one will see his car. When he gets out of his car, he notices his hands are shaking. Tom uncaps a fifth of bourbon takes a deep swallow and pitches the bottle on the ground. He kicks it under the tire of another car parked near his.

Keeping to the shadows, he begins looking for Harry. After skulking around in the mud Tom wishes he had not drunk all the bourbon. A man needed bracing for this kind of work. He just wants to get Harry someplace he can ambush him. He has dreamt of plunging his knife into Harry's belly. He wants to watch the look of horror on the Nazi's face as he twists the blade.

The warm night air, heavy with humidity, sweats some of the liquor out of him. His thoughts go back to Harry telling him the Gestapo would kill him if they suspected he killed Harry. He stops cold when he sees his quarry scraping the mud off the bottom of his boot. From his viewpoint Tom can see a yard crane next to the ten-foot sections of four-inch thick armor plate Harry stands next to.

"Jesus Christ, I've got 'im!" Tom exclaims. Harry's in the perfect position. It's just too good to pass up. He looks around to see if anyone can see him, then hunches over, staying the shadows, crabbing toward the crane. Tom starts the crane; as soon as it fires, he backs it into the stack of armor plating. There is a huge crash of metal to metal that rings throughout the scrapyard.

Men stop what they are doing; some duck and cover their heads. It is, to some of the men, a sound of death, one they have heard before: heavy steel plating that crashes making that sound usually kills men. Tom jumps from the crane to fade into a shadow.

When Harry heard the crane's engine race, he ran around the armor plate stock pile to see what was happening. The steel plates missed him by inches. He cupped his ears to keep the sound from deafening him. Harry is sure it is Tom he sees jump from the crane.

Harry pulls a pistol from his pocket as he heads for the shadows that consumed Tom. Scrapyard men gather to see what happened. One of them cautiously approaches the crane. He shines a flashlight in the crane's cabin, then climbs up to turn the engine off.

Larry, the Moose, hears the sound and sees men run toward the area the sound emanated from. He is to one side of the metal bins when he sees a form dart from the shadows going in the opposite direction. The big Marine flicks on his flashlight and lifts the beam to freeze Tom's face in the cone of light.

Tom is only momentarily distracted before he puts on speed to flee from the area. He changes direction to put distance on the beam of the flashlight. He runs hard for ten yards when he splashes in deepening water. The west side of the island is a vast lake several feet deep after the week's hard rains.

He can't gauge, in the dim light, if there is any way through. He sees the red lights atop one of the tall radio towers. Cold water pours over the tops of his boots as he makes for the tower. Hunched down behind one of the towers' concrete legs he can see Moose, the big Marine, playing his flashlight over the area at the edge of the water.

Harry was twenty yards behind Tom when he saw someone catch Tom with the beam of his flashlight. He is amazed by how quickly Tom disappears into the darkness. Harry watches as the flashlight plays over the area searching for the man.

The cold water completely sobers Tom; hate and anger boil his blood when he sees Harry come into a light from the scrapyard. Tom mutters under his breath. "I'm gonna kill both a you bastards. Maybe I can make it look like you assholes killed each other." He wades over to another leg of the tower to wait out the search for him.

Moose switches off his flashlight, hoping Tom will think he's stopped looking for him. He thinks about firing a shot to warn Keys. The thought quickly passes; Moose turns back to the scale house to wait in the shadows for Tom to show himself.

Tom waits to see if anyone comes for him. Adrenalin courses through his body; the cold water quickly overcomes hot blood and makes his teeth chatter. He decides to make a break for his car. Wading across to the eastern radio tower, his heavy boots fill with water, twice pulling him under. He pushes his head above the water wanting to scream with the rage that pulses in him. He is coming into bright light but he no longer cares.

Tom takes two knives from his coat, then pulls the wet, heavy thing off. The coat floats on the water, the sleeves spread out like drowned man. Wind coming in from the Bay chills him to the bone. Tucking the knives in his belt behind his back, he fails to notice a Helix House guard.

"Hey, what the hell are you doin' here? Get your hands up. You look like a drowned rat. Come on over here. Do you have a yard badge?"

"I'm just a little drunk, boss. The boys throwed me in the water. I lost my jacket. You got a blanket or somethin' I can warm up in?"

"You know there's a war on, don't you?" The guard growls. "You guys better knock off the shenanigans before you get yourselves shot. I gotta report you, but come on inside, I'll get a blanket for you."

Tom stands meekly before the guard who lifts a blanket to drape over him. He draws a knife from behind his back. With the guard's arms outstretched, his chest unprotected, Tom stabs the guard through the blanket. He quickly thrusts up under the ribcage into the man's heart. The guard is dead before he collapses to the ground.

Tom quickly pulls off the guard's clothing before there is much blood. He strips off his own wet muddy clothes to pull on the guard's dry clothes. The pant legs are too long, and he has to roll the cuffs under. The guard's wallet and ID are in the back pockets.

Tom puts his own wallet in his shirt pocket thinking the guard probably wouldn't have much money but he could sell the ID. He searches the room for a coat and hat. On the rear wall is a row of hooks with the guard's hat and coat. Tom grabs a duffel bag crumpled against the wall to stuff his clothes in.

He drags the guard's body across the room to a cot. Sitting on the floor he uses his legs and feet to shove the body under the cot and covers it with the blanket. Tom surveys the room wiping away spots of blood and drag marks on the floor.

Satisfied anyone looking in from the doorway won't immediately spot trouble, he slowly opens the door. Finding the way clear, he pulls the hat low over his brow, hoists the duffel bag over his shoulder and heads for the parking lot.

Chapter 32

Tom can hardly believe he made it to the parking lot unchallenged. The harsh lights and increase in shipyard noise begin to unnerve him. Unsettled, he starts to think he should climb in his car and get away from the yard right away. His blood lust overpowers any rational thought. Yanking up the rear seat he drops the duffel bag in the hidden compartment. He takes a small bottle of bourbon from the glove box and uncaps it for a deep pull. Before putting the bottle back, Tom decides he needs more.

With his courage fortified, his thoughts go to Harry. When he sees the Nazi bastard's face in his mind's eye, raw hatred overcomes him. He stands by his car clenching and unclenching his fists. Tormented by Harry's superior attitude, Tom thinks of his painful beating and all of the humiliation the Nazi forced him to swallow. Firing up his emotions helps to bolster his resolve.

He knows if he does not kill Harry, the Nazi or his Gestapo friends will kill him, sooner or later. The liquor takes hold. He twists his head, popping the tense knots from his neck. Tom takes his favorite knife, gauges the gleaming razor-sharp edge with a grin, and puts it in his pocket. Filled with hate and purpose, he heads back to the scrapyard. Harry is going to die.

On his way out of the parking lot, Tom spots Harry's pickup truck. He uncaps the valve stem of the left front tire. Then, using the point of his blade, he lets the air out. Recapping the tire valve, he is about to leave when he stops in mid-stride. Tom opens the driver's side door to get under the dash panel; he yanks the ignition wire from the back of the switch then tucks the wire back up so it won't dangle down.

"That'll hold 'im till I get 'im." He shuts the door, acknowledging his cleverness with a grim sneer.

Tom skulks into the scrapyard hunting for Harry. Staying in the shadows as much as possible, he searches for his quarry. He is fearful of going too far into the western end, not wanting to run into Moose without finding Harry first. Going back to Cedar Avenue, he skirts around the scrapyard to plod through the mud off Dump Road.

Moving quietly, he makes it to the scale shed unnoticed. Tom takes his boots off to climb upstairs. Creeping up, he stops to listen for any movement. Harry would be cornered and very dangerous. The nerves in his neck knot, he angrily tries to control the tremor in his hands. Reaching the top, he is relieved to see no one is there.

Pulling on his boots, he thinks again of getting out of the yard. He needs to surprise Harry, to make his attack before Harry can defend. He crosses the road back to the scrapyard.

Tom just misses Harry as the Nazi bastard circles around the scrapyard, then back to the parking lot to check Tom's car. The car's hood is cold so Tom is still on the yard and dangerous. He is certain Tom will try to ambush him. Returning to the scrapyard, he stays in the bright lights. He sees Moose still on the west side of the scrapyard keeping watch. He turns to go back toward Cedar Avenue and sees a man coming from the scale shed.

Harry moves back under the shadow of a tall bin. The man he sees is familiar but in a Marine uniform. *It's Tom! What the hell's he doing in a Marine uniform?* Harry wonders. Harry presses back against the bin and watches as Tom passes no more than ten yards away. This not the place for gun play, he will wait to see where Tom is going.

Tom moves slowly, his head swiveling right to left. He slows at the end of the second bin, then moves around it. Harry waits a moment, then follows. When he rounds the second bin, he sees

246

Tom step out of the way of an oncoming truck. The headlights wash over Tom, who seems to shrink in size. From the far side of the truck Harry hears Moose call out.

"What the hell are you doin' in a Marine uniform, you creep?"

Tom scurries to some high piles of railroad ties. He ducks down between the piles out of Harry's view. The spy sees Moose come around the truck and head for the railroad ties.

Tom crouches down behind the pile of railroad ties, pulling out his long blade. He can hear Moose approaching over the muddy ground, the mud sucking at his boots. Moving back a few feet, he lets his eyes adjust to the darkness. The big Marine swings around the corner. Tom springs forward plunging the blade deep into the man's belly. Moose instinctively grabs Tom's throat with both hands, strangling him. Tom frantically uses both hands trying to work the blade up to pierce Moose's heart.

Moose knows he's been stabbed but can't understand why Tom does not stop struggling. His great strength has never failed him. His senses shut down as Tom's flailing knife finally rips into the Marine's heart. The Moose falls forward bending Tom backwards. The Marine's weight crushes Tom to the muddy ground.

Tom's horror intensifies when he is face to face with the dead Marine. He quickly realizes his head is sinking into the mud. His hands and arms are trapped under the weight of Moose's body. He squirms under the Marine, desperately trying to free himself. Muddy water is getting into Tom's eyes; he opens his mouth to scream only to swallow gritty water. With all his strength, Tom frantically kicks with his legs.

Harry watched the big Marine go after Tom. He almost called out to him; to warn him against going after Tom. The Marine disappeared into the darkness behind the ties. Harry hears a grunt, then splashing and an odd whining sound. When Harry gets into the darkness between the piles, he sees Moose lying on top of Tom in the murky light. Tom's face is almost under water, but Tom is kicking free.

Harry jumps on top of the lifeless Marine, then spreads his arms and legs to keep the dead man from rolling off Tom. Harry stabilizes the body, then moves his head to look into Tom's face. Tom's horrified face, eyes shut tight, flails side to side in time with his legs. Larry's dead eyes stare back at him. Harry whispers to Tom.

"Stop struggling, Tom. Let the dirty water take you; it's what you deserve."

Chapter 33

Harry pushes Tom's head under, watching the bubbles of air finally purge from his lungs. He climbs off Larry after Tom stops breathing. He wonders if Tom has his bankbook, but doesn't have time to move the Marine's body off. A voice calls out. "What's goin' on in there?" He can't get to Tom's pockets. Wiping his muddy hands off on the Marine's coat, he sees a small notebook half out of the coat's pocket. Harry puts the notebook in his pocket and backs out from between the tie piles.

Coming out of the darkness, Harry sees two men who are standing together, sheepishly keeping their distance.

"Looks like two Marines got into it. You better go get the police. I think they're both dead."

"Uh, why don't you go?" one of the men says to Harry.

"I'll stick here till you get the police. You better get goin'," Harry says.

"Yeah, okay. Let's go, Georgie." The two men head off toward the yard's interior.

Harry starts back into the murder scene but sees more yard workers gathering.

***

Keys, standing by Building 679, looks impatiently at his watch when two men, their eyes wide, obviously rattled trot toward him.

"What's the hurry, gents?" Keys calls to them.

"There's two dead Marines back by the railroad tie piles. We're goin' for the police," one of men says as they trot by Keys.

Keys looks at his watch again. Larry is always on time. He knows in his heart it has to be his friend. He looks to the heavens, "Oh, Christ, please don't let it be Larry."

Keys takes off in a run to the tie piles where yardmen gather in groups. He yanks out his flashlight, moving in between the wood beams. Shining the light down, he sees immediately it is Larry.

"Larry, Larry, oh, not you Larry. Goddamn it, I told you. Sweet Jesus, why didn't you fire a shot. You didn't even have your pistol out. I hate this, damn it, a good man; you make it outta Guadalcanal only to end up like this. Damn it, Larry, I really liked you man. I…aw hell."

He gently rolls Larry off of the other man; the bloody knife hilt juts out from his friend's stomach. Keys bends down to go through the other man's pockets. He finds a wallet and yard badge in the shirt pocket. Patting the front pants pockets, he feels a ring of keys.

Getting the keys out of the pants pocket is awkward. Anxious to make an identification he makes no attempt to turn the man over for further inspection. Standing up he shines the flashlight on the yard badge.

"You're no Marine." He pockets the badge and keys, then opens the wallet.

"Tom Walsh," he reads. "I'll bet you're the same one from Larry's bar fight. God damn you to hell, Tom Walsh."

Keys turns, hearing the yard police coming to the entrance of the tie pile.

"Come on out of there," one of them says to Keys.

Keys flicks his flashlight off and comes toward the police, holding his hands out. "I'm Keys, let me get my ID out."

He shows his ID and the commandant's letter.

"Okay, we've been told about you," the lead officer says.

"The big Marine is my friend, Larry Mazurki. You guys call him Moose. He deserves the best treatment you can give him; he's a Guadalcanal Marine, a real hero." Keys hands the yard badge to the officer. "This other guy is a bum; he sure as hell isn't a Marine. Here's his yard badge. I'm sure he's one a the bums we're after. I'm gonna get over to the address on his driver's license before anyone else beats me to it. I'll make a full report as soon as I get back."

Keys wastes no time getting to his jeep and hurrying across the causeway. There is no pleasure in this drive; Keys fights to keep his mind on the case. Larry's lifeless face keeps jutting into his brain. The address on the driver's license is on Kentucky Street. Keys counts down the address numbers coming to the right one. From where he parks under the street light, he can see a two-story place hidden behind tall shrubbery. Walking up the steep driveway, the entire building comes into view.

The old rectangular house sits on a knoll. Even in the faint light he can see its flaking gray paint, which may have been blue sometime in the past, is cracked and curled, baring the old dark wood beneath. A wooden stairway leads up to the second story under a flat roof. The upper floor has been divided into two apartments. Keys bangs on the doors of both apartments. No one answers at either apartment.

He tries the door of the B apartment. Finding it locked, he uses the keys he took from the dead man to unlock two dead bolts to open the door. The interior is dark with the curtains drawn. Keys leaves the door open to cross the main room to open the curtains. With dawn just breaking, he closes the door. Dust from the curtains floats in currents on the early light. Keys stands in the middle of the room for a moment to take in its content. The furniture is unremarkable; it probably came with the apartment, he thinks.

A big Zenith radio phonograph stands out from the otherwise drab room. To his right is a small kitchen. He thinks an open door off the main room must be the bedroom. The smell of cigarette smoke, spilled bourbon and vomit is pungent in the now-closed space. Keys moves to a window to bring in some fresh air. The window has a hasp screwed to the sash with a padlock.

There is one other window in the room, also padlocked. He decides he can live with the odor and checks in the bedroom, bathroom, and kitchen to make sure there are no surprises. Returning to the main room, he scans the walls, his eyes resting on a fresh plaster patch at the phone cord. He removes the plate around the cord then, with his pocket knife, digs out the new plaster. There is nothing but wood lath behind the plaster, no room to hide anything.

He pulls off his coat, taking his time to make a thorough search. Going first to the usual hiding places, he then removes all the switch plates and electrical outlets, finding nothing. Next the drains in the kitchen sink and bathroom, the toilet, and tank; again his search turns up nothing. After hours of searching, the place has grown hot and stuffy; the stench becomes overwhelming.

Keys once again stands in the middle of the main room rubbing his jaw. *Why would this crummy little man who killed Larry lock every window and door in the place if he had nothing to steal, nothing to hide?* Keys' anger grows. *Could the little bastard outsmart him? Would he let that happen?*

Keys goes to the door, opening it to welcome in the fresh air. Taking a breath, he looks out at bright sunny day, a day Larry would never see. Droplets of water clinging to the grass sparkle like diamonds. There he sees a peaceful beauty even while a burning anger smolders in his soul.

He turns back to the room to scan it again. His eyes go over the walls with the electrical outlets still hanging out. The light fixture in the ceiling hangs down on its wires. Keys rummages in his cigarette package for another smoke. Finding the last one in the pack he sticks it between his lips crumpling the pack to throw it on the bare wood floor. He curses remembering his lighter is out of flint.

In the kitchen, he takes a box of matches out to the front room. He entertains a brief thought of setting the place on fire wondering if he would find any satisfaction in it. Angrily running the match head across the wainscoting by the door to strike it, he watches the flame flare. He drops the match on the floor and smothers it with his foot.

The wainscoting is in this room only; there is no other wall paneling in the whole apartment.

Keys excitement builds; he closes the door to look over the paneling. He goes down one wall examining each panel. On another wall, he comes back to a panel near the center where there are faint scratches on the wall above the panel. Just able to get his fingernails under the panel's edge he pries it back on his knuckles.

The panel comes away enough to get his fingers behind it and pull it out from the wall. The wall laths have been cut away leaving a recess. Stacks of cash are held together with rubber bands. A journal and a bankbook are among some papers. Keys opens the bankbook. George Booth's name is printed in ink at the top of the first page.

"You murderous little bastard. You must have thought you were so very clever. I wish you could see me take your hoard. I wish I could pay you back for stealing Larry's life. You killed a good man, but at least he put an end to your lousy life, too."

Keys grabs a pillow from the bedroom; he sheds the pillow to use the pillowcase to carry the cash and papers to the jeep. Locking the apartment door, the triumph he feels quickly diminishes with the thought of going back to Mare Island and taking care of Larry. He groans inwardly, thinking of telling Mary that their friend is dead.

Across the street from Tom's place, the angry Nazi saboteur pulls his car to the curb. After killing Tom, Harry hurried to his truck wanting to get to Tom's place before anyone else. He was sure Tom had plenty of money hidden away, and he had to have that money. It took him a long time, thanks to Tom's sabotage, to change his flat tire and then find the cause of the truck's refusal to start.

He is reaching for the key to turn off the truck's engine when he notices movement across the street. His blood boils as he watches Keys toss a lumpy pillowcase in his jeep. Harry takes a pistol from his pocket, keeping it from view below the windowsill of his truck. He wants the bag, knowing it must contain whatever Tom had stashed in his apartment. Grinning maniacally, he snicks the truck in gear, planning to drive alongside Keys, kill him, and take the bag.

Harry pulls away from the curb to make a U-turn. He glances behind, then cranks the wheel over to pull out. A horn blares, snapping his head around. An oncoming bus is almost on top of him; it blocks his turn, then stops several yards behind Keys' jeep. Men and women disgorge from the bus on their way home from a war plant shift. The jeep is gone by the time the bus pulls away.

Harry hammers the steering wheel in frustration.

Chapter 34

Returning to Mare Island, Mary is on Keys' mind. He will have to break his rule of not seeing her on the yard. Telling her of Larry's murder over the phone is no good. Driving through the causeway gate, he thinks of Tom Walsh, wondering if he could have been the leader of the black-market gang. *How could he have benefited from stealing a torpedo? Was the murderous dog a saboteur also?*

When Keys walks into the administration building and sees the back of a big Marine in the hallway, he rushes forward, his arm outstretched. "Larry, Larry." The Marine turns with a puzzled look on his face; Keys turns away without a word to climb the stairs to his office.

Keys enters his office and closes the door behind him. Dropping the pillowcase, he sits heavily in the chair behind the desk. With his elbows planted atop the desk, he cradles his head in his hands. He needs a moment alone before he can see Mary. "What the hell, Larry?" he says to no one, then slaps the desktop as a tear rolls down his cheek.

Staring at the wall seeing nothing, Keys struggles. *How could the Moose let himself get killed?* When he looks down at the tear on the desktop he angrily pounds the desk; he can't remember the last time he cried. His shoulders shake and the tough detective lets himself mourn.

Rubbing his eyes with the heels of his hands, Keys gets up from the chair to pace the office. Hands behind his back, head down, he paces. Suddenly his head snaps up; *the Marine uniform! It had to be the Marine uniform. The Marines were Larry's life; his commitment to America and the Marines was without question. When Larry saw Walsh in that uniform it must have driven him crazy.*

"It's all right, Larry, I'm gonna get 'em," Keys says out loud. "I promised Mary I wouldn't go lookin' for trouble, but I can't sit by and do nothing." Keys realizes he's talking to himself and shakes his head.

"*I've got to find a way*," he thinks to himself. "*I can't lie to Mary but I can't let 'em get away. I have to go after the rest of the gang.*" He tilts his head back, eyeing the ceiling. "*But I can't lose Mary either.*"

Keys takes a breath, then strides purposely out of his office to find Mary. Descending the stairs, he sees Mary in the hallway talking to a Marine. Keys goes to her and when he is closer, he sees her dab her eyes with a handkerchief. Keys clinches his jaw, steading himself. Mary looks away from the Marine, her eyes meet Key's, she stiffens, choking back the tears. Keys motions her to follow him back upstairs.

When they enter his office, Keys turns to Mary, he reaches out to hold her close. As soon as they embrace, her body begins to tremble and he feels her warm tears on his neck.

"I was going to be so strong, Barry. I just can't help it; he was such a nice boy. He was so full of life; he wanted to be like you. I can't believe he's gone. I can't believe we won't ever see him again."

"Mary, I'm sorry you got the news before I could tell you. He was a very brave man, and, in the end, too brave. He should never have gone after that bum. I told him to fire a shot if he saw trouble. He never took the pistol out of his holster. I'm not trying to blame him; it was the way he thought things should be done. I think when he saw the bum in a Marine uniform he just lost his head.

"I'm pretty sure the guy was the same one who tried to knife him in a bar. Larry handled him easily then; he probably thought he wouldn't have much trouble. They called him Moose because he was big, strong, and a good-hearted man. I was going to talk to you about asking him to work with us after the war's over."

"Oh, Barry, he would have loved that. Who was the man that killed Larry? Did you know he killed another Marine?"

Keys holds Mary before him searching her face. "What do you mean? When did he kill another Marine?"

"Mitch told me the man that killed Larry had a Marine guard's uniform on. The police found the guard's wallet in the pants pocket. After they checked the duty roster, they found the guard's body in a radio station building. He was knifed the same way Larry was killed."

"That murderous little son of a bitch. A bum like that wasn't fit to walk the same earth with Larry," Keys shouts, then pauses taking a breath. "I think he killed George Booth, too. I found Booth's bankbook in the guy's apartment. I'm sorry, Mary, I can't let this go. I know I promised to stay clear of danger but I can't let those guys get away. I've got to talk to Mitch and the yard police before the trail goes cold. We need to know how many more of those guys are out there."

Mary squares her shoulders looking up into Keys' anguished face. "Your promise was genuine Barry, I know that. I needed a guarantee then, but I know now more than ever there is nothing certain in life. I want the men involved in Larry's death brought to justice, too.

"That sweet man would have charged through the gates of hell to help either of us. He has to be avenged. Please, just try to be extra careful. I know you're the best man for the job but I don't want to lose you...we have a good life to live together. I want that to be our future, Barry."

Keys face visibly relaxes. "Thank you, Mary. That's just the tonic I needed. I'm gonna get 'em, you can bet on it. I'll be as careful as I can. Stay strong, Mary, that's what Larry would want." He looks down into Mary's teary eyes. "Give me a kiss for luck."

After Mary leaves, he copies the ID information from Tom Walsh's wallet then takes Booth's bankbook from the pillow case. Bundling the money up, he puts it in a file cabinet drawer.

Keys enters Morsey's office to talk to Mitch.

"I got a question for you, Mitch."

"Hey, Keys. Man, I'm sorry to hear about Moose."

"Me too, Mitch; they don't make better men. I found a stash of money and George Booth's bankbook in the guy's apartment. The guy that killed Larry I mean. He musta killed Booth and was surely one of the black-market men we're after. One thing bothern' me is, what would he do with a torpedo? Is it a big secret? Would our enemies want it?"

"I don't think so, Keys. You know we've had big problems with our torpedoes. The electric model is supposed to be better than the steam model. The way I hear it, we stole the electric's design from a captured German torpedo. So, it wouldn't have anything they don't know about."

"Is Morsey in?"

261

"Naw, he's down on the building way with his sub."

"Okay. Tell 'im I'm gonna find every one a these bums an' put 'em outta business permanently. Whoever's in that gang I'm holdin' responsible for Larry's murder. I gotta go find out what the yard police found. See you later, Mitch."

At the police station Keys hands over Walsh's wallet and Booth's bankbook.

"You can keep the wallet but I'll need the bankbook back."

The police chief, a burly dark-haired man, sits behind his desk flanked by two of his officers. Cigarette butts overflow an ashtray atop the desk's scarred wood. The chief scowls fixing Keys with narrowed eyes.

"I've had my officers out looking for you, Keys. You're impeding my investigation. This is my bailiwick; I don't take kindly your interference."

"Chief," Keys interjects, "before we get too far down that road, let me say I have the utmost respect for your office and staff. That said, you have read the commandant's letter that makes it clear that I am in charge of this investigation. I told the officers on the scene that I would report as soon as I searched Walsh's place.

"I intend to run down the rest of the gang Walsh was with. I hope, with your cooperation, we'll bring to justice the men responsible for the murders and black-marketing. Larry Mazurki was a good friend. I'd like to see his personal effects."

"That's a nice speech, Keys," the chief says. "We all liked and respected the Moose. What we found on his body, and Walsh's, is in our evidence room. You're welcome to look through it.

"I don't like cowboys, Keys. A one-man vendetta is not going to the get results that my department can. You need to work with us, bud."

Keys, clearly anxious to get back to his case, turns his attention back to the chief. The chief waves his hand in dismissal. "I can see this is falling on deaf ears. You keep me in the picture and I'll do the same for you. How's that?"

"Sorry you see it that way, chief, but I've gotta see this through. I have to report to Morsey and my FBI boss daily. You'll get the same reports. Is there anything on the car that went into the bay?"

"Not yet, Keys. The weather is clearing. I'll have a grid search by as many boats as I can muster."

Keys stands, then he leans over the desk to shake hands."Thanks, Chief. Where are Larry's and Walsh's bodies?"

"In the morgue at the base hospital." The chief shakes Keys' hand with a firm grip. Looking Keys over, he shrugs his shoulders then says, "Good luck, Keys."

"You didn't find a notebook in Mazurki's coat?" Keys asks the evidence room matron.

"No sir," she replies.

"He had it in his coat pocket when we started out; someone must have taken it."

Keys goes back to his office, leans back in his chair, hands behind his head, staring at the ceiling. He leans forward, picking up the phone to call Mary.

She answers her phone saying she was about to call him.

"I have the license number of Walsh's car."

"Excellent, baby, that's my next move."

Keys hurries out to his jeep to search the scrapyard parking lot. Driving down a row of cars checking the license tag numbers, he stops at a '36 Ford four-door humpback sedan. He brings out the keys he took from Walsh's pocket and slots the Ford key in the door lock. The key turns in the lock allowing him to rotate the door handle. "Bingo," he says.

In the glovebox, he finds two small knives, dice, and three boxes of playing cards. The registration on the steering column is to the same address where he found Booth's bankbook in Vallejo. Opening a rear door, Keys sees a trail of muddy splatter on the floor but nothing on the rear seat. He yanks on the rear seat but it won't move.

Bending down to look under the bottom seat cushion, he sees a catch in the center above the driveshaft tunnel. Releasing the catch, he raises the seat, revealing the hidden compartments on either side of the tunnel. One compartment is empty; the other has a muddy duffle bag in it. He pulls the bag out, yanking it open to dump the contents on the floor.

The clothes that come out of the bag are muddy and reek badly. They are clammy to the touch. He finds nothing in the pockets. He stuffs the clothes back in the bag and looks down into the compartment. This compartment extends farther back to the rear. Keys has to duck his head into the mouth of the compartment to be able to reach the back wall.

Feeling with his hand, he traces the walls of the compartment. A crumpled damp paper is stuck to the back of the metal compartment. Keys gets out of the car to bring a flashlight from the jeep. Shining the light into the compartment, Keys can see writing on the paper.

He carefully peels the paper from the metal wall. The type written note contains a list of what Keys recognizes as black-market items to be delivered to Jake's Auto Parts in Stockton. He puts the seat back, closes the rear doors and gets behind the steering wheel to see if the car starts. It fires up and settles to a smooth idle.

Keys slots his jeep in a parking space and returns to the Ford. At the locksmith's, he bangs on the counter, calling for Smitty.

"Hold your britches on, will ya?" Smitty calls from the gloom in back.

"Oh, Keys, I shoulda known from the bangin' it was you. So what can I do for you, my hurried friend?"

"I need a favor."

"That don't surprise me much, Keys. What's it this time?"

"I'd like you to pick up my jeep from the scrapyard parking lot and bring it back here. If I'm not back by tomorrow, give this note to Mitch; he'll know what to do with it."

"You fixin' to get into trouble, Keys?"

"I hope not, Smitty, but you never know. It's a lead to a black market gang and the people that killed Moose. I'm gonna weed the bums out an' make 'em pay. I'm not sure what I'll get into, but I don't wanta spook 'em with an army a guys until I know more."

"I'll go with you. Let me get my shotgun."

"Hold up, Smitty. I can't let you do that. I appreciate the offer but I need to play this by ear. I want to learn what I can without makin' anybody nervous. If I spook 'em, I just wanta be able to back away with no fuss. I'm gonna leave my ID with you just in case my new friends get curious."

"Okay, Keys, I'll play it your way, but you owe me breakfast tomorrow, you hear?"

"I hear you. Thanks, man."

Chapter 35

Walsh's Ford has a full tank of gas that is unusual in the face of gas rationing. Keys enjoys the car's engine: it has very good power and response. The ride, however, is quite harsh. Although this car is not raised off the ground like the Pontiac he chased into the bay, it is stiffly sprung. By Keys' map, Stockton is almost seventy miles from Mare Island along Route 4.

Keys hopes to be at Jake's on the southern side of Stockton before late afternoon. Where the road is smooth Keys steps up his speed: the Ford romps ahead with a light touch on the gas pedal. Keys stops at a diner, orders coffee and a piece of pie, then goes to the phone at the end of the counter. He opens a phone book that hangs on a chain, running his finger down the page to J.

He notes the address of Jake's New and Used Parts listing and returns to the counter. The sweetness of the pie knocks the edge off the battery acid taste of the coffee. Back in the car, he stops down the road from the diner to spread his map out and pinpoint Jake's. Turning left at a railroad track intersection, he follows the road to the auto parts yard.

As he turns into the yard, he can see the black stained earth where scrapped cars once sat. A huge sign atop a worn wood building has "Slap a Jap, Give Us Your Scrap" painted in large letters. A man is out in front of the building, helping a woman unload a bicycle, some worn out tires and metal pans from a wagon.

After piling up the scrap, he takes some bills from his once white grease-stained overalls to give to the woman. When the woman turns away with her wagon, the man looks at Keys and waves. Moving forward slowly, the Ford crunches across some gravel, then jounces over the uneven ground to stop by the man in overalls.

The man bends to look into the car. "Howdy, feller, ain't this Tom Walsh's car?"

"Yes, sir," Keys answers. "Ol' Tom got hisself killed in a knife fight."

"Huh, I ain't too surprised. Him and them knives…always showin' off. I'm Jake. So Harry send you ta get them batteries?"

Keys takes a moment, lighting a cigarette. "Yeah, sure did; where they at?"

"Drive on around back. Don't get outta the car, I'll be there shortly."

Keys drives slowly to the back of the building, taking his gun out and putting it on the seat by his right side. He wonders if Jake is calling Harry. At the back of the building, a man stands up from a barrel he was sitting on as Keys stops the Ford. A sawed-off shotgun lies on a bench within easy reach of the man. Keys waves to the man, then puts both of his hands in plain sight at the top of the steering wheel. The man returns to his seat atop the barrel, arms folded across his chest. The detective glances up at the rearview mirror to see if anyone is coming up in back of him.

Within minutes Jake comes out of the back of the shop, holding some papers. "I can't get Harry on the phone; I reckon he's out makin' his money. So, I guess he's okay, Petey. He's here ta pick up them batteries. You can come on out now, feller. What's your name anyways?"

"Frank's what they call me," Keys says. He slides the gun in his pocket as he opens the car door.

"Okay, Frankie, here's the paperwork for them batteries. You tell Harry I can only get twenty more a 'em an' he's gotta come up with a lot more dough ta get 'em. Maybe we can trade for more a them tires he gets. I could use some sugar an' coffee, too. I got people clamorin'."

"You get lots a business here, Jake?" Keys asks.

"I do all right, Frankie. There's lots a ways for a smart man ta get rich in this war. I'll bet ol' Harry's doin' good, am I right?"

"Right as rain, I guess," Keys replies.

"Tell Harry I'll call 'im tomorrow. Come on, Petey. Give Frankie a hand loadin' them batteries up."

Pulling out of Jake's lot, Keys breathes a sigh of relief. The Ford, loaded down with the batteries, doesn't have the pep it had before, but he keeps the speed up where he can, anxious to get back to Mare Island. Jake named Harry as the head man; now Keys has to put a face to the name. When Harry finds out someone stole his batteries, Keys is sure Harry will come looking for the man that took them.

His thoughts are of how he is going to let Harry find him. It is growing dark by the time Keys enters the shipyard. He drives the Ford to Smitty's locksmith shop, parks the car under the building's eaves, locks it and walks warily down to the ferry slip. The water on the bay is calm and the night warm, without rain. Keys is eager to be home. To be with Mary, have a hot shower, a pleasant dinner, and sleep in his own bed.

Keys wakes from a dreamless sleep. He yawns, then stretches out his arms, lifting his left arm up before jostling Mary. She is sleeping on her side facing away from him; he leans to her, taking in the scent of her hair. Getting out of bed slowly, he makes his way in the darkness to the bathroom.

After shaving and brushing his teeth, he opens the bathroom door. Mary is in the hallway, rubbing the sleep from her eyes.

"Morning, Sprite. How 'bout I treat you to a good longshoreman's breakfast before we go to work?"

"Are you sure you want to be seen with me down by the docks? What if someone from Mare Island sees us together?"

"Well, okay, you've got a point. I'll make us breakfast here. I want to ask you about how the vehicle files are organized anyway."

"Go easy on the hot sauce, Barry, I don't need to be on fire."

"Captain has the word," Keys says. He kisses Mary's cheek on his way to get dressed. After breakfast, Keys takes the plates and cups to the sink. "I'm gonna go see Frank Gray before I go to the shipyard this morning. He's usually early and I need to bring him up to speed. I'm wondering if there is any way you could check the vehicle registrations by date?

"We have three names, Rian Murphy, Tom Walsh, and now Harry, which I'm takin' as a first name. Maybe those guys all registered their cars at the same time. I know it's slim but it's worth a try if you think it can be done."

"I don't know, Barry, but I'll get on that first thing. I have the registration cards for Murphy, and Walsh, so I can check the dates to see if they're close. If the dates are the same or real close, I'll see if there's any way to cross check."

"Thanks, Mary, if anyone can do it you can. I'll be home tonight and not so worn out. Let's have dinner out somewhere and an early night in by ourselves."

"I'd like that, Barry. We could snuggle up in bed and listen to the radio."

Keys winks at Mary with a wicked grin. "I like the snuggle part."

"Ooh, I do like it when you play the big bad wolf," Mary says.

"Oh, you kid," Keys growls.

Keys has some delicious daydreams dancing in his head on the way to the FBI office.

Keys bursts into Gray's office, grinning madly.

Startled, Gray barks at Keys, "What the hell's gotten into you Keys? You're grinning like an idiot. Knock on the door next time or you're liable to get shot."

"Sorry, Frank. I guess with Mary back I'm just a happy boy."

"Good for you, Keys, go find someplace else to be silly. Have you got something to report or are you just lost in your delirium?"

Keys hands Gray a typewritten sheet of paper.

"I found Walsh's car in the scrapyard's parking lot. This note was crumpled up in the back of a hidden compartment. I drove the car to

Stockton and went to Jake's New and Used Auto Parts like it has on the note. Jake's an older guy that makes money on the black market. He thought I came for some car batteries he had for a guy he called Harry.

"From the way Jake talked, Harry's gotta be the head man we're after. Jake said he's got twenty more batteries comin' and that Harry was gonna have to pay big money to get 'em. Those batteries gotta be for the stolen torpedo. I took the ten batteries Jake had and brought 'em back to Mare.

"I figure Harry's gonna be lookin' for me as soon as he talks to Jake."

Gray looks up from the note paper. "I'll round up some agents and bust Jake's place before that happens."

"No, don't do that, boss. One sure way to find this Harry character is to have him find me."

Gray rubs his chin. "Well, as much as I'd like to use you as bait, what's to keep our new friend Harry from doin' you in?"

"I'm glad I can bring some light to your life, boss. Unless Harry's a complete idiot, he'll want those batteries I have. I also have all that money I found in Walsh's apartment. I'll have Mitch and Smitty start up the shipyard's rumor mill that I've got the money and the batteries."

"That's a dangerous play, Keys. I'm going to have a couple of agents shadow you."

"I've got one man dead now, Frank, and he was a good man. If you've gotta do it, let me have

273

Jerry. He knows how I work and I trust him. He won't walk into anything half-cocked."

"He's in L.A. on a job. I can't pull him off until I have someone else to cover the job."

"Maybe I'll hold up a coupla days till Jerry gets here."

"No maybes, Keys. Stay outta trouble. Watching you dangle might be fun but I'm not going to have that be your funeral. Besides, Mary would kill me if anything happened to you. I'm amazed a good-looking intelligent woman would take up with a miscreant like you."

"Gee, Frank, you say the sweetest things."

Chapter 36

In the Vallejo barn, Harry's knuckles turn white gripping the phone. "Gottverdammich!" he rages into the phone, completely forgetting to speak English.

Jake, on the other end of the line, puzzles for a second.

"What the hell was that, Harry?"

Harry, trying to recover, says it was an old Polish curse his father used to say.

"You know, Harry, I was in the Great War and that sounded like German to me. I always thought there was something off about you. So, quit yellin' at me. I tried to call you when the guy showed up here. He was drivin' Tom's car and knew all about you and the batteries.

"Batteries ain't easy to come by, Harry. I gotta pay my man a lot more dough to get twenty more. There's a long list a guys that gotta get their

Mike Downs

palms greased. So right now, the deal's gonna be another 50 per cent for the rest of the batteries."

"You lousy bastard," Harry screams. "We have a deal. If you go back on it, I'll come take the damned batteries!"

"Come right on, Harry. I'll be waitin' right here ta fill your Nazi ass full a buckshot. You want them batteries, it's gonna cost you double."

Harry takes a moment; eyes tightly shut, his fingers squeezing the bridge of his nose. Puffing his cheeks, he expels a breath.

"I'm sorry, Jake. I'm just upset about someone hijacking my stuff. We need to come to a reasonable agreement for the batteries. I am willing to pay more, but you have to be reasonable."

"I don't gotta do nothin', Harry. Double is the deal, take it or leave it."

"Look, Jake, I need those batteries. If you don't be reasonable, you won't get anymore goods from me. I know you make a big profit from the goods I supply you."

"That ain't gonna work, Harry; I got other places to go for that stuff. I ain't real thrilled sellin' batteries to a Nazi no how. Whatta you gonna do with all them batteries anyways?"

"I have several customers I've promised those batteries to. I need to supply them, Jake. They are very good customers."

"Tell you what Harry; you pay double for the ten batteries I just sent and I'll think about a deal for the rest."

"I didn't get those batteries, Jake; you let someone steal them from me."

"Well, I don't really know that do I, Harry? Maybe you got 'em and just don't wanta pay me. It don't matter none to me anyhow, it's your problem now. Maybe you oughta go find 'em. You send me cash money and maybe we can deal."

"You're a pirate, Jake; a real son of a bitch of a pirate. I have to have those batteries. I'll get the money."

Jake's face breaks out in a huge grin. "A real pleasure doin' business with you, Harry."

Harry slams the phone down. Pacing the floor, he repeatedly smacks his fist into his palm. Standing by a rough-hewed wood column with his fists balled, his brain churns with rage. He suddenly lashes out bashing his fist into the column. Pain seems to satisfy the rage; he watches as blood from his torn knuckles drips to the floor.

"What ya do to your hand, boss?" Alby asks.

Harry has a bloody handkerchief wrapped around his hand."Just a little accident, Alby. How come you're late?"

"My Mom's sick. I had to call a doctor to come see her. I've been tryin' ta get her to go see him, but she won't go. He says she's got a bad heart, the beat's irregular or somethin'. She's in bed by herself, I wanta go home before our shift tonight to check on her."

"Sure Alby, sorry to hear she's ill. I need you to take this envelope to Jake for me; you can go home when you get back, okay?"

"Okay, boss, I'll see you tonight."

Harry parks in an alley behind Alby's house. He hops over the backyard fence making his way to the back door. Slowly turning the doorknob, he carefully opens the door entering the kitchen, then stops to listen for any sound of movement. Creeping down the hallway, he peeks in a bedroom, seeing the thin form of an old woman lying on a bed.

Her eyes are closed; he studies her shallow breathing for a moment to make sure she is sleeping. Harry continues down the hallway to the other bedroom. Lifting the mattress, he smiles seeing several thick manila envelopes. He opens one confirming it holds money. Holding the mattress up with one arm, he puts the other envelopes on the floor.

"What are you doin' here?" a raspy voice questions. Startled, Harry turns to see Alby's mother leaning against the doorframe. She is much thinner than when he last saw her. Alby had invited Harry and Rian to the house for dinner last summer. Alby's mother made a shepherd's pie with potatoes and carrots from her garden and some mystery meat she hounded from the butcher.

"My goodness, Mrs. Kelly, you scared the dickens out of me." Adding a sugary tone, Harry spills the words out. "Alby asked me to get these envelopes for him. He's doing some important chores for me and needs something from them for work tonight."

"That's my son's money you got there. Why would Alby send you to get it?"

"I don't know, ma'am, he just told me to be real quiet and not wake you. I think he might be wanting to surprise you. Let me help you back to bed."

"I hate bein' in bed so much; maybe I'll make me some warm milk."

"Please let me make it for you, Mrs. Kelly. We have to get you back to bed first. Alby will be mad at me if he knows I woke you up."

"He's such a good boy; his father was a real mean cuss but it didn't rub off on Alby."

Harry holds the frail woman's elbow as he ushers her back to her bedroom.

"That's right, Mrs. Kelly, he's a real gentleman. Here now, lie back; I'll fluff the pillows up for you."

"Thank you, Mr. Harry. Don't forget my milk, will you?"

"No, ma'am, I won't forget."

"I'll tell Alby you were real nice when he comes home."

"No, you won't."

Harry uses a pillow to cover her face. The thin little woman fights back with astonishing strength, her arms and legs thrashing. Harry turns his head away from her flailing fists and pushes down harder on the pillow.

Chapter 37

As soon as he arrives at the shipyard, Keys heads for Smitty's shop. Smitty is at the counter, with a steaming cup of Mare Island's own roasted coffee, reading a newspaper when Keys comes in.

"Your humppity-back Ford is sittin' low, Keys. Whatta ya haulin"?

"I've got ten 6-volt batteries in that thing. I'd like to unload 'em; you got someplace I could store 'em?"

"We probably outta take 'em to the battery shop. That'd be right after you buy me breakfast."

"I'll be happy to buy breakfast, Smitty, but I need ta get the batteries someplace safe. The people that stole the torpedo are gonna want those batteries. I hijacked 'em yesterday and I don't want anyone to get 'em."

Smitty, his face upturned, Adam's apple working, downs the last of his coffee. "I pity people that can't get this good coffee; I can't get

281

goin' without it. Okay, Keys, I'll get a hand cart an' we'll put 'em under the stairs an' cover 'em with a tarp. I came by here late last night and saw the Ford so I ate breakfast at home anyway."

After unloading the batteries, Smitty brings two mugs of coffee out to the car.

Smitty hands a mug to Keys. "Somebody put a lotta work in this buggy."

Keys pats the car's fender. "I wouldn't mind havin' this car. It rightly flies; it's too stiffly sprung, but it'd be a good thing to have."

Smitty goes to the front of the car, lifting the hood. "Let's see what she's got for an engine." Looking down on the gleaming bright metals of the engine, Smitty hoots, "Wahoo, a Slingshot manifold an' Denver heads. Yeah, I bet she's a runner all right. You outta keep this one, Keys."

"I might just do that, Smitty. I'll have to see what my boss says. I need another favor from you."

"You know, Keys, for a guy I don't know much about you sure ask a lotta favors."

"I'm willin' to pay my way. How 'bout a coupla bottles a good scotch?"

Smitty grins up at Keys, scratching the back of his neck. "That'd be enough to tempt the Pope."

"I need to start the rumor mill goin' full speed," Keys says. "I want everyone to know I've got the batteries and a load of money I found at Tom Walsh's place."

Smitty closes the Ford's hood, squinting into the morning sun. "You lookin' ta get killed, or just robbed, Keys?"

"I'm lookin' for the man that's responsible for getting Moose killed. I don't mean Walsh, I mean the head man. The fastest way for me ta find him is for him to find me."

"'Scuse me for sayin', but that don't sound like the safest way to go about it."

"I need to put an end to this thing, Smitty. I'm not sure that bein' safe is gonna get the job done. Will you do it?"

"Yeah, Keys, I'll get it goin'. I hope you know what you're doin'."

Mitch is next on Keys' agenda. At Morsey's office, Mitch sits behind his desk, elbows splayed, fists balled under his cheeks, reading a Navy manual propped up against file baskets.

"Hiya, Mitch, looks like you're into some heavy stuff."

Mitch looks up over the edge of the book. "Hey, Keys, just the man I wanted to see. You got a coupla minutes to spare?"

"Sure, Mitch, I need a few minutes too." Mitch closes the book, getting up from his chair. "Morsey's down with his sub; let's take a walk."

Out of the administration building, they cross the street to Alden Park. The sun, bright in the sky, is a blessing after all the rain. The park is named after Commodore James Alden who in 1868 was the Commandant of Mare Island. It was he who had different varieties of exotic trees from all over the world planted on the barren island.

Keys leads the way, anxious to find a place in the sun. The noise of the shipyard that makes it necessary for the men to speak with raised voices, is incongruous with the placid setting of the park. The different colors of trees and flowers in the park, embellished by the bright sun, tug at the viewer's senses.

"Let's have a seat on the bandstand, Mitch. I wanta feel the sun on my face."

Seated on the steps of the bandstand, Keys turns to Mitch. "I take it you're close to a decision."

"You some kinda mind reader, Keys?"

"Nah, it's a simple conclusion of circumstances. Morsey's sub's almost finished which means it's gonna get outfitted and then be shipping out in about two months. You don't have much time before you stay or go."

Mitch, stares absently, then turns to Keys. "You make sound like a pretty simple problem."

Keys lightly punches Mitch's shoulder "No, what I mean is, it's not difficult to know what you're thinkin'."

"So, whatta you think I should do?"

"You have to follow your head and your heart, Mitch. You make this yard work better, which means the war effort here gets the job done. The guy that replaces Morsey is gonna take time to figure the place out. That'll slow things down.

That's on one hand; the other hand is fighting the enemy in a shooting war and being able to tell your grandchildren that's what you did in the war.

"Here's my take for what its worth. I have a friend who's almost like a son to me and Mary. His entire being is dedicated to the submarine service. He told me that every man on the boat has to be able to run every system on the boat. A slip or screw up on the part of any of the 80 men on the boat means they all die.

"That's not to say you can't do it. But you can't be thinkin' of this shipyard. You can't help anyone here. You're livin' in a glorified sewer pipe, either bored to death or scared shitless. I'm sayin' you gotta be totally dedicated to the submarine service. Have you ever been to sea?"

"No, and I'm readin' the Navy sub manuals wonderin' what the hell they're talkin' about. I've never been good with machinery, I just don't get it. But I don't wanta look back on this and think I didn't do my part."

"Mitch, I think you're needed here. Submariners gotta feel like there's nothin' else in the world. I was told that the modern submarine is the most complicated war machine ever built. If you feel unsatisfied in the future, you can blame it on me. I hope that helps.

"Now, I need a favor. I gotta shake out the bastard that got Moose killed. Smitty's spreading a rumor that I got Walsh's money. I took Walsh's car to a black marketer in Stockton and got the batteries a man named Harry is after for that stolen torpedo. I need you to help spread that rumor."

"That doesn't sound too smart to me, Keys."

"I put it to you, Mitch, 'cause you've got a good mind for this stuff. If you think of a better way, I'm all for it. But right now, I need to bring this thing to an end before anyone else gets hurt. I'd be lyin' if I told you I didn't care who got this Harry character. I want 'im, and, by God, I'm gonna have 'im. He's gonna pay for Larry the Moose."

"Do you just want me around to help you out with this, Keys?"

"Mitch, I've watched you with people here. You get things done. You gotta a talent for getting' people to work together. You get along with the highest officers and the lowest yard worker. I think you could make 'em dance together if you wanted. This place is the busiest, most productive repair shipyard in the world. It needs you, man.

"There's plenty of men and women workin' here on the home front to make it possible for our troops to fight the enemy. Right here, every day, I see ships repaired and sent back to the fight. New ships and equipment go outta this place by the ton damn near every day. That's a war record worth a lifetime of being proud of, Mitch."

A Marine guard from the administration building waves at the men, catching their attention. Mitch gets up to walk toward the

Marine. After a brief conversation, Mitch comes back to Keys.

"The police chief is looking for you. They found the Pontiac."

Keys says goodbye to Mitch and walks out of the park. At the yard's police station, he asks to see the chief.

The chief comes out of his office, dons a hat, and motions Keys to follow him. "One of the Navy divers found it. The water cleared up enough after the storm for the man to find it. They had a hard time getting it unstuck from the mud."

The chief pulls off a tarp uncovering a battered, mud-encrusted car that is hard to recognize as a Pontiac. The windshield and side windows are broken out. The door frames are dented and scared with marks left by chains.

The chief yanks open a rear door. "I've got an inventory list of things we found in the car. We found a dead Marine guard we thought had gone AWOL in the trunk. It's no wonder the guy driving this thing was tryin' to get away from you."

Keys bends down to look in the car. The seats are gone and the hidden compartments exposed. A layer of smelly silt covers the rest of the interior.

Keys backs away from the car. "I still don't understand why in such a short period of time three Marines had to die. Was there any paperwork or journals that the water didn't destroy?"

287

"We found a waterproof box bolted to one of the hidden compartments. There was a home title, a bankbook, a birth certificate, and a little over twenty thousand dollars in cash in it. The paper in the glove box was ruined; there's nothing legible."

Keys thumbs back the brim of his hat. "Twenty grand. I guess business was good. Too bad he didn't keep any records in that box. Thanks, Chief. I found out yesterday that the head man of this gang is a guy named Harry. That's all I got, just Harry. I'm gonna try to smoke 'im out by lettin' him know I've got his money and his batteries."

"You got any back-up, Keys?"

"Not yet, the FBI is sending my old partner when they can."

The chief eyes Keys with a hard look. "Okay, hero, I'll need your report so I can pick up the pieces when you get yourself killed. Bein' a lone wolf here just ain't smart, Keys."

"Come up with a better tune, chief, an' I'll play it."

"No, you won't, Keys; it ain't your style."

Chapter 38

Harry licks his thumb, paging through the bills he stole from Alby's house. He throws the money down; the bills scattering across the table. It is not going to be enough to finish his grand scheme of launching the torpedo. He broods, adding up the costs in his head. There are the batteries, and their wildly inflated cost, then battery chargers, wiring, testing, a war head, and a boat to launch the torpedo.

Wandering around the barn's interior, his mind spirals out of focus. He kicks a loose ration box around the dirt floor; the musty smell of old earth rises with the puffs of dirt. Harry's mood grows darker. He thinks of the man in the jeep leaving Tom's house with the bulging bag that must have contained Tom's money. No, his money.

Harry decides to go to the yard and look for Tom's car and see if there is any money stashed in it and then find the jeep. The man in the jeep is now the target of his inability to complete his mission. With a rush of resolve, he retrieves the keys to his pickup truck and heads out the door.

Going through the yard's parking lots is tedious and time consuming. Tom's car should have been in the first place he looked, in the scrapyard lot. There are hundreds of places Tom could have left it and even more where he could have hidden it.

Harry begins to feel conspicuous, traveling slowly down rows of cars, parking lot after parking lot. He pulls out of a lot, craning his head back for one last look, when he hears a shrill air horn. A big truck screeches to a stop inches from Harry's door. The truck driver yells, "Watch where you're goin', you idiot."

A bit unnerved, Harry parks his truck and walks to the cafeteria for something to eat. He selects some sausage, piles on peas and potatoes, then pours coffee after he pays. He finds a table by himself and starts in on his food.

"Hey, Harry, ain't seen you around lately. Mind if I sit?"

The man sits before Harry can answer.

The man, who works at the scrapyard, forks a mouth full of food, chews ardently, then begins to talk.

"I hear'd about Tom an' Moose. Ya'all worked together didn't you? Rumor has it some railroad inspector found out he was black marketin'. They say the 'spector found a bunch a money at Tom's place an' a mess a car batteries. Guy's struttin' round like a peacock, I hear."

Harry pushes away his plate. "You hear what the peacock's name is?"

"Yeah, Harry, Keys is his name. He's the same guy that got Casey an' Biff sent ta jail."

Harry pushes back his chair to stand. "Yeah, I remember the guy."

"Ya'll gonna finish them taters?"

Harry wipes his mouth with a paper napkin. "You can have 'em."

"Keys, you bastard. Keys," Harry says aloud on his way back to the Vallejo barn. Now it fits. The same guy he saw when he tried to burn Booth's office. The same guy he saw at Tom's house, and the same guy Moose wrote about in the notebook Harry took off the Marine's body.

Harry pounds the steering wheel.

"I've got you, I've got your secret, Keys, and I'll use to it to get my money and get even, too."

Harry drives down the dirt road to the barn, dust billowing up from the drying ground behind the truck. Alby steps out from the barn, tears streaming down his cheeks. Harry stops the truck and bends forward to turn off the ignition as Alby comes to the door. Alby puts his hands on the doorsill, his red face streaked, tears still falling.

"My mama's dead, Harry. I came home to see her an' she's dead. I called her doctor an' he come over an' said she had heart failure. I was ballin' so loud he said ta go find some flowers for her an' he'd take care a her. I came over here, Harry, 'cause I couldn't think a anywhere else ta go."

"Golly, Alby, I'm really sorry to hear that. Is there anything I can do?"

"I don't know, boss. I just really don't know what to do. I know we all gotta die, but I just didn't see it happenin' to my mama. I wish it was me instead. I wish I could trade places with her."

"Let me out of the truck, Alby. What you need is something to take your mind off your troubles."

Alby backs away, wiping the tears from his face on his shirt sleeve.

"Did you get the money to Jake?"

"Yeah, he said he'd be talkin' at you."

"Okay, then, Alby. We've got an enemy we need to take care of. He's the man that got our friend Rian killed; he's the guy that chased Rian to his death. Your mama liked Rian, maybe you told her he died. Well, maybe that hurt her heart, Alby. This guy, Keys, he's making all the trouble, my friend, an' I got a plan to stop him. You wanta help me, Alby?"

"Yes, sir, boss, I'll help. You want me ta squeeze the life outta the guy? I can do it."

"No, Alby, I want you to go to the yard and grab his wife. She works in the administration building. I'll give you her office number. You wait for her to go home and then grab her. I want you to bring her here. We'll make Keys pay; you can squeeze the life out of his wife just like he hurt your mama."

"I don't wanta hurt no woman, Harry, it ain't in my nature."

"He hurt your mama, Alby; he's gotta pay."

Alby looks down at the ground, shaking his head. "I don't wanta hurt no woman, Harry."

"Okay, Alby. If you grab the woman, then I can get Keys to come here for her. We won't have to hurt her, Alby. Just bring her here and we can get Keys here. Then we'll make him pay. I'll bet your mama would want to see him pay, wouldn't she?"

"I don't know, Harry. She hated some folks but I don't know why. She said Jews killed Christ; she didn't like them none at all."

The Nazi saboteur, grinning fiercely, his eyes alight, emphatically nods his head. "There you go Alby; I'll bet Keys is a Jew. I'll bet he meant to kill your mama."

"We'll make 'im pay, Harry? You an' me, we'll do it, Harry?"

"We'll do it together, Alby, for your mama. I'll go type a note for you to give Mary Keys."

Harry returns with a folded paper and a notebook.

He hands the note to Alby. "Take this to the administration building and ask for Mary Keys. If anyone asks…" Harry thumbs through the notebook. "Ah, here it is, tell them Mitch sent you. Mitch is Commander Morsey's aide. Okay, Alby? Can you remember all that?"

Mike Downs

"Can you write it down for me, boss?"

"Sure, Alby."

Harry writes on a page of the notebook before ripping it out and giving it to Alby.

"We're getting close to quitting time at the yard. I'll give you an hour, then I'll call Keys to tell him we have his wife. I need to set up a plan to make sure he doesn't have anyone following him. When I'm sure he's not followed, I'll direct him here and we'll have him. If I'm not here when you get back, I'll be out checking up on Keys. Tie the woman to a chair so Keys can see her when he comes in."

Alby checks his notes, putting each in a separate pocket. "Okay, boss."

Chapter 39

Keys reaches for the phone on the desk of his office. He has been pacing the floor waiting for Harry to call him out.

"Oh, hi, Mary. What'cha up to?"

Keys glances at his watch as he listens to Mary tell him that she is leaving early to catch a bus to Marinship. She says she promised her old roommate that they would have dinner and catch up on what each has been doing since she left.

"That sounds like fun, Mary. I may be late tonight anyway. The police have the Pontiac that I chased and I need to go over it. I want to check with the morgue. I'll bring you up to date tomorrow. I'm glad you have a friend to chat with. If you bring up Larry, please think of him with a smile. He would have liked that."

The change in Mary's voice tugs at Keys heart. After a pause, she says, "I am sad about Larry, but my old roomie won't let me be dog-faced for long. I just need to get away for a little while. Don't get into any trouble will you please? I love you, Barry."

"I love you too, Mary. Have a good time, and say hello for me."

Keys finishes his daily report and is thinking of asking Mitch if he is free for dinner when his phone rings.

The unfamiliar voice on the phone immediately commands Keys' attention.

"I've got your wife, Mary. You will bring the money you stole from Tom Walsh's house and the batteries you stole from me and go to the Owl Drug Store on Florida Street and wait for my phone call. I will call there at precisely six o'clock."

Keys waits a beat before answering. "Two things, friend. I've got no way to transport batteries and how do I know you have a Mary I might know?"

"If you want to play games, Mr. Keys, tell me what part of her body you would like to identify. You bring the money and the location of the batteries and maybe you'll see your wife alive. I'll call the drug store at six with your instructions. You have the money, be alone and unarmed."

The phone goes dead in his hand. Keys brings his arm up to look at his watch wondering if the man on the phone, (almost certainly Harry) really had Mary. He has little time to call Mary's old roommate. He yanks out his desk drawer for an old note book that has the roommate's phone number.

There is no answer to the phone. Keys looks at his watch again. He takes his snub-nosed .32 ankle gun and straps the gun and holster to his ankle. Rolling up his left shirt sleeve he uses adhesive tape to secure a six-inch blade under his forearm. He hopes if he is patted down the ankle gun will end the weapons search.

He phones the Marinship housing again. Keys' grip on the phone intensifies when a voice answers.

"Is Mary Keys there?"

"No, but I think I saw her get off a bus a little while ago. You wanta hang while I look for her?"

"No thanks, I just wanted to make sure she got there okay. Thank you."

Hanging up the phone, Keys expels a breath; he wanted to be sure Mary is not in danger. Time is running out.

When he calls Frank Gray at the FBI offices, it comes as some relief to find the boss has left for the day. Instead of having to explain why he is not waiting for a backup team, he leaves a message saying he is meeting the head of the black-market gang in Vallejo.

After looking up the address of the drug store, Keys takes Walsh's money from the file cabinet and heads for his jeep.

Harry leaves the barn after quickly devising a plan to make sure Keys is not being followed. He is anxious to get moving before it gets dark. His nerves jangle, doubts begin to clutter his mind, maybe things are moving too fast. "No!", he cries aloud. He has to have that money. Keys has to be eliminated. Harry's resolve strengthens; he will not allow anything to stop his assault on the Navy yard.

The drug store will be the first stop where Harry will get a good look at Keys. He will make Keys stop several more times on the way to the barn to make sure no one follows.

Keys parks the jeep in front of the drug store; the phone booth is just inside the entrance. Harry watches with field glasses from a phone booth in a camera shop across the street.

Keys pushes a man away from the ringing phone and closes the booth's door. Keys recognizes the voice on the phone as the same man he spoke to before.

Harry speaks into the phone. "I hope that wasn't a friend of yours, Mr. Keys. Yes, that's right, look all around you; I'm watching every move you make. We have several more stops to make. Do not call anyone after I hang up. Go to the next address I give you and wait for my instructions. Any deviation and Mary will pay dearly."

After more stops, Keys picks up the phone. "Okay Harry, enough of the merry-go-round; let's get to it."

"How clever, Mr. Keys, you know my name. There will be one more stop and I will give instructions on our meeting place."

Harry rushes back to the barn to make the last call to Keys. Alby's car is not there. Harry enters calling out, "Alby, are you here? Damn it, where the hell are you?"

He goes to the phone, counts down the minutes on his watch, then places the call. "Ah, right on time, Mr. Keys. You will drive east on Benicia Road until you see my signal, turn left into the dirt road and drive to the building. I'll be watching."

"What's the signal, Harry? How will I know it?"

"Don't worry, Mr. Keys, you won't miss it. Get going."

Keys drives east on Benicia Road wondering what the signal might be. He slows, looking to both sides of the road for the sign. Behind him the sun is sinking. Keys' hand flies up to shield his eyes when a great ball of light flashes directly into his windshield. The light moves to his left, resting on the entrance to a dirt drive.

Harry, in the loft of the barn, directs the sun's light with a large mirror. Grinning wolfishly, he rests the light on Keys' jeep and back to the drive several times.Keys turns into the drive heading toward a big barn under a stand of old live oak trees. As he comes to a stop by a pickup truck, a Ford sedan pulls up behind him.

Harry comes out of a door pointing a pistol at Keys. "Get your hands up, Keys. Alby, check the jeep for the money." Harry motions with the pistol. "Come inside, Mr. Keys."

Keys moves to the door as Harry backs away, keeping the pistol trained on the detective. Keys takes in the cavernous interior of the big barn; it is well-lighted with rows of fluorescent fixtures.

Crates of Navy goods are stacked neatly along with tires, lumber, metal plate, paint cans, and numerous other items on the dirt floor. Stairs lead up to what was a loft and is now divided into separate rooms with closed doors.

"Taking it all in I see, Mr. Keys. Where are my batteries?"

Keys, standing almost a head taller than Harry, looks down at the man, contemptuously. "Where is Mary?"

"You don't ask questions here, Keys," Harry growls. "You are here to answer my questions when I demand it."

"Got that Napoleon complex, Harry? I'll tell you what I know after you produce Mary and let her go. You'll get nothin' from me till then."

Alby bounces in on the balls of his feet, holding the bag of money up like a happy terrier.

"I found the money, Harry."

"There ya go, Harry. Now you show me Mary and I'll tell you where the batteries are."

Alby offers the bag to Harry, then looks downcast. "I couldn't get her, Harry, she left before I got there."

"Oh, for Christ's sake, Alby, shut the hell up. Where the hell have you been then?" Harry fumes.

Alby puts the bag down on the table in front of him. "I went home to see if the doctor needed me, Harry."

Keys watches Harry and lowers his hands.

"I said get your hands up, Mr. Keys. I will not hesitate to use this gun."

Keys' hands stay by his sides. "You shoot me, Harry, and you can kiss those batteries goodbye. Now that I know you don't have Mary, you've got nothin' to trade."

Harry studies Keys a moment, then grins. "I'll just keep you here, Mr. Keys. We can get your Mary tomorrow or the next day, or next week. You do think you're so very clever, but after I finish with you, you'll tell me everything I want to know."

Keys tries a bluff of his own. "If I'm not back at Mare Island by midnight, you'll never be able to set foot there again."

Harry's grin dissolves. "I don't believe you. Alby make sure Mr. Keys isn't armed. I'll keep him covered."

Keys raises his arms out from his sides as Alby pats him down.

"Check his legs," Harry commands. Alby reluctantly bends to run his hands down Keys' legs. He stops at Keys' ankle. "He's got a gun on his ankle, Harry."Alby unsnaps the holster to hold the pistol up for Harry to see.

"I told you to come unarmed, Mr. Keys."

"You told me you had Mary, Mr. Harry," Keys says.

"Alby, go back and check his crotch. Pull his pants down, make sure he didn't bring some other weapon."

Keys closes his hand over his belt buckle. "You gonna enjoy watchin', Mr. Harry? I read the reports about you Nazi boys dressin' like girls for each other."

"You insolent pig," Harry shouts, his face turning crimson. The money bag jumps on the table top as Harry bangs his bandaged fist down. "We are the master race, all others are inferior. You are a mongrel, not fit to utter a slur."

"Well, Mr. Master race, your hand bleeds red just like everybody else's," Keys retorts.

Alby watches the exchange, a puzzled look on his face. His face clears, then grows stern staring at Harry's hand.

The pitch of Alby's voice rises, his speech coming fast. "Harry, there was blood on the back of my mama's pillow. The doctor said it wasn't from my mama. The money's gone from under my mattress too; I checked it. You killed my mama, didn't you, Harry? I'd a given you the money, Harry; all you had to do was ask." His pistol comes up, shaking slightly with the intensity of his grip.

"Put the gun down, Alby. It was an accident. I was just trying to help her. Put the gun down, Alby, or I'll have to shoot you."

The muscles stand out on Alby's face as his jaw tightens. His eyes blaze with hatred; the pistol bucks in his hand. Harry is only a few feet away; his right hand goes to the wound on his hip, then he fires twice. Keys dives under the table, frantically tearing at the adhesive tape to get at his knife.

Alby staggers backward, then lurches forward. He fires the pistol until the hammer snaps on empty rounds. Harry tries to raise his pistol but Alby is on him. Alby's weight crushes Harry to the ground, the big man's hands are at the Nazi's throat.

Keys hears shots that seem muffled, then silence. He gets to his feet, knife in hand, then cautiously approaches the two bodies. Alby is face down to one side of Harry. Two large nasty looking holes are bored through the back of his shirt. Blood pools at an appalling rate, leaching into the ground.

Keys bends down to check Alby's pulse. The big man's heart is still. Keys rolls him off Harry revealing multiple wounds to the chests and sides of both men. The muffled shots Keys heard were delivered to Alby at point blank range. Harry had fired his pistol jammed into Alby's side.

To Keys surprise, Harry's eyelids flutter. Keys leans toward him, speaking into his ear. "What were you going to do with that torpedo?"

Harry's eyes slowly open. He tries to raise his arm and in a low, raspy voice says, "Heil". A shallow breath wheezes out, his eyes close, his deadly scheme dying with him.

Chapter 40

"I told you boss, he said he had Mary and I had to get to his first phone call in a hurry. I did call your office but you'd gone home; I ran outta time."

Keys and his FBI boss, Frank Gray, are outside the barn, their breath visible in the cold pre-dawn light. Gray jabs his finger at Keys' chest. "I think you just had to play it on your own. Damn it, Keys, I told you I don't want you killed on my watch."

Keys face is haggard, red-eyed from being up all night, making it difficult for him to control his temper. He pushes Gray's hand away.

"Come on, Frank, gimme a break. We got the bad guys, the goods, and I found the torpedo in the back of the place. I've searched for a journal but haven't found one yet. If we're lucky, maybe we'll find who they dealt with when your guys finish searching the place. Those two mutts killed each other so there's no trial, no muss, no fuss. I need to call Mary; she was expecting me home last night, okay?"

"Yeah, go call her. Tell her you're outta the dung heap smellin' like a rose again. I'll tell you this, though—if I ever put you on another job, we're gonna have a serious talk first."

"Thanks, Frank."

"Boss, Keys, boss. Can't you get that into your thick skull?"

"Oh right, sure thing," Keys says as he turns away, headed back into the barn. Gray shakes his head, "You're a real piece of work," he says with a grin.

Keys has to push one of the FBI men aside to use the phone. "Mary, I'm glad I got you before you left for the yard. I've got the case licked; there's only the paperwork left for us to do. When the FBI guys got here, they stopped me searching Harry's barn. I'm too tired to knock sense into 'em. Besides Gray's here and grumblin' already."

Mary has the phone receiver gripped in both hands. "What happened? Are you alright?"

Keys smiles, still delighted with the sound of Mary's voice. "I'll tell you all about it when I get home. Stay there, please, an' after I take a nap, we'll go out an' celebrate."

"Hurry home, hero. I'll have breakfast ready when you get here. We have to go back to the yard to finish our work and say goodbye to everyone."

"Yeah, you bet, we'll do that. We both met people there we don't wanta lose touch with, and I need to clean out the office they gave me. When we get back to our office in the city we can make out our bill to the FBI. I'm kinda lookin' forward to battlin' Gray over it."

Keys drives the jeep back to the city knowing he will soon have to give it back. He lies on the sofa, his head in Mary's lap. She runs her fingers through his hair, then smoothes the strands across his forehead. His eyes pop open when she raps her knuckles on his head. "You knew I was at Marinship and safe. Why did you have to go to that barn alone? Damn it, Barry, do you really love danger so much you'd risk our life together?"

"Jeez, Mary," Keys says rubbing his head. "Gray was after me for the same thing. Look, I called your old place at Marinship; the woman I talked to said she *thought* she saw you. I had very little time to make a decision. What if it wasn't you she saw? I couldn't live with myself if I hadn't made sure. I went there because I want our life together more than anything else on this earth."

"I wonder if you really believe that, Barry. I wonder if it's me or the chase you love more."

Keys hesitates for a moment. "You are my only true love, Mary."

Mary looks down at him smiling. "That's the right answer."

Epilogue

Some weeks after the excitement of the Mare Island case has died down, Keys and Mary have returned to their Mason Street office.

Keys enters and pitches his hat toward the hat rack. He bends down to give Mary a peck on her cheek. "The walk didn't cure my boredom any."

"Well, go pick up your hat off the floor. Frank Gray wants to see us. He says he's got another job for us."

Keys snatches his hat off the floor on his way out of the office. Mary hurries to catch up; she takes Keys' hand with a gentle squeeze. Keys smiles down at her, slowing his pace. They walk together down Sutter toward the FBI offices in the Hunter-Dulin building.

Finis

Coming Up Next

Jack Novac is back in *Novac's Way*. The Nazis ended his auto racing career but Jack's back racing his own airplane. He's still battling bad guys. He and his wife Maddy have plenty of adventures to keep you entertained.

Barry Keys next adventure is still in the plotting stages. Tentatively titled *Roosevelt's Riddle*, Barry and Mary are under orders from the president to look for war profiteers.

Reviews

Sounds of Deception

"By far your best! --- way best!" Kas Kastner

"You kept me on the edge of my seat!" Peggy
Kastner

The Artimus Box: Great Read

"Heard this book was a great story and was
not disappointed."

Novac's Race: Five Stars

"Enjoyable tale of intrigue and murder set in
an auto racing genre"

Novac's Run: Not too Short, Not Too Long

"Once I started Novac's Run, I didn't put it down!"

Acknowledgements

Thank you to Kathy Downs for her untiring work with editing (a daunting task) and the artwork she does so well.

Heartfelt appreciation also to Kas and Peggy Kastner; Janice Torbet, San Francisco's best librarian; Phyllis Gurney; and Mare Island Museum. I couldn't do it without you.

About the Author

Passion is a sustaining element in Mike's life. After a forty-year career of professionally racing factory sports cars, writing became that passion. As an avid follower of American history and early Auto Racing, Mike combined the two in novels.

He finds bringing to life fictional characters in historical events and locations fulfills his passion. Making the stories and characters exciting is a grand challenge. The many hours in crafting a novel are enjoyable ones spent trying to become a better story teller. Finding innovative ways to illuminate a scene to bring the reader into the moment is a lovely satisfaction.

Connect with me on online

Mike Downs Mysteries website;

http://www.mikedownsmysteries.com

Facebook: Mike Downs

Twitter: #Mike Downs Author

Goodreads: Mike Downs

Lenka's List: Author List, Mike Downs

Amazon Author Page: Mike Downs

www.ingramcontent.com/pod-product-compliance
Lightning Source LLC
Chambersburg PA
CBHW061129200626
46817CB00016B/437